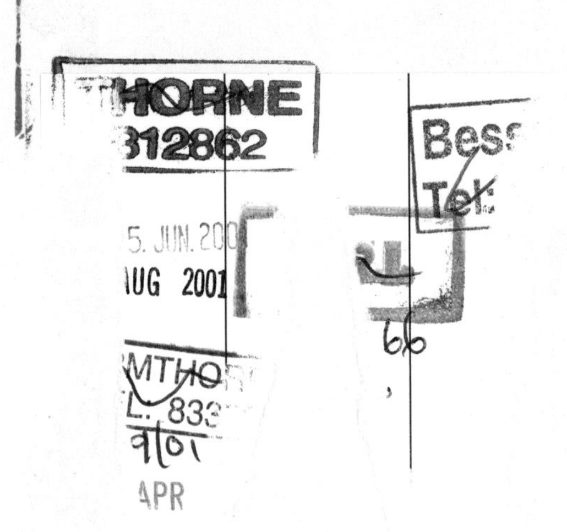
THORNE
312862
5. JUN. 200
AUG 2001
APR

WITHDRAWN
FROM
DONCASTER
LIBRARY SERVICE

DONCASTER LIBRARY SERVICES
30122 01269216 2

5 JUL

SPECIAL MESSAGE TO READERS

This book is published by

THE ULVERSCROFT FOUNDATION

a registered charity in the U.K., No. 264873

The Foundation was established in 1974 to provide funds to help towards research, diagnosis and treatment of eye diseases. Below are a few examples of contributions made by THE ULVERSCROFT FOUNDATION:

A new Children's Assessment Unit at Moorfield's Hospital, London.

•

Twin operating theatres at the Western Ophthalmic Hospital, London.

•

The Frederick Thorpe Ulverscroft Chair of Ophthalmology at the University of Leicester.

•

Eye Laser equipment to various eye hospitals.

If you would like to help further the work of the Foundation by making a donation or leaving a legacy, every contribution, no matter how small, is received with gratitude. Please write for details to:

THE ULVERSCROFT FOUNDATION,
The Green, Bradgate Road, Anstey,
Leicester LE7 7FU. England

Telephone: (0533)364325

I've travelled the world twice over,
Met the famous: saints and sinners,
Poets and artists, kings and queens,
Old stars and hopeful beginners,
I've been where no-one's been before,
Learned secrets from writers and cooks
All with one library ticket
To the wonderful world of books.

ANGELL & SONS

Mary Angell has pulled up by its bootstraps her Irish husband Fred's failing grocery business — carried on in Marylebone since 1720 — for the sake of their son, Johnny, and daughter, Cis. When Fred's nephew, Horace, comes to help in the shop, he and Cis fall in love, marry and have a number of children. By modern times, many things have happened in the annals of Angell & Sons — by now a flourishing supermarket — and Hilary, a descendant of the family, wants to find out all about them.

Books by Pamela Hill
in the Ulverscroft Large Print Series:

DIGBY
VOLLANDS

PAMELA HILL

ANGELL & SONS

Complete and Unabridged

ULVERSCROFT
Leicester

First published in Great Britain in 1992 by
Robert Hale Limited
London

First Large Print Edition
published May 1994
by arrangement with
Robert Hale Limited
London

British Library CIP Data

Hill, Pamela
Angell & Sons.—Large print ed.—
Ulverscroft large print series: general fiction
I. Title
823.914 [F]

ISBN 0–7089–3077–8

Published by
F. A. Thorpe (Publishing) Ltd.
Anstey, Leicestershire

Set by Words & Graphics Ltd.
Anstey, Leicestershire
Printed and bound in Great Britain by
T. J. Press (Padstow) Ltd., Padstow, Cornwall

This book is printed on acid-free paper

Part One

1

BEHIND the respectably drawn Nottingham lace curtains of the Angell living-quarters above the Marylebone shop, Mary Angell was somewhat anxiously going over her husband's accounts. It was necessary to do this while Fred was out to avoid hurting his feelings, and as Mary had married him out of mild affection and a certainty that she could manage him, neither of which states of mind had been altered by twenty-seven years of marriage, she adhered to first principles. Her smooth, only slightly greying dark head, in its scrupulously laundered plain linen cap, bent itself accordingly over the current ledger. This contained entries concerning butter, best and second grade; tea, ham, meat extract, strawberry preserve and other such items, all entered in Fred's strange spiky handwriting; she had, come to think of it, never known him very well. In a second ledger were the

outstanding bills from delivery customers, and therein lay Mary's present worry; she firmed her lips, closed the first ledger, got up and went to where a kettle simmered gently on the kitchen range, made herself tea in a brown pot, and while it underwent infusion returned, almost thankfully, to the letter received that morning from her husband's sister's son, Horace Cicero Trevelyan.

Mary frowned a little, and surreptitiously eased the stiff armpit-high corsets which restricted her ample frame. She recalled Horace Cicero as a small boy whose elder sister, Theodora — both children had been pretentiously named, their father, Fred's sister's husband, having been an usher who died early of consumption after imbibing a certain degree of classical knowledge at his thankless occupation — had, one remembered, been a great gangling girl of fifteen, calculated to lead dear Cecily into unladylike pursuits almost immediately. Caught out one day playing cricket with the rest behind the stables, Theodora had been promptly marched to Mrs Udney's Registry to be interviewed and put down

for future employment as a governess; the references from paternal connections had helped and Theodora had remained in steady employment elsewhere ever since; nothing more, in fact, had been heard from her. As for Horace Cicero, it had been decided, with the timely birth of young Johnny Angell, that there was no future for a nephew in the family firm despite apparent mathematical brightness, and Horace Cicero had been set instead to schoolmastering. Now, it appeared that he wanted to give it up.

* * *

Keighley, Yorkshire, May 17th, 1851.

My dear Aunt,

I am sick of keeping order, or failing to do so, among little wretches who invade my privacy and even disturb my sleep. The owners here are as abominable as most and take their pound of flesh for very low pay indeed. I should greatly prefer, if you will permit it, to return to London and hopefully assist you and

Uncle Frederick in the shop at least meantime, and if you were dissatisfied with me could then find something else from there. I trust, however, that you might discover a permanent use for me. I could keep accounts, can slice ham thinly, write clearly and please most. I have not, I may add, seen any ham at all for over two years; the food here is unspeakable. I propose leaving the wretched trade at any rate, and failing all else could no doubt sail before the mast to Australia. I trust however that such a step will not be necessary. Remembering your early kindness, I would hope, as the newspaper advertisements say, to give satisfaction by strict attention to business, if only you will permit me to undertake it. This profession is without hope and turns men into slaves.

Your affectionate nephew, and with regards to my uncle and cousins,

H. C. Trevelyan.

Mary folded up the letter and put it back in its envelope. It was time to

go down to the shop, give Alec Frame the assistant his hour to feed himself in the back lower premises, and oneself serve such customers as might come in. Mary looked briefly into the small scullery, where Hannah the servant was cutting up vegetables to put in the stew; swiftly into the small parlour, where Cis was, very suitably, seated glueing shells on a small box, the sunlight filtering through the curtains on to her lank and carefully combed fair hair; called upstairs to Johnny, who was recovering from measles in bed; and went down. As she descended the stairs, Mary smoothed her apron and patted her hair where it lay disposed in a tidy knot on her neck beneath the cap. She was still a handsome woman and customers respected her; there was no nonsense about unexpected credit the way there would be with Fred; that was part of the trouble. Perhaps, for the moment at any rate, Horace Cicero would be a good idea.

She took up her place behind the counter, at the same time scanning the shelves. They weren't as full as they

ought to be, as they had no doubt been in the days when the first Angell, whose name happened also to be Horace, had retired from being Robert Walpole's footman after the South Sea Bubble business, with Walpole's blessing and a sizeable vail culled from withdrawing the money early on. Old Horace's portrait, still wearing the Houghton livery, hung with its full-bottomed wig in the parlour upstairs where Cecily was glueing shells on her box. If things got any worse, they might have to sell the portrait, which might be worth something by now. That would be a pity; one had to keep up appearances, especially in business. She hoped Fred wouldn't be late getting back with the delivery cart; the other day he'd gone to sleep in it and the pony had brought him home.

Alec Frame, the assistant, departed for his beef and beer sullenly; he was a thin creature of no particular appeal, and had been thinking for some time of handing in his notice. It was all very well having a sign waving outside saying *Angell and Sons, Family Groacers*, the way they'd spelt it in the old days; that kind of thing

didn't bring customers in by itself, and Alec by now had ideas of his own.

* * *

Cecily Angell, Mary and Fred's only daughter and, until Johnny's surprising advent when she was aged about fourteen, their only child, sat somewhat dispiritedly glueing her shells on wood, an occupation which Mama considered ladylike. Cecily had never been brought up to do anything unladylike, and left to herself would probably not have done it anyway; she was predictable, placid, somewhat unimaginative, and constantly obedient. She had only given her mother a single hour's trouble long ago in moments which, now and again recalled, were still glorious; making the runs while HC batted and Theodora, briefly an entertaining and terse companion, looked on from the side; one's body a trifle breathless from lack of such accustomed exercise, running round and round with skirts flying and laundered pantalettes most improperly revealed above one's active ankles; cheeks flushed, fair hair

disarranged, and a feeling of escape which had never, even in the more enlightening intervals of Mr Smithers' sermons at church on Sundays, been surpassed. Mama had come out, of course, almost at once and had ordered everything to stop, and they had all three gone in, regretfully leaving the sunshine, to gaze instead at the aspidistra at which Cis herself gazed now, alone like she was, sitting in its brass pot by the window. It occurred to her that she and the plant had some general matter in common, but Cis was not certain what. It sat there and she sat here, and Mama watered it daily and would presently, as happened each day at one o'clock, call out to Cis to be sure to wash the glue off her hands before sitting down at table with Papa. Cis' hands were large, purplish and somewhat plump, although her body itself was tall and thin. She was not pretty and knew it. She had no friends, because Mama would never permit her to serve in the shop and there was no time to meet anybody otherwise. Cis would have liked to marry and have children, but by now, at twenty-six, the

prospect seemed remote; she never met any young men. No doubt the whole of life would be spent in this way, regarding pallid shells or doing woolwork for sale for the missions. Cecily was pious in a Low Church way. She trusted in God to look after her and, also in due time, her brother Johnny; Johnny was a friendly boy and fond of everyone. No doubt she would keep house for him when he was older.

Cecily selected a shell, which happened to have a few freckles on its surface; stared at it, duly applied its portion of glue, fixed it in place and suddenly remembered a thing Theodora had said long ago when she had briefly stayed here before disappearing. Her narrow eyes had stared at exactly such a box as Cecily was glueing even then, and her voice, which was somewhat sharp, had uttered, with an extra edge to it, "Whatever do you do that *for*? It spoils the shells, doesn't do any good to the box, and makes it difficult to dust. Why not leave it the way it was?" But all that had been too hard to answer, and anyhow Theodora had shortly been taken away.

* * *

Fred had arrived, more or less awake, with the delivery cart in time for midday stew. He had a long aimless face, pale blue eyes behind metal-rimmed spectacles, and hair of a strange inherited apricot colour worn rather low and receding slightly from his forehead. He put the old pony back in its loose-box up the lane, passed his tongue round his deplorable teeth in anticipation of the stew, which could be smelt agreeably beyond the house, and went in, regarding his wife's bustling form, returned from the shop now Alec had safely eaten, a trifle warily. Fred was not very clever, but mild enough, and his processes were strictly animal. He had spent his childhood on a farm in Ireland.

"Where's Cis?" he asked, as he sat down at the scrubbed table. His spouse replied that their daughter was washing her hands; it took a little time to get the glue off. While they waited, Mary broached the subject of Horace's letter.

"It's difficult," she said, "when you think of Johnny. In a year or two he'll

have left school. This lot of measles'll have kept him back, though, a bit. What d'you think, Father?"

It helped Fred in some way to be addressed in this fashion, and he looked up, his eyes vaguely fishlike behind the glasses. "Difficult to say," he echoed. "Do whatever y'think, Mary."

Mary, who had hoped to be given this accustomed freedom, helped him to stew as Cis came in and sat down. Fred applied himself to his food, almost forgetting the matter; Mary had always decided everything, and always would. Fred remembered, vaguely, having an affection for his only sister, who had married, for reasons not immediately evident, the consumptive usher who had left her with two hopeful children, but Em had not long survived him. Fred tried to remember what had happened next; hadn't there been a girl who was rather bright?

"What became of Theodora?" he mumbled. Mary, who had no intention of having Theodora unduly remembered, returned to the more pressing matter of their nephew. "He could help out, at least

until Johnny's ready to come in," she said. Fred nodded, wiping his mouth routinely with the back of his hand. He was tired and wanted to go to sleep. No doubt it didn't do to have the whole family in the shop. He really didn't know.

"I think we could use another hand, if he'd work," he ventured. Cis spoke up, a thing which seldom happened, and both her parents turned their heads.

"It would be pleasant to have some company," she said quietly. Mary pounced on her daughter at once.

"Your cousin's here to work, remember that," she said. In a somewhat unfair addendum she stated, "I've brought you up with advantages, Miss. Most girls your age are turned out by now as governesses. You wouldn't like that, I can tell you."

Cecily, who had not in any case learned very much at school, made no reply. She was fond, she knew, of sewing. How difficult Mama sometimes was! Despite everything, it would be pleasant to see Cousin Horace again. Perhaps he remembered the cricket in the lane. He couldn't possibly spend all his time in the shop.

* * *

Some weeks later, at the end of the school term, a stocky young man with a determined countenance and a good head of curly brown hair was walking purposefully, carrying a moderately sized yellow hair trunk by its handle, along the Marylebone Road towards the familiar Angell sign. He regarded it critically. In his opinion, shortly to be reinforced, it should have had underneath *In business for more than a century*. One would see.

Horace Cicero Trevelyan expended his lungs with a last breath of the doubtful air of outer London, firmed his already firm mouth and walked into the shop. Mary was serving behind the counter, knew him at once and nodded amiably. Horace Cicero walked round behind the customers, deposited his hair trunk meantime out of sight, and at once commenced to serve, as it happened, a stout lady in bombazine carrying a small dog on one arm. He chucked it under the chin. "Nice little fellow," he observed amiably. "What may we do for

you today, madam?"

By fortune, the lady demanded a pound of thinly sliced ham; she kept a nearby boarding-house. Horace Cicero turned to where a large naked pink block stood among the cheeses, seized a carving knife, flourished it expertly, and sliced on. It was his chief, in fact his only, social talent and earned immediate praise. "My," said the next woman, "see them slices, just like paper. Makes it last." She also ran a small boarding-house. Both women paid agreeably, then went. There were not many others in the shop, and when the rest had been dealt with Mary turned to her nephew by marriage and asked if he would like a cup of tea. Horace Cicero's behaviour on arrival had heartened her; it would be pleasant to have somebody who didn't need telling. Alec had given notice that same morning: there hadn't, since then, been time to think.

"Call me HC," said its owner. "Saves time." He retrieved his trunk from under the counter, carried it upstairs, was shown his small attic room, washed his hands at the jug and ewer after

relieving himself, then smoothed his hair, and went down into the living-room. In front of the aspidistra, which he remembered, sat a young woman with fair hair, glueing shells on a wooden box. This must be Cis; he remembered trying to teach her to play cricket. She looked up, and smiled.

"I expect your tea's ready," she said. "It's keeping warm on the range." This made HC feel immediately at home.

* * *

Immured upstairs all this time with the most unfair attack of measles caught at school from which he was recovering just in time to miss the holidays, was Johnny Angell, Fred and Mary's hopeful only son. He was a bright, good-natured and willing boy of twelve who took after his mother except that he was thin. He had grown remarkably during his illness and was still a trifle languid, a fact which caused Mary to keep him in bed and continue to take him up jugs of her own excellent home-made lemonade and calf's foot jelly long after it was

necessary. Johnny, however, was anxious to get back to the Saturday delivery round, when he was allowed to help his father hand in the orders at service doors and, on return, while Papa dozed in the emptied cart, gloriously to drive the old pony himself back to the stables and its hay. Johnny insisted, therefore, despite his mother, on coming downstairs as soon as he could; and shambled into the parlour, to blunder upon HC and Cis seated holding hands on the sofa in front of the aspidistra. Cis blushed, which Johnny realised made her almost pretty, and tried to draw her hand away; HC kept firm hold of it.

"You'll be Johnny," he said. "Feeling better? You were a baby when I left."

"Yes, thank you," said Johnny. Being a polite child he made no comment on the evident situation, then or later; and as the days passed was able to return, as school was still closed, to help in the shop, which he liked to do, and stack the delivery orders in their cardboard boxes, feeling a trifle shaky still at first when his thin arms lifted them into the cart; but there didn't seem as many boxes as usual,

and at the last minute HC, who seemed to be everywhere, handed Johnny a pile of envelopes bearing customers' names. On top was that of Mr Larkin, who often gave Papa tips about horses, wore a perpetual bowler hat on the back of his head, and also often winked. Johnny stared doubtfully at the pile.

"You may as well know what's in them," said HC. "Customers who haven't settled their bills for six months don't get more goods till they're paid. If anyone asks questions, tell 'em Mr Trevelyan says so."

Johnny dared to speak up. "Mr Larkin won't like it," he ventured hesitantly.

"Then Mr Larkin will have to lump it. You get away with your father on the round, my lad. A customer is worth as much as his money; remember that."

Johnny drove off beside Papa with his heart sinking, somewhat taken aback at being called my lad, and certainly it wasn't as pleasant as usual on the round; some people objected to the notes and said they'd go elsewhere in future. Returning from such encounters, Johnny glanced more than once at his

father for guidance; but Fred Angell as usual had nothing to say, and held the reins as he would have held them in sleep. Mr Larkin hadn't answered the door.

2

THE discovery that Cecily wanted to marry her cousin disturbed Mary Angell for no immediate reason she herself could fathom. Certainly marriage was every girl's ambition, and Cecily at twenty-six was fortunate to achieve it, though marriage between cousins was perhaps not a good thing. Why she should have preferred to keep Cecily upstairs by herself, engaged in ladylike pursuits into a predictable spinsterhood, was not clear; Mary merely had a vague feeling that she would rather things had remained as they were. Things had, however, altered already, discreetly but with certainty, at least over the accounts; HC's determined treatment of the non-paying customers had brought about a trickle of money at last and one or two sullen returns of certain persons, the rest being no loss. Moreover, HC's swift and schoolmasterly arithmetic in adding up the ledger columns and making out

bills surpassed her own, and Mary was honest enough to admit it and to be glad of time to do a little more housework and keep an eye on Hannah. Alec Frame had gone, and nobody missed him; Johnny by now was strong enough to help in the shop every day, though HC himself proved more of a lure to customers with his dexterous slicing of paper-thin ham and a certain stolid and predictable presence across the counter. There was no doubt that he was happier as a grocer. Also, he devoted his spare time, apart from steadfastly courting Cecily, to the improvement of the shop; he had given up one whole Saturday evening to whitewashing the shelves, which made everything look much better, and he and Johnny rearranged the stock very early on Monday morning. HC also had suggestions to make.

"Now you have more time, Aunt Mary," he said one day, "what about some of that honeymoon jam? I remember it well. It would make a special line nobody else has; keep the recipe to yourself, perhaps let Cis have it in time for the wedding, but that's all."

He winked at Cis, who was seated regarding him adoringly; it was as though a god had come into her life, ordering everyone about, herself and even Mama. And the wedding would be quite soon. Cis was aware of a small flutter in her stomach. She didn't, of course, know anything about marriage or the duties of a wife; no properly brought up young woman did until after the ceremony; but Cecily looked forward to everything, and to babies, which came somehow. HC would tell her about it. They were going to Epping for the honeymoon, and Mama could perhaps later on teach her to make jam. What was a special line? HC was full of such unencountered phrases. Cis loved him more and more as each day passed.

Mary pursed her lips. She hadn't the least intention of giving away the recipe, at least not yet. However she made the jam, and was somewhat taken aback when HC put it in the window, with a carefully lettered notice saying MRS ANGELL'S SPECIAL HONEYMOON CONSERVE, 1/9d PER JAR. The whole thing, in fact, seemed a trifle vulgar. Fred, when consulted, had said he supposed it was all right for

the couple to be engaged; his nephew seemed steady enough, and could stay; as for the wedding, it might as well take place whenever anyone liked. Fred spoke absently, being in some dejection; he missed Harry Larkin and didn't know what to put on where. Mary was getting very managing. He would miss Johnny when he went back to school. There didn't seem much else to do but drive the delivery cart. As for HC, he had jumped to his feet on discovery and made his declaration, but admitted that he hadn't intended to speak quite yet.

⋆ ⋆ ⋆

The wedding itself having been arranged for mid-October and Cecily herself having sewed diligently for it, there presently arose a contretemps. One night, with the Marylebone Road muddy and dark after autumn rain, a knock came to the back door, which was situated near the pony's stable. Outside stood a woman of perhaps thirty, a trifle stout, carrying a small portmanteau and a bundle circumspectly wrapped in a grey knitted shawl. The

bundle presently revealed dark curls covering its head like snail-shells, eyes somewhat too close together, a nose that would become rather long and, already, a determined little infant's mouth. He was in fact the double of HC. Mary stared accusingly: of course, she and nobody else had gone down to the door.

"I want my rights, that's all," stated the woman, whose name, as might have been predicted, proved to be Nellie. Taken inside, as it was raining hard, Nellie was given a seat to nurse the baby while HC was sent for from upstairs. Meantime Nellie admitted that she had been the cook at the Yorkshire school; something terrible, the food there had been, worse than most; nobody could have made anything of it. HC, arriving downstairs, admitted that the whole thing was true. He hadn't, he admitted modestly, been given to such things as a rule, but conditions in general had required some relief. Nellie made excellent toast and dripping by habit in the gloomy cellar behind the school's official kitchen. It had all been perfectly private: nobody else knew.

"*He* knew the way I was before he left, because I told him myself," said Nellie, refreshed with tea. She proffered a nipple to The Stranger, who sucked vigorously. Interrogated, it turned out, to Mary's relief, that Nellie was married, but that her man had gone off to sea years ago and had never come back. Mary thought swiftly of Cecily, upstairs sewing by lamplight. She oughtn't to be told, and yet she ought. It was difficult to know what to do. HC, as usual, took the initiative.

"If we give you some money and a character, you can find work easily in London, Nell," he said kindly. "*He'll* have to be put in an orphanage where they can look after him. You wouldn't get a situation otherwise, and he can't stay here."

Mary echoed that The Stranger could most certainly not stay. She permitted mother and child to remain in the stables for the night, on some straw; Nellie wasn't very grateful and said Mrs Angell was hard, they all were, it was a hard world. Next day she departed with her reference. Mary had meantime decided

to tell Cecily, if not Fred; Fred wouldn't know what to make of it.

Cecily proved adamant; the episode shook her far less than it had done her mother. "Where have they put the baby?" she asked. Mary replied with some sharpness that The Stranger would be put in an institution where he would be reared, moderately educated and taught a trade. "It shouldn't be necessary to tell you such things," she said. "The best thing is to break off the engagement. I dare say you're disappointed, dear, but a man who would behave in that way isn't worth marrying; you're far better by yourself, getting on with your nice embroidery."

Cecily was white-faced; she had not previously stood up to her mother. "I said I would marry HC, and I will," she said.

"What? A girl like you, brought up as a lady and *this* — "

"If I can't marry HC, I'll leave home and be a governess. You did that to Theodora. HC told me about it. I'd rather get married." Cis's eyes filled with tears; all that sewing, and the hopes she'd

had! It shouldn't come to nothing; HC was somewhere in the house, perhaps down at the shop. She wouldn't abandon him, or he her. Mama didn't know everything she thought she did.

"You haven't any notion of the kind of life a governess leads, treated like dirt," Mary bridled. She was outraged; what a way for a girl to speak to her mother! But Cis proved obstinate, even to tears, and merely kept saying she would marry HC or else leave home. In the end, after a promise extracted from HC that he would not err in such ways again, Mary was, in a manner, reconciled.

* * *

HC and Cecily Angell were married in a prim understated ceremony at the church Cecily frequented on Sundays, with few guests present and the bride in a grey bonnet and pelisse she had made herself. Afterwards HC signed himself in the register Horace Cicero Angell-Trevelyan, by arrangement with his bride, who thought it excellent. Mary and Fred had not been consulted, and

neither, of course, had Johnny.

Mr and Mrs Angell-Trevelyan journeyed to Epping for a brief stay, then returned quietly, HC to take up his duties again in the shop. If events had already taken place which were to split the firm of Angell into two halves, nobody, not even Mary, guessed it as yet. The customers were glad to see the return of HC, whom they had meantime missed for his solid presence and his self-appointed slicing of ham; and the special line had already sold exceedingly well, perhaps out of sentiment. In fact, business was picking up.

* * *

Cecily began to entertain Hopes almost as soon as she and HC had returned from Epping, where everything had no doubt been set on foot on the wedding night. Less notice was taken of the pending event than might otherwise have been the case, as everyone was meantime exercised over the ungrateful behaviour of Alec, who having walked out without serving proper notice had had the impertinence

to set up a stall of his own on the Chiswick Road; nobody had had time yet to enquire further. Meantime Cis, in her placid way, gave up glueing shells, learned housekeeping, and began knitting herself a pélérine on the advice of somebody at church. This was a comprehensive garment in mulberry-coloured wool which covered the shoulders and waist, kept one warm, and boasted a pattern of small woollen protuberances among which one more would hardly be noticed. It was to last for the many years Cis bore, one after the other, a surprisingly pretty daughter and then, after an inexplicable interval, a posse of fine upstanding sons only one of whom turned out to be weak in his wits. They named the daughter Emily after HC's mother; Mary was slightly offended. It was as though she herself was no longer of any importance. It was almost irritating to see how quickly Cis changed from a useless and ladylike creature to a good practical housekeeper and manager of the linen. One thing HC never permitted his wife to do was serve in the shop, and this seclusion became almost the only echo of Cecily's

former life. On Sundays, bonneted and pélérined, leaning on the arm of HC in his best suit of clothes and tall hat, she would duly attend church, piloting an increasing number of handsome small boys with hair varying from brown through apricot to very fair indeed, like Freddy's. Freddy Angell was the eldest son, the best beloved, the one allowed to do things the rest were not; it was tacitly assumed by everyone that he would better himself. Meantime a subtle change came over the Angell household, heralded by the advent of HC's sister Theodora, evidently freed from governessing. She brought, however, an enchanting eight-year-old charge with her from a world none of them yet knew; Lady Rose Purslove, only daughter of the Earl of Quayle.

* * *

Mary Angell had of course demurred at the prospect of having one more inmate in the house, let alone two. If Cis was going on the way she was, they would have to build on soon. However it was implied at the beginning that Theodora's

visit would be short; nobody expected her to stay on and on the way she did. Mary, or rather Cis by then, had arranged for a truckle bed to be placed in the attic room for the Earl's daughter, beside the iron bedstead, already to be found there, for Theodora. It wasn't very grand, but if they didn't like it they could leave. It had formerly in fact been slept in by Alec Frame, but the increasing prosperity of his roadside stall made his very name unmentionable now; also, Cis at the time was again in a state of imminent parturition, on that occasion with Mike. Grandfather Fred Angell was as usual no help; asked if he hadn't remembered about Theodora, he merely said he hadn't. "Well, I don't like it at all happening for Johnny's sake," said Mary mysteriously. This remark could not have referred to the charms of Theo, for she had none: a thin upright close-eyed spinster, who said very little and could add up accounts with suspicious ease. The fact that she took this job away from Mary was softened by the timely offer she made to educate Johnny at home, to save expense. This was agreed, and left more

time for Johnny to help with deliveries as he liked to do. It was fortunate, as Fred had lately more than once fallen asleep over the reins and the horse, like General Montcalm's, had brought him home.

* * *

Theodora Trevelyan-Angell — of course she took the name as well — had so marked a talent for mathematics that she had survived the customary rigours of governessing early on and had procured a number of posts less humiliating than usual, latterly with the children of peers of the realm. Once these latter entities, or their wives, took one look at Miss Theodora it was clearly evident that nobody would want to seduce her and nobody, not even themselves, would manage to bully her; it was in fact like trying to make a dent in a stone surface with one's thumb. Theodora had, in fact, no affection for anyone except her brother, whose fortunes she would continue to promote to the utmost of her considerable powers. Lord Quayle, a widowed recluse devoted to his library

and anxious to see as little as possible of his two children, had suited her very well indeed and she him; they would dine together each evening in complete silence, which the Earl found restful. His late Countess, being inbred, had been given to hysterical spasms during the marital act and the ensuing one of giving birth, during which last-named process she had died. The whole disturbance had been such that, despite the efforts of every unattached female in the county to entrap the noble widower immediately after the funeral, nothing of the kind happened again or ever would. The heir was not very bright, but adequate for the purpose at fourteen years old; as for the small Lady Rose, she was all and more than an afterthought should be; curls, dimples, large blue eyes, and a nature initially fractious but, by now, resembling refined West Indian sugar under Theodora's grim care. Theodora knew a good thing when she met it. Lady Rose seldom spoke by now, but smiled always; even Mary, sourly admitting the pair at last to the attic room, gave vent to the opinion that her young ladyship

was a little love, to be sure. Lady Rose made no complaint about the truckle bed, for she never complained nowadays about anything; and that night and other nights slept as sweetly as a cherub, disturbing nobody either late or early. At lesson times she and Johnny shared the kitchen table, presided over by Theodora in her plain dark gown, on which the Earl had permitted her to keep the braid trimmings, less as a sign of trust than of the fact that he had never noticed that they were there in the first place.

HC himself was as devoted to his sister as she was to him. If he wanted advice on any matter it was to Theo he went, never Cis; Cis, busy with her appointed tasks one way and another, and having an unsuspicious mind, did not realise the situation till it was too late. She consoled herself by admitting that she had never after all been very clever; she had been lucky to marry HC; if *he* was happy, that was the main point. "You ought to assert yourself," said Mary, but Cecily was not by nature assertive. The state of affairs became accepted; Theodora stayed, and nobody questioned

her fiats, issued with all the command of a schoolteacher released from bondage.

Mary was no longer in any case a paramount influence at Angells. For one thing her sight was beginning to be bad; she found herself fumbling between tea and coffee and once mixed them up together in the weighing-machine; this episode reduced her privately to angry tears. Wisely, in view of HC's superior capacities in such ways, she had allowed him more say in ordering, packing and selling than had originally been intended. By now, it could be said that he had taken over the shop. Again, Fred was no help; leaving the deliveries more and more to Johnny, he mostly slumbered upstairs in an armchair prudently covered some years previously with holland. "It's Johnny's business," Mary would say fretfully. "He'll be the owner one day, or should be." But Fred showed no interest in this oblique reference to his own demise, and meantime a thing happened to strengthen the hand of the Trevelyan-Angells.

* * *

The premises next door, which happened to be a haberdasher's, were suddenly announced to be for sale owing to the undoubted age of the owner. The sale had not yet been advertised, and the old woman, quavering, came round to consult HC and fortunately met Theodora. Working it out quickly in her mathematical mind, Theo decided that it might be possible to touch the Earl for a small loan. She knew exactly what to write. "It will pay off," she remarked to HC, "in increased business; there's no doubt it is a *chance*." The thought of Alec along the road, now in possession of a cover for his stall against the rain by means of increased carriage-custom, caused HC to reflect; besides, Cis was expecting again. "It'll impress the customers," he said cautiously. Theodora knew that it was in order to write to Quayle, and did so at once, with a report of the excellent health and progress of Lady Rose. Great Quayle, without children — the heir was at Harrow — was a peaceful place; his lordship no doubt wanted it to remain so, and would almost certainly help out to this end.

3

LADY ROSE PURSLOVE had never been as happy in her life as during the time she spent with Miss Trevelyan's relations in Marylebone. It was all quite different from the gloomy Tudor pile, with an earlier abbot's tower behind it which was said to be haunted, and a chapel where certain ancestors' remains were appallingly manifest, that she had lately left; and from her father, who she never saw if the latter could help it. To do him justice, Lady Rose had, before the advent of Miss Theodora, been a wailing nuisance, prone to incontinence and nightmares. The governess had applied certain time-honoured remedies, and over a very few years had somehow produced a silent and presentable little girl. Nevertheless in Lady Rose's recollection there still writhed certain memories; the great-grandfather who had been so convinced that he would be buried alive at eighty

years old that he had instructed a glass dome to be inserted in the lid of his coffin after death so that any moisture would be seen condensing on the inner glass; fortunately the coffin itself, which had by the same instruction to be left unburied for a hundred years, reposed in the chapel at too high a level for anyone to gaze down at the unsavoury contents; but imagination was perhaps worse. All of it had been relayed to Rose, at the age of seven, by an upper housemaid who had been employed, and her mother before her, long enough at Quayle to remember a great many things either witnessed or experienced. The old lord in the glass-domed coffin had been the husband of poor Lady Em, and hadn't been kind to her; and this interested Rose, as Lady Em's portrait, in the becoming garb of the late eighteenth century, reposed in one of the draughtier corridors upstairs and greatly resembled Rose herself. The child had in fact developed a habit of staring at it for so long that even the Earl noticed, and presently applied to Mrs Udney's Agency for a suitable governess. Theodora had come, and apart from

relieving the unpleasant tedium of the only other company Rose ever had, that of her brother when home for the holidays, she managed to fill her young charge's mind with other things to the exclusion of Lady Emmeline Purslove, who had died young and who for some reason was never otherwise spoken about by the family. Theodora also, and this was an achievement of which she need not have been as proud, procured the dismissal of the gossiping upper housemaid, who had departed with weeping and gnashing of teeth.

Accordingly, it was now a joy, when lessons were over, to ride round with everyone's full permission in the delivery-cart with Johnny Angell. Johnny was always kind to her, quite differently from her brother who had used to pinch Rose's arms or pull her hair to divert himself. Johnny even allowed her to hold the reins while he delivered boxes and even, sometimes, to drive the pony. If Rose had known, the sight of her exquisite little face, bright hair curling beneath its velvet bonnet, white lace stockings and tiny kid slippers perched on the

box, glimpsed from door to door by increasingly contented customers, was enough to raise the status of Angells to quite a degree. Well-heeled persons began to call at the shop itself and to leave orders, including an eccentric viscountess who preferred to choose her own groceries.

Johnny himself was devoted to his small companion; it was better than having a dog. He had in fact made up his mind to marry Lady Rose when they were both old enough. It was true that she was an earl's daughter and he himself only a grocer's heir; but although Johnny already knew of the prevailing upper-class objections to any kind of alliance with trade — his mother had warned him in a general way already — there should, in some way, he was determined, be a straightening out of odds in that respect in proper course. Once HC had been somehow removed — this prospect was not immediate or even, one had to admit, very likely — and had moved on somewhere else, he, Johnny, would come into his rightful inheritance. In the meantime, it was a matter of pleasing

everybody, and Johnny was good at this. He also imbibed what instruction was available from Miss Theodora: it would come in handy, and he didn't miss school one bit. He was by now again a healthy, handsome, fresh-faced boy, still too thin, but having shed the temporary delicacy left by measles and the adverse effects of his mother's undue pampering. Johnny knew what he wanted from life and assumed, meantime, that he would get it.

One day, driving back along the Chiswick road, he and Rose had espied a loaded barrow and a nearby covered stall. Behind the stall was Alec, whom Johnny remembered clearly. The barrow was selling toffee apples separately. Rose expressed a desire for one, very sweetly; Johnny handed her the reins, leaped out, and purchased, out of his day's tips, one for her and another for himself. The two young creatures bit with relish into the white flesh of the fruit through the sticky outer layer, which shortly left Lady Rose's face in a brown mess round her pretty little mouth. Johnny took out his handkerchief — his mother gave him

a clean one every day — spat on it, and carefully wiped Rose's face clean. "Otherwise, Miss T will scold you," he remarked protectively. Rose smiled on like a cherub. It was the first toffee apple she had ever eaten or guessed at. Life with Johnny was great fun.

From his stall, Alec Frame the erstwhile assistant at Angells watched them sourly. Trade was picking up, and he kept a boy now at the barrow for odds and ends; but he had married a wife, too soon as it turned out, or perhaps not soon enough. One way and another, Alec was disgruntled; it disturbed him to see the two children happy.

"Remember me, I s'pose," he had said grudgingly to Johnny after the apples were paid for. Johnny said he did. "You used to work for us," he added pleasantly. "You went away while I had measles. I'm better now."

Alec's unrelieved aspect informed him, for he was a sensitive boy, that his own concerns were not of as immediate interest to everyone as they were to his mother. "Doing all right?" he enquired kindly of Alec. The other shrugged.

"More or less, s'pose. Got married, though; should've waited, maybe. Two to feed costs more than one, and now there's three," he added with evident depression.

Johnny showed interest; it sounded exactly like Cis and HC. "Is it a boy?" he asked. Cis generally had boys. Alec reached sideways and spat, as a routine measure.

"Naow," he said. A boy would have meant some hope. As it was, the wife, who'd been able to help for nothing earlier on, had to feed the little rat, now three months old, and stay at home, saying she still didn't feel up to anything. As for the rat, it howled all night. They'd called it Belle, for no apparent reason."

"Perhaps it'll be a boy next time," said Johnny encouragingly. "My sister had a little boy last year and — " He choked back the statement that there might shortly be another; Cis was wearing the mulberry cape again. Ma said it wasn't proper to mention such things, even to another man. He nodded farewell to Alec, got into the trap once more, and he and Rose drove off, the latter

beaming angelically. Johnny thought the name Rose Angell would suit her very well. It would be necessary, of course, to make enough money to keep her in pretty clothes like she was wearing now. That kind of thing needed strict attention to business, which he himself was prepared to apply. Pleasant manners were a part of it, such as looking cheerful when delivering heavy goods at the door. Three people today had tipped him half a crown, which as a result had meant he could afford the toffee apples; but in future he supposed he'd better save up.

He turned to Rose, to clinch matters. "I think you're awfully pretty," he said shyly. "When we're old enough, I'd like to marry you, if you think that's a good idea. It wouldn't be for some time." His handsome face had flushed a little. Rose's smile reached her eyes, and she nodded. It would be fun to go on driving with Johnny in the cart, all her life; and never again have to go into the chapel where great-grandfather lay blowing bubbles under his glass dome, unless perhaps she would have to be married in there; but as long as Johnny

was with her she wouldn't mind.

"Don't say anything to Miss Theodora," Johnny told her prudently. Rose promised not to, still smiling, and the old pony clop-clopped on his worn shoes back again towards Marylebone.

* * *

Mary Angell toiled upstairs one day to find Fred absently stuffing shirts into a Gladstone bag. She stared incredulously; it was unlike him to undertake any activity at all, especially these days.

"What are you doing?" she said sharply. Fred did not look round; she stared at his bald head, surrounded by the fringe of apricot hair. Some of the grandchildren had it, especially Emily; but on her it was pretty. Fred had a dejected look; he always had had, come to think. He did not answer at once.

"I'm going home," he told her. "To Ireland."

Mary's mind whirled. "You can't do that," she said: she was aware that he had relations there, but they never wrote. "What d'you want to go to Ireland for?

You've got a good home here." She heard her voice rising in the shrill way it often had nowadays; with one thing and another, there was a lot to put up with. Fred closed the bag with a snap; he'd forgotten his slippers, however; Mary could see them lying by the bed. The fact heartened her; he'd never manage by himself for five minutes.

"I'm coming with you," she said firmly. The back of Fred's head looked, if possible, more dejected than ever; he drooped like a wilting stem left out of water.

"There's no need," he told her dully. "Better stay to keep an eye on Johnny."

Mary's conscience tore at her, but after all, as she swiftly calculated, Johnny by now could pretty well manage for himself; Fred couldn't, and never would. She wasted no more time in words, but made him sit down, clutching his bag with the slippers now included, and herself packed a few things; she didn't need much, a nightgown or two, caps, stockings; no need for a spare gown, they'd be back soon. "We'll be back," she said loudly to reassure herself and, if it was needed,

Fred, who did not reply. They left by the noon mail; neither HC, his sister, nor Johnny asked any questions. Now she thought of it, everything would go on perfectly well at Angells without her. There hadn't even been time to take a last look at the shop.

* * *

Fred's relations lived on a farm in County Wexford, where they had been since the seventeenth century; they made Mary and also Fred, who had been sick on the crossing, extremely welcome in the hospitable Irish way. There were more relations living up in the hills a few miles off, including some who remembered the last grandmother recurring on the Fiske side; she had been very beautiful and had been known as the Belle of the Ball. Her name had been Sarah. Mary took in this information in a dazed fashion, drank the good Irish tea, and surveyed a framed early photograph of Fred's parents on their wedding day; the bride wore a pork-pie hat and the groom looked solemn, as befitted the

occasion. Beyond the farm was a pleasant countryside where primroses grew in the lanes, also a bog and a field which was the family graveyard. Mary found none of the attention to business which pertained of late years in Marylebone since the brisk arrival of HC; everything here was slow and peaceful, and nobody asked how long they were going to stay. She wrote home an account to Cis of all of it, asked at last for her own second-best gown to be sent across, and sent her love to Johnny and the grandchildren. She was still in a slight daze at the way everything had turned out; Fred didn't often think of things for himself. There was one respect in which HC missed his mother-in-law. Mary Angell had been an excellent maker of all kinds of jam; it was not that the firm had hitherto sold much of the home-made variety on its shelves, most self-respecting households continuing to make their own. However, with the departure at last of the elderly haberdasher and the resulting expansion of the premises made possible by the Earl's loan, wider horizons were contemplated, including even the sale of wines and spirits. A licence for the latter

was obtained with ease, again through the Earl's quiet influence; such matters operate in unseen ways, and although it would not have been becoming to have the Purslove name associated with trade in any open way, it could be admitted among the Angells themselves that Lord Quayle was by now virtually a partner. As regarded jam, this had in fact been the notion of young Johnny, who still occasionally raised his voice after the departure of his mother.

Johnny had several times noticed, on his forays for toffee apples on the Chiswick road, jars of marmalade being sold rather unsuccessfully at the covered stall. On the day he and Rose had last stopped there it had been raining, and the drips had settled drearily on the lids of the half-protected goods through an unforeseen leak in the tarpaulin. Johnny had thought at the time that it was a pity, and wondered in any case what they did about the marmalade at night; probably they had taken home any of it that remained unsold, it being difficult to lock the stall successfully against marauders.

"Why," he said in his innocent way

one day to HC, "don't you come to some arrangement with Alec? You could sell the marmalade in the shop to keep it dry."

HC grunted that they didn't have much truck with Alec Frame after his behaving as he had. Theodora however pricked up her ears. "Why not ask him?" she said to her brother. HC grunted again; he was by nature conservative and preferred to bank his assets. "Johnny can do it, then," he assented grudgingly, "but don't let 'em make a favour of it at that rate."

Alec however showed no signs of doing anything else. "What you stoppin' here for again?" he greeted Johnny sourly. "You stay away and mind your own business." There were reasons for his lack of too much joy in living; by now, a depressed-looking woman stood beside him again at the stall, with a small, skinny and rather dirty child clinging to her skirts with one hand and picking its nose with the other. Johnny smiled his radiant smile; might as well cheer everyone up.

"We'd like to come to an arrangement

about the marmalade," he said pleasantly. "I noticed the other day that it was getting wet. It'd save you carting it home at night if I took it and sold it for you at the shop, that is if you'd agree."

Phyll Frame — nobody ever knew her very well — spoke up shrilly. "For Gawd's sake let 'em," she said. "I'm sick of carrying the stuff back and forth, and 'er to mind as well." She looked down with malevolence at the nose-picking child, and slapped it. "I told yer not to do that in public, Belle," she said. "Do as you're bid." Belle promptly set up a howl. Alec, almost shuddering away from his spouse and offspring, gave in, not too easily.

"No discount, mind," he said. Johnny bought two jars at customer's price — HC would disapprove, and so would Miss Theodora, but something might be arranged later if the whole enterprise worked out — and took them home. He put one on the family breakfast table, it was sampled and pronounced to be good, and the other sold in the shop at once. Thereafter HC himself called at Chiswick and contrived to beat Alec down a trifle;

multum in parvo, as he announced unarguably at the beginning. It was also the beginning of an Arrangement. The marmalade was to be collected, by Johnny in the cart, at Alec's modest one up, one down in Brixton; a regular order received its agreed price; sugar would be sold to the Frames at cost; and Alec's stall was to discontinue sales of that particular commodity. This, as it happened, suited everyone very well. Bee became quite fond of Johnny, who never took Rose as far as Brixton. Once or twice Phyll invited him upstairs for a cup of tea. He played with the small Belle agreeably, as he would have played with any child. Had he been able to see into the future, nothing would have induced him to enter the house. Meantime, Phyll Frame progressed to strawberry, greengage and plum, all to be sold under the agreed Angell label. It was almost as if the two establishments had become one, except that Alec and HC never did get on. Phyll began to indulge in dreams. She knew she couldn't have any more children. As for Alec, he consoled himself by operating a baked potato brazier whose products sold

hotly in winter. It saved carting anything home; the brazier was easy to lock up at night, and nobody in any case was going to break in for the mere sake of a possible cold potato.

* * *

Rose was not permitted to go out quite so often nowadays with Johnny in the cart; Miss Theodora used various excuses to keep her at home. The girl was growing into a pretty young thing, almost nubile, and it had occurred to the prudent former governess that the Earl might well withdraw his subsidies from her brother's business if it became evident that there was any possible entanglement of another kind. Also, she was determined that HC, rather than Johnny, should prosper; Johnny could remain the errand-boy as long as he chose. Meantime the Angell sign, newly gilded as to *Groacers* in the spelling of Walpole's day, and with a flying angel above it, waved invitingly on the fitful breeze of a Marylebone spring. More and better customers stopped their carriages to enter the new, refurbished

premises, with their alluring jars of jam and other delights, and good Mr Angell — the Trevelyan had gradually disappeared — amiably and reliably slicing his excellent ham and exchanging predictable remarks about the weather. Besides, nobody could purchase the kind of goods sold here without going much further into town, paying more for the look of the thing, and encountering rival horse-traffic.

* * *

It was as well that Johnny had the growing interest of promoting jam sales and enjoying the occasional cup of tea at Brixton. Various events were set on foot about then which were to change, disturb, and grieve his young life. In the first place, a concatenation of events, of the kind which can only occur in these islands and almost baffled the College of Heralds, suddenly caused Lord Quayle notably to increase his substance; in fact, he became almost unique. There had only been one Duke Marquis before, in Scotland at the turn of the recent century; and now

the former Earl was another, shortly to become known, by those few persons who had much acquaintance with him, as the DM. This meant that his unworthy son fell heir to the former title of Quayle. Unfortunately the young man did not long enjoy it; on return from Harrow, and being about to take up an unwanted residence at Trinity for the usual obscure purposes, he went out, in late autumn, to the hunting-field. No more than anything else in his life did he enjoy hunting, and it was a part of the irony of things that his not particularly mettlesome horse bucked at a stone wall and promptly threw its rider, breaking his neck. Lady Rose, accordingly, became a person of great importance and was sent for at once, not only to attend her brother's funeral.

She and Johnny parted with tears and kisses, promises to write, soon to be together again, and other such fondly expressed hopes, watched somewhat cynically by Theodora Angell-Trevelyan, who had made her own plans. Deep in mourning blacks, the woman and the young girl travelled by closed carriage to Great Quayle, where the few relatives

left alive were duly assembled and the DM had for once emerged from his library. Beside him, near poor Quayle's coffin, stood a tall cold-eyed young man in correct blacks. He proved to be a second cousin and the nearest heir to the title after Rose's demise. His mother, a fearsome dowager, was present also, her eye firmly fixed on the DM; at one point it swivelled to focus briefly on Rose, then on her son, then back again. The funeral took place, in the chapel; afterwards, Rose was discovered to be missing when everyone had assembled in the erstwhile solar, which was panelled in oak from the time of Henry VIII, to drink marsala and condole in general terms. Rose was searched for, and finally discovered standing on top of a pile of kneelers which she had purposefully dragged from their places behind the chapel pews, gazing down at last on her long-dead ancestor beneath his glass dome. On being rather roughly pulled down, already white-faced, the pile of kneelers collapsed too soon and Rose sprained her ankle. It could not, Miss Theodora assured herself, have turned

out more fortunately. There was now no question of Rose's returning with her to Marylebone, the girl being laid meantime on a striped sofa with a carved mahogany head, her ankle bandaged after being steeped first in very hot, then in very cold, water. On being addressed, she had silently turned her head aside to be sick. The dowager was in charge of her.

"No," said Miss Theodora firmly aloud, "there can be no question, I fear, of my remaining. I am essential to my brother's business, and must return immediately." It was quite true that HC would be hard put to do without her; he was solid, but hardly constructive except for providing Cis with more and more sons to help, in due course, in the shop; but it was early days yet for that. The dowager expressed polite regrets, Miss Theodora was seen off, and Rose was left in a place she hated, with people she did not know and of whom she was already afraid; and there was the memory of what she'd briefly seen under the glass dome. It would have been much better not to try to look.

It was, in fact, the last expression of independence Rose ever made. Her ankle having recovered, the dowager thereafter did not spare her the rod. Nor did that lady fail — she never failed in anything — in becoming the Duchess Marchioness at last, but that could, in the nature of things, produce no tangible result. In fact, Rose found, to her horror, that she herself was to sleep beneath the embroidered tester in the master bedroom with her new stepmother, who guarded her thereafter every instant of the day and night, the DM having returned to his library, in the cataloguing of which he was by now ably assisted — everything the young man did was able — by Leonard Purslove, the dowager's only son and fervent hope from the beginning. Leonard had never disappointed his mother, and had been educated carefully for his position; his cold prudent nature was an echo of her own. It would not be necessary to bring Lady Rose out, or in fact to let her be seen very much beyond the purlieus of Great Quayle by anyone who might take a fancy to her.

As far as that went, the dowager shortly

purloined a letter Rose had somehow written, while unsupervised. *Dear Johnny, I hate everyone here, I wish I was back with you in the cart. Love, Rose.* Stern measures were used to prevent a repetition, and any return messages from this Johnny were confiscated and never delivered; as a result Johnny himself, pining in Marylebone between increasing cups of tea, thought Rose had forgotten him, and grew bitter; he played more and more with little Belle in Brixton. She was by no means growing into an attractive child, but was better than nothing; someone had to fill his empty heart, and his mother was still in Ireland and hardly ever wrote, except to tell her Johnny to be sure to mind the shop, as it ought to be his one day.

Time passed, and in the newspapers there was at last an announcement, not of Lady Rose's betrothal, but of her recent marriage, to her cousin Leonard Purslove, privately at Quayle: the marriage of a pale and spiritless girl of sixteen, all resistance long beaten and bullied out of her; all it meant was that, on the night of the wedding, the old woman didn't come

into bed and Leonard did. Rose was uninstructed as to what happened next, and regarded it, then and later, with a horrified loathing that caused the entire household to assume that she was beginning to resemble her late mother. However this state of affairs was shortly discovered to be due to her condition. Leonard had continued to perform his duties coldly, by day in the library and by night upon his young wife, to whom he never by any chance spoke during the process. It was a fitting conclusion that, less than a year later, a further notice appeared in the papers; Lady Rose Purslove had died in childbirth at Great Quayle. The child was a son, was doing well, and would inherit. His grandmother would bring him up in her own way, with the result that he turned out, at least superficially, to resemble his father.

Meantime poor Rose's remains had been laid beside those of the glass-domed ancestor down in the family crypt. The hundred years had not quite passed, and in fact added up to only ninety-nine; but the DM's lady, who by now

ordered everything, decided that it would save expense to have a double funeral and, by now, really ought to do. In the coffin closeby lay Lady Emmeline Purslove, who had endured almost the same experiences, though not quite, as her young descendant.

For some days, after that, Johnny Angell at Marylebone went about delivering his parcels red-eyed. He never spoke of Rose again; after all, she had betrayed him. From then on he lost a certain fresh appealing innocence he had had, and instead became one of life's failures; whatever he might do in the future, somebody would get the better of him; but this Johnny did not yet know.

* * *

All this time Belle Frame was growing up; she was one of the minor creations that attain an early maturity. She had stopped picking her nose in public but still did so in the lavatory. She would never be pretty, but had a certain sexual attraction, chiefly odour, very early. Johnny was unconscious of it, but others were not; in

fact, by now Belle was commonly referred to as the Golden Wonder because her father's baked potatoes were achieving a notable commercial success. Most suitors were however discouraged; it had been privately agreed by Belle's parents, if as yet by nobody else, that it would be an excellent thing if, in time, she and young Johnny Angell should make a match of it. "It'll run things together, after all," said Phyll. Alec said nothing. His words were, as a rule, few. The only danger, as Phyll then put it, was that meantime young Johnny might meet somebody else. The matter, therefore, was shortly mooted, not this time to HC but to Johnny himself, with certain sub-clauses relative to the Chiswick stance. "You want to keep your end up," Phyll told him; they had become almost matey over the years and cups of tea.

Johnny said he would think it over. He felt no enthusiasm; Belle wasn't a little thing any more and he wasn't attracted to her as she was now, but then he couldn't seem to feel much interest in girls. "It'll come when you marry," Phyll assured him. When he was twenty-five and Belle

much less, there was some kind of formal engagement. After that it was difficult to get out of it; they were married in due course. Part of the reason, from Johnny's point of view, was that by then the preponderance of HC and his sons was becoming hard to bear, not to mention the unvarying bossiness of HC's sister Theodora. He and Belle somehow fitted into the enlarged Marylebone house. By then, there was a new coachman.

Part Two

1

"IT'S all very well for you, Freddy," expostulated the latter's immediate junior, Mike Angell, bitterly. "You're at school at Westminster being turned into a gent. Later on you say you want to go to Woolwich to be turned into an officer. If all that's to be afforded it means the rest of us are supposed to serve in the shop. It isn't going to be me, I can tell you. If Papa won't run to Dartmouth for me, I'll go to sea as an A.B. as soon as I'm fourteen."

His jaw, already strong, set firmly beneath the head of dark brown curly hair inherited from HC; not all the sons had turned out apricot. Freddy, the blue-eyed eldest, his hair blond as an angel's, stretched his long graceful limbs idly, lifted his classic profile in the air and pretended not to hear. Mike was always going on like that, talking of going off to sea as a common sailor. If he wanted to, let him; there were plenty of others

left at home. Freddy, home himself at the week's end from his present status as an Oppidan at Westminster, to and from which the Angell carriage conveyed him daily, somewhat to his discontent as he would much rather have boarded with the other fellows and not come back, raised his celestial gaze to where his mother and only sister Emily sat side by side, sewing grey calico to clothe the heathen. Freddy saw no reason for this activity. He was unaffected by religion despite the efforts of the choir tutor and others at Westminster, and saw no reason why the heathen should have their brown bodies hidden after a great deal of unnecessary work: they looked better as they were, at least one supposed so. When he, Mike and Raph were alone in their shared bedroom upstairs above the newly built wing, they would caper about naked and survey themselves in the glass, Freddy with open satisfaction. His broad shoulders, slim waist, fair unblemished flesh and tall height made him a young Achilles, most suitable later on for The Shop, as those in the know already called Her Majesty's Royal Military Academy,

Woolwich. There had never been any question of Freddy's appearing in the shop here. He was his mother's pet, perhaps also his father's secret pride, and knew it. Even now, Cecily's glance flew up from the dreary calico to survey this godlike being she and HC had created together, long ago at Epping. The rest had her mild and dutiful affection, and Emily had certainly turned out very well. Emily's apricot head, arranged in symmetrical curls on either side a neat white parting, was bent now uncomplainingly over the sewing task, her busy hands — they were a better shape than her mother's, less large, and had never turned purple — making commendably even stitches in the long dull seam. Emily always did as she was told and never asked questions. She was, accordingly, restful company and Cis was glad of any; the boys were usually busy with their own concerns, except of course poor Horace; and Horace's father was, as a rule, closeted with his sister Theodora over accounts. Cis was aware of a very faint pang of a kind that had assailed her now and again over the years, despite all

wifely resignation. She consoled herself, as always, with the thought of her children; after all, Theodora hadn't any. The sight of poor Horry, dragging his hobby-horse aimlessly round and round the floor, staring at nothing, however brought Cis up short. Horry was her only failure, not quite as he ought to be. She'd been getting on, after all, when he was born; perhaps that was it. The rest were healthy, handsome and a credit to her. After Freddy's birth — of course the eldest had had to be named for dear Papa — a fellow-worker in the calico-for-heathens ladies' group at church had suggested prettily to Cis that as the boys' surname would be Angell in any case, the rest, expected to follow in natural course, could perhaps be called after the four Archangels if HC agreed? There had, accordingly, since then been Michael, Gabriel, Raphael in undisputed order; but when it came to Uriel HC put his foot down. No poor child, he said, could be saddled for life with a name like that; certainly not any child of his. This raised a dilemma, but by good fortune one of the regular customers in the shop, apprised

of the situation, informed everyone that when she had travelled in Germany some years before she had visited a church, and inside had been a marble angel blowing a trumpet, called Jeremiel: the name had been gilded underneath. This was thought satisfactory, and Mike, Raph, Gaby and Jerry grew up healthy and active little boys, the hopes of the firm. As for Horry, he would have to be looked after for life.

Cis looked at her ultimate disaster again and realised that the dragging sound of his hobby-horse was beginning to tell on her nerves. She had opened her mouth to ask him to stop when HC himself, in grey side-whiskers and growing a trifle paunchy these days, came through the doorway, looking grave. He had a letter in his hand bordered in black.

"What is it, my love?" asked Cis gently. She had a sudden picture of them as they both were now, especially on Sundays going to church: HC, his legs looking a trifle short by contrast under the tall hat, his stomach prosperous and ponderous under his watch-chain; and

herself, surprisingly unchanged in figure after it all, tall and still slim except for rather more bosom, with her grey hair carefully curled under a lace cap, and her gloves and shoes of the finest kid, a lady's. It was what dear Mama had tried to make of her, after all. She —

"I fear," said HC, "that it is sad news. Put down the horse, Horace. Your grandfather — " and he drew himself up with ceremonious dignity, the same used on occasion with valued customers who nevertheless showed no signs of paying their bills — "is dead in Ireland. We must all put on mourning; the younger boys may wear black bands. The shop must not reopen on Monday; the shutters will be drawn and a testimonial fixed above the door."

He handed his wife her mother's letter, which had in fact been addressed to her. Cis felt no resentment that it should have been opened and read; it was the accepted habit of husbands. Theodora, however, must have been informed of the death before herself, and she did mind that. "When is the funeral, dearest?" she asked placidly. Later she admitted that

she could hardly remember dear Papa at all; his demise had of course shocked one, but when he was at home he had after all hardly ever had anything to say and was mostly asleep. However HC would know what was to be done. "What of poor Mama?" she enquired timidly. HC did not answer at once, but stated majestically that the funeral itself was already over; Fred senior had been buried in the field adjoining the farmhouse of his maternal ancestors, the Fiskes of Leskinfere. Studying the letter, Cis informed herself that others had been buried there from, evidently, early times. Papa would not be alone.

"As for your mother," HC was beginning ponderously, but Raph, who had an independent mind and was seldom to be intimidated, spoke up.

"If the funeral's over, why shut the shop?" he demanded pertly. Raph liked the shop; he enjoyed seeing money handed over the counter and frequently helped on Saturdays, thereby learning aspects of the trade denied to Freddy, officer and gentleman. As for the black bows pinned over shop doors when their

owners died and were buried with a lot of hired mourners in black weepers and horses with nodding sable plumes, he'd seen them. There was no need for any of that. He glanced at Mike, who winked. HC looked disapproving; he would speak to Michael later.

"Suffice it that that has already been decided by persons more responsible than yourself, Raphael," he pronounced grandly. "The firm of Angell has shown constant respect to its founders over the generations. I assume that an equal respect will be shown to myself in proper course. Frederick Angell, your mother's father, must be honoured with the rest."

At this point Johnny Angell's face gaped through the door; he had learned the news from Belle, who'd been listening outside the counting-house and told him to assert himself for once. It was true that he, not HC, should have made the mourning arrangements. However it had been done by now, evidently, and there was no need to make a fuss. Johnny insinuated himself into the room, for the sake of telling Belle he had been present.

It didn't make any difference; everyone ignored him as usual.

Fred Angell, senior, lying peaceably in Irish soil, was duly honoured with black bows and drawn shutters, also the sight of all his descendants clad in black for some time. A few customers who hadn't read the papers turned up at the shop on Monday, found it closed, and went along instead to Alec Frame's potato stall, buying other goods there as well while they were at it; as a result, business there was brisk. Also, within a matter of days, and without warning, old Mary Angell came home: and that was the beginning of open war.

2

AS sometimes happens despite the increasing miseries of old age, Mary had returned from the years in Ireland refreshed. Life in the damp cottage she and Fred had finally rented on his relations' farm had certainly left her with arthritis in both knees, but she used them fiercely to climb up and down stairs once more in the enlarged version of her remembered house in Marylebone. Her temper was short these days, but on the other hand she had, during the pleasant leisurely Irish years, garnered considerable energy and had also taken some time to reflect. Her accrued wisdom she now used to assess, and if possible correct, the situation as regarded HC and his all-pervading family. It was impossible not to be fond of one's grandsons, but at the same time Mary knew them to be usurpers of what should by rights be her own son Johnny's. Cis was now beyond redemption, a placid cowlike creature

devoted to her man; even the constant presence of Theodora seemed to arouse no response in her. HC was happy, she would say, if asked, and that was all that mattered; but was it? Mary did not hesitate to ponder other aspects of the question, glaring at the obtrusive spinster whenever they met one another in the passages, on the stairs, or at meals. On one occasion Theodora went down into the counting-house to find the old lady already looking through the ledgers but, evidently, unable to find anything there about which to find fault. Mary — her hair had not yet turned grey — looked up through metal-rimmed spectacles at HC's sister with an expression that conveyed no liking.

"Well?" she said defensively, as the other remained silent. "I dare say I've as much right to look at these as anyone else. I ran Fred's affairs for more years than you can number, even yet." This was unkind, but Theodora did not flinch. No one, she remarked pacifically, was stopping Mrs Angell from looking at the books if she so chose. There was unlikely to be anything wrong with them.

"That's for me to say," Mary insisted. "It's not certain what you think you're doing here at all, miss, or ever were, and there it is."

Miss Trevelyan-Angell replied coldly that she was here at the invitation of her brother.

"Yes, and a good thing *he's* made out of all of it for you both," replied Mary with prejudice. "There's enough of them now eating their heads off out of the profits, and getting on and upwards. My son's the owner, not your brother; Johnny can take it to law if he likes, I dare say."

Theodora smiled with closed lips, knowing Johnny would never take anything to law; he hadn't the guts, to put it coarsely.

There was, moreover, the defensive alliance lately established between Johnny and Raph in the shop. Since the expansion of the premises, and the employment of the coachman for actual deliveries, two at the counter was better than one, and while Johnny was obliging by nature Raph was sharp, which made for an excellent working partnership. It

was unlikely that Johnny would agree to the removal of Raph, or that Raph would in any case agree to go; he was like a duck in water among the ham and marmalade and cheeses, knew exactly where to find everything and how much it cost, and could serve with utmost despatch. The customers however liked him less than Johnny, whom they knew of old and pitied somewhat for his openly useless marriage; and so, in such ways, the two men complemented one another and it was better not to interfere.

Mary did, however, interfere in the matter of Johnny's unwelcome wife. She had been aghast at news of the wedding, and suspicious from the moment of setting eyes on Belle, who seemed to spend her time riding back and forth in the carriage to Chiswick, dressed up as she shouldn't. Stall or no stall, that marriage hadn't brought any good to Johnny. It was too late now to undo it, but if something was wrong it should be put right by her, his mother. Johnny himself spent his evenings counting the stock, which showed he wasn't suited. She'd see about everything, when she

could; and kept an eye meantime.

Theodora had stalked off at last out of the argument over the ledgers; foiled as to any victory there, Mary closed them, and thought instead what to do about Belle. Next day, in her bonnet with its jet beads, and a small black boa, she appeared without warning at the coach-house door, demanding to ride to Chiswick. "It's time I met your ma," she said firmly to Belle, who replied sullenly that Ma wasn't there every day now, they had an assistant instead.

"Well, I'm coming just the same, and most days too," said Mary. Seated squarely at last beside the sulky Belle, she surveyed, with native suspicion, the broad back of the young coachman driving the pony. For some reason its contours reminded her strongly of HC, and Mary told herself she must be getting fanciful; it wouldn't do to imagine him in everything. Nevertheless, when the driver jumped down at Chiswick, Mary observed his face; and a memory rose of a woman standing outside the door long ago in the rain, with a recognisable bundle in a shawl. This young man was in fact so

like HC it was impossible nobody had noticed it. A sense of fury rose in Mary's upholstered bosom; one was kept out of everything, no doubt on purpose.

"Where," she asked the young driver without ceremony, "was your last place?"

The Stranger shuffled his feet, slightly intimidated by this old woman with the angry eyes and bristling bonnet; she reminded him of the matron, back where he'd come from long ago. He answered truthfully enough. He'd been in an orphanage, where they hadn't taught much book-learning. "I had a way with horses, though, and after one thing and another I came to Mr Angell, and he gave me a place." The Stranger shut his mouth firmly on the no doubt expected whinings about hoping he'd given satisfaction; that was none of the old bitch's business. The visit to Chiswick was made, Alec encountered, duly shaken hands with, and the carriage then drove home. Once there, Mary went straight to HC, who for once was not with his sister but with his wife.

Bearded, HC told all; Cis of course knew about it already. The young man

had appeared one day at the door, bearing a letter signed by Nellie before she died, saying who his father had been. "I couldn't refuse to help him," said HC defensively. "It seemed only fair to give him a chance. If I hadn't, he might have talked. It would have been bad for trade." He champed slightly at his new porcelain teeth, which fitted not too comfortably, feeling one way and another a slightly unheroic figure despite Cis' loyalty. As a rule, conveying as he did the image of a calm and benevolent paterfamilias, nothing could unnerve him; but it was true that the episode with Nellie was best left buried.

"Well, if you must have your bastard here, keep an eye on him," said Mary uncharitably. She was uncertain why she still had to nourish suspicions of the young coachman; after all, he did his job. It was only that she didn't like the way Belle had been going off alone with him, day after day. It wasn't as exciting as all that merely to go and see old Alec. At any rate — Mary grinned to herself — there'd be fewer carriage-rides to Chiswick now; the young woman knew

when she was beat.

Shortly after that, Mary caught Belle out, or as near as made no difference. A length of straw was clinging to the back of the latter's dress. There wasn't any straw, nasty stuff, in the house; it just might be out of one of the back shop packing-cases, and again it might not.

Mary kept her counsel, and soon obtained proof positive; spying constantly, she came at last upon the guilty pair, making the two-backed beast, as Rabelais puts it, in the stable-quarters. Belle screamed, sat up at once, and tried to pull down her dress; but her bodice gaped unmistakably. The Stranger, maintaining more than ever a stolid likeness to HC, refused to be abashed. "Can't say a word, can yer?" he jeered. "Bad for business, that's what it'd be." Whatever was said, the old man wouldn't refuse him a reference, perhaps even money; if so, he might go to Australia and start up on his own. They said it was a country where it didn't matter what you'd been before. The more he thought of it the better it got.

Leaving him thoughtfully fastening his

trousers, Mary marched Belle back to the house and locked her in her room, saying she would tell Johnny everything the minute he was finished in the shop. "And here you'll stay till you've had your monthly, then we'll know where we are," Mary added roundly. "If you get what you deserve, my girl, Johnny'll beat the tripes out of you, and you know it." Privately, she herself knew Johnny would do nothing of the kind.

Belle snivelled. It wasn't any good saying to this old woman that her precious son was hardly any bloody use and never would be. In fact, as she admitted presently, the monthly hadn't come in any case. They might as well know, soon as late.

"Is it Johnny's, or is it not?" demanded Mary, for the moment resembling Mrs Siddons as Clytemnestra, if it ever happened. Belle prudently said she wasn't sure.

Thereafter, with a white-faced Johnny occupying his dressing-room, the pregnancy pursued its unwholesome course and, finally and with much yelling and screaming beyond the necessary,

produced a son. He should, as Mary put it to herself, have been the heir of Angells; but now nobody would ever know one way or the other. The child resembled neither Johnny nor The Stranger, still less HC or even old Fred. It was in fact, and remained, the image of its paternal grandfather Alec Frame of the hot potato stand at Chiswick.

All of the above having been assimilated, tension hardly ceased to exist among the crowded Angell-host, as young Freddy impiously described conditions at home: and it became increasingly evident that either one side of the family or the other would have to remove itself elsewhere.

3

HC had maintained cautious relations with the DM over the years at Great Quayle. In addition to the money originally loaned but in plain fact invested in the business, the two men had the common interest of classical quotations, particularly those of Horace and Cicero. HC had from time to time absented himself briefly from the shop, leaving matters in charge of Theodora, had visited Quayle itself, and had on one glorious occasion been bidden there for the Saturday to Monday, never described as a weekend shoot. He ventured now, presuming on this closer. acquaintance, to take Cis and Emily with him, ostensibly to discuss the growing necessity of removal to other premises than Marylebone while still retaining that earlier outpost of empire.

Emily had grown remarkably pretty, as her father had noted complacently for some time. He could not clearly have

described his present intentions as other than a calculated laying of one's cards on the table. The old Duchess Marchioness was by now moribund, having after two strokes become a wordless ancient vegetable hulk looked after by nurses in her own Tudor wing, and could not, therefore, as she would without doubt otherwise have done, put a spoke in anyone's wheel. That the wheel might not begin to turn at all was possible. However, the whole thing was at least worth a try.

They set out together in the spare Angell carriage, driven by the safe middle-aged coachman who had replaced The Stranger and had a safe middle-aged wife who shared such private moments as the exercise of his duties allowed. Raph had been left in the shop with Johnny. Mary, torn between the books downstairs and the act of maintaining a hawk's eye on Belle and nasty little Alec upstairs, had no time to accompany them. Theodora was not feeling well and had gone to lie down. Freddy was already at Woolwich, Mike away at sea; they had heard from him lately in Barbados. The younger

boys were in the charge of a servant. Cis therefore, looking handsome, fulfilled and pleased, had put on her best dark-grey satin and a cap from France, with lappets. Emily, by contrast, wore a new pale-blue dress and hat with a feather which greatly became her, deepening the rather pallid colour of her eyes and flattering her apricot hair. She had been sedulously brought up, sent in the end for six months to a finishing school for young ladies newly opened in London, which was not yet too particular about admitting only the daughters of upper-class houses. In any case Emily's manners had always been naturally impeccable. Her innocent gaze surveyed the passing roads now under the blue hat's brim, while the feather waved gently with the mild unavoidable jolting of the well-sprung carriage. "Country roads are not like town ones, dear," said Cis instructively. Emily smiled gently. The sight of the countryside pleased her. Once, when she was a child, she and her elder brothers had been taken by Papa to spend a day in Sussex. She had liked the trees, the wild flowers and small scurrying animals

seen on the way, and there had been a farm where they all drank milk. Perhaps today would be something the same. It was pleasant to have Mama with them on this occasion; on the last, now one remembered, either Jerry or Horry had been born at home while they were out. Emily, like most properly brought up young women of her generation, knew nothing of the processes of birth; when one returned, there was another baby. She would very much like to have a baby of her own.

* * *

The DM received the party somewhat testily: he had not expected the women. However having taken a sighting of Emily as a damned fine girl, and being told that the two ladies would go for a drive before lunching with HC at an inn, he grew almost amenable and offered everyone madeira. This being drunk, and polite converse duly exchanged, Cecily and her daughter drove off. The two men repaired to the library, where the DM suddenly began to relate his woes.

"Not often I'm awake during the day," he explained. "That damned son-in-law of mine is constantly in here, never leaves the place, and I like it to m'self. What I do as a result is to sleep all day and read all night, then get m'self out of sight again before Leonard comes in. He's the biggest bore in the county, perhaps in three. Luckily m'grandson's bright." He ended with a non-committal grunt, and HC then launched into his own troubles, forthrightly enough.

"It is becoming impossible to continue," he said, "under present arrangements. The constant enmity of my mother-in-law would, granted, not be of great importance by itself; I can deal with that matter." He inflated his stomach consciously under the watch-chain, which rose and fell, gleaming golden in the faint light. "However," HC continued, "there is no doubt that any legal aspect declares the property to be my nephew's. Any goodwill I continue to bring to the business" — here an image of thinly-sliced ham rose before both men, like certain Old Testament writing on the wall — "any such goodwill accrues in

the end to him, not to myself or my sons. I should like, frankly, to remove with my family to more suitable premises. However the question that raises itself is one of capital." HC's close-set eyes gleamed a little, but otherwise his habitually unexpressive face did not alter. The DM surveyed his fingers, which rested meantime on a cherished copy of Melanchthon. He then raised his non-committal glare beneath a pair of tufted grey eyebrows so thick he had lately had to resort to pince-nez, which irritated him.

"I have," he vouchsafed slowly, "certain property in Piccadilly." HC had known this perfectly well. "At present it don't earn its keep," said the DM dolefully. The building in question had, in fact, lain empty for some years and he had been wondering at intervals what to do about it. Piccadilly was no longer a commendable residential quarter; everybody had moved out west and the prostitutes had moved in. This fellow — one couldn't entirely dislike him, given a permanent eye to the main chance, but who hadn't? — could

hang his Angells sign outside, bring in custom, and perhaps pay rent or convey other perquisites. It would be better than nothing, but one didn't of course want too much of a damned favour made of it. At the same time, in face of HC's transfigured countenance — the last announcement had been exactly what he had hoped for — the DM remembered the fine girl he had lately seen and who had drunk his madeira. Certain aspects of a possible situation flitted through his mind. Firstly, poor Rose's son was healthy, but there had after all been an accident to the earlier Quayle. A second heir in the offing wouldn't be a bad thing at all, if that stick Leonard could manage it again; at any rate, it might take his mind off the library for a bit at any rate, and oneself would be left in peace. The DM reflected again that Leonard was such a liability that none of the young women of the county would look at him twice, title or no title in the remote offing and in the event of two deaths, one his own. What he had already in mind might serve very well; the young woman had had presentable

manners and a pleasant voice.

He murmured something of it in his direct fashion. It was after all no different from the marketing of a young mare, let alone a first edition. HC, naturally, hummed and hawed. He had seen Leonard Purslove at the shoot and had disliked him at sight as much as everyone else did; but perhaps Emily would have a softening influence. Certainly it would cement relations between his firm and the aristocratic Pursloves, precisely as he himself, long ago, had taken on dear Cis to cement them with the early Angells. That had had a most successful outcome; no doubt this would also.

"I shall have to consult my wife," he said. Cis would almost certainly have to be brought round; but HC knew by now how to do it. Nobody else was liable to raise any valid objection. By the time the interview ended and the paterfamilias left to join his womenfolk for luncheon, two things were virtually settled. The first was that a new gilt sign, entitled HC Angell and Sons, should wave shortly over Piccadilly. The other was that Emily Angell should be married

to a still uninformed Leonard Purslove, whom she had never met. This, all things considered, was as well.

⋆ ⋆ ⋆

Cecily shed tears, of course, and at first would not hear of such a thing: Emily should be allowed to choose for herself, as her mother had done. Reminded that in their circle it was unlikely that Emily would meet any very eligible bridegroom at all, Cis grew thoughtful for her daughter's sake. It was true they didn't go anywhere much, there wasn't time. Anyone as pretty as Emily ought to better herself. "Well, that would happen once she was this fellow's wife," said HC reasonably. He added that Em might even be presented at Court, in feathers, on her marriage. This was a shrewd shaft which struck home in exactly the right quarter; a mind-picture of Emily attired in low-cut white satin, with a train, and high ostrich plumes nodding above her undoubtedly beautiful hair, was one no mother could resist. Cis prevaricated meantime, but HC knew

that she was won. He clinched the matter by making love, in far more ardent a fashion than was his custom, to Cis once they were in bed together that night. This she was unable to resist, even though HC announced in a somewhat humdrum way in course of proceedings that it would, of course, be a useful contact in the business as well; the very best people would call at the Piccadilly shop.

"But wouldn't they come anyway, dearest?" asked Cecily adoringly; it had all been exactly like their wedding-night; she felt twenty years younger. "After all you're known by now, and can slice that beautiful ham." She had never ceased to marvel at this particular dexterity, given all the other attributes dear HC possessed. He himself allowed his small tight smile to manifest itself privately beneath his nightcap; it was easier now it was dark and his teeth were out.

"We will consult Theodora about the whole thing," he said, and Cecily, her nightgown not yet pulled down, felt unwonted stirrings of unwifely rebellion.

Emily was *her* daughter, after all, not Theodora Angell's. It was for a girl's own mother to decide such things, never her aunt. However, she said nothing as HC gave her his final goodnight kiss, turned over and slept with a clear conscience. The notion of asking Emily herself had not yet occurred to anybody.

Cis lay awake for some time, at last realising this aspect. It would be only fair to tell Emily what was happening; she'd do it tomorrow. Em would do as she was told, naturally; she would remain as she had always been, a good and dutiful daughter. There would certainly be no doubts about her ability to fill the suggested position; what else had the finishing school been for? Cis began then to dream, reprehensively, of county visits to be experienced somehow by herself, the relative by marriage of the great DM. This however she recognised at once as worldly ambition, and controlled her imagination severely before she went to sleep.

* * *

The prospect of consulting Theodora did not, this time, occur, as Theodora was found dead in bed next day, sitting bolt upright against the pillows as if in protest. The doctor, consulted, said it must have been heart. Nobody except HC pretended to be very sorry, but he was so depressed for days that even the matter of Em hung fire. From then on, Cecily assumed her rightful place as his helpmeet and occasional adviser, although her capabilities did not even then extend to the ledgers. Mary saw to those, and was regrettably so jubilant that she refused to attend Theodora's funeral. "And to think," remarked HC lugubriously after that event had taken place without a hitch, "that my poor sister will never now see the new sign waving over Piccadilly. She would have been understandably proud."

Cecily smiled, and went on with her sewing. It was no longer grey calico, but an almost transparent lawn nightgown for Emily's marriage-night. She wanted that to be as successful as her own.

* * *

Theodora's demise made this difference to the already strained household; the influence of Mary Angell, and, in his way, of Johnny, grew paramount. Mary kept firm hold of the accounts, as formerly, with a chastened Belle by her side, the latter's condition again making it unsuitable for her to appear in public. This time, the cause of the pending happy event was certainly Johnny: Mary had seen to that. It was perhaps too much to say that Johnny now reigned supreme, because Raph had decided to stay on at Marylebone. It didn't matter what the old man took into his head, Raph had already told himself; he had hitched his wagon to the original Angells, and there he would remain. He had other ideas as well, but they would keep. He watched as unemotionally as his father when a series of carts trundled the family possessions towards town at last by the autumn; if the firm was split in two, the altered identity belonged to the lesser branch, not the one founded after the South Sea Bubble long ago. Longevity was the thing; old Horace Angell's portrait still hung upstairs in its wig. Raph planted his feet squarely on

the floor behind the Marylebone counter, smiled on, and served customers as usual. Yes, it was true they were expanding, he answered enquirers; but he himself, and Mr Angell here, would certainly be available: there was no question of closing down. Also, the Chiswick branch under Mr Frame was prospering enough to be about to call itself an emporium, but nobody mentioned that.

* * *

By then, Emily's wedding was about to take place. There had been a meeting, unenthusiastic on both sides, with the middle-aged bridegroom, who had said and done nothing to endear himself to his bride and had looked her up and down as though she were a servant. He had earlier been persuaded by cash. Emily herself spent some hours in tears afterwards, but her mother, now an apostle of the cause, comforted her. At the beginning all brides felt like this, she assured her daughter; later on it would be different, and there would be the babies. "Look at how happy I am with Papa," she pointed

out, "and all of you. Before he came I used to sit upstairs in the parlour all day, glueing shells on a box."

Emily nearly said "But you knew Papa from long before; you told me yourself you used to play cricket with him in the lane." However that was not the kind of thing one said to one's parents; Emily supposed they knew best; they always had. The ceremony was to be before Christmas, and Em passed her time sewing somewhat dispiritedly at a white silk wedding gown.

* * *

The marriage of Leonard Purslove and Emily Angell was distinguished less by the presence of the unhappy bride and the drily uninterested groom, and a scattering of the county who were for the time being in search of diversion, than by the glorious figure of Freddy Angell in the uniform of a third-year Woolwich cadet. He was by now Adonis rather than Achilles, and the county raved. At the reception, which was held at Brown's Hotel after a dim ceremony in the same church with Low

leanings in which Cis and HC had been married, Freddy was promptly invited to two house-parties, at the second of which royalty would be present. Less interesting in appearance, his brother Gabriel also made a presentable showing; having not yet decided what to do with himself, the contacts he made on that particular day later helped him to attain to a certain position in the City. Mike, who might otherwise have had something adverse to say, was of course absent with his ship. Raph kept in the background, as befitted his trade. Jerry, young enough to be a page in turquoise satin, was greatly petted at the reception, looking as usual pretty, virtuous and sly. The bright hair prevailing in the family was much remarked upon and the name of Angell made subject to several puns. It was secretly hoped that the Purslove looks, growing drearier since the time of Lady Rose, would be enlivened by the present injection of new, if parvenu, blood. HC himself, majestically leading in the bride, had looked so dignified that many persons resolved soon to call in at the new Piccadilly premises on purpose to

encounter him again. On the whole, the ceremony passed off uneventfully. The bride — her maintenance of Low Church leanings had been secretly admired by many who would never have admitted to them — shed tears on going away, but that was to be expected.

Mike would certainly have made strong objection to the dreary marriage: but Mike was far away and uninformed. None of the rest thought of saying anything. Freddy himself, with the mind of a butterfly, was flattered and pleased to be taken, at last, into the bosom of the society to which he felt himself, by some unspecified right, to belong. At the house-parties in question he was made much of by the ladies and his morals, if any, corrupted for life. His eye for a target at the butts, like his father's, was noted and approved of; he would be asked back. Freddy Angell was, in short, launched in polite society.

* * *

Emily's marriage would have been even more wretched than it was had she not

been possessed of a certain rectitude of character, much sweetness, and a deep if narrow piety. Her husband sneered at this as he sneered at most things about Emily. From the beginning, as she did not satisfy him physically and he despised her origins, he neglected her even more brutally than he had neglected Rose. Time passed and it became evident that there would be, in any case, no children. Emily was bewildered and grief-stricken; she had taken her mother's word for it that there would be this compensation, at least. For the rest, she was glad to be left alone. She had dutifully tried to love her dry stick of a spouse, also her stepson; neither prospect was at all rewarding. Young Quayle had been taught already that a grocer's daughter was to be ignored; in any case he was mostly away at school, then Cambridge.

The county had called politely at first, but found Emily naïve. Left mostly alone in the great draughty house — young Quayle already talked of rebuilding it — she passed the time in wandering back and forth about the passages, staring at the portraits of long-dead Pursloves from

the time of the Civil Wars which hung there. There was one, painted much later, which intrigued Emily more and more; it reminded her of Lady Rose, whom she remembered in the cart with Johnny when she herself had been a small child. This woman had Lady Rose's face, her great appealing eyes, the brightly curling hair, the tenderly curved rosebud mouth; but her dress was, naturally, of an earlier time. Emily nerved herself to ask her husband about it when he was next met with. "It is Lady Emmeline Purslove," replied Leonard coldly, but would say nothing more except that it was true his first wife had been said by some to resemble her. No, there were no portraits of Lady Rose in existence.

Emily got herself pencils and paper and sat down to draw; she had an aptitude for this, which had been remarked on at the finishing-school; young ladies were expected to execute water-colour before they left. Emily drew what she remembered, a heart-shaped face beneath a velvet bonnet, and coloured it in carefully. She did not dare show it to Leonard, who had evinced no

further desire to talk on the subject; but, greatly emboldened, she showed it to her father-in-law. The DM peered at it through his pince-nez. "Yes, it's like Rose," he admitted, "what I remember of her. Better frame it." To her pleased surprise, he ordered a small gilt oval frame, with a hook at the top to hang the portrait up; thenceforth it occupied a place on the wall in Emily's own room, where Leonard never now came.

It was one achievement, but Emily's conscience told her it was not enough; she must do some good in the world by whatever means. She had tried to love her stepson, but had received none in return; Rose's son was like his father. In due course he would pull down the old Tudor house almost completely and rebuild, in ugly fashion, a Victorian Gothic mansion, complete with pepper-pot turrets, vestibule, billiard room, cloakroom, sixteen bedrooms, three drawing-rooms, quarters for the housekeeper, butler, and servants both resident and visiting; also a Young Ladies' Corridor and a number of water-closets. However these glories were not quite

yet to arise. Meantime, as there was nothing she could usefully do for the dying old horror upstairs, his rebuffed young stepmother turned to charity. At the beginning, especially towards each Christmas, Emily would merely pay visits to the cottagers, taking them jelly and other comforts in a covered basket carried on her arm. The fact that the children seemed to have nothing to do however disturbed her; there seemed a great many of them somehow, later, presumably, to be fitted for service. The idea came to Emily to start a sewing-class for the girls as soon as they were ten years old. Her own apprenticeship in clothing the heathen at Marylebone was very useful for the purpose. Shifts, caps, chemises, even gowns in proper course, were duly cut out and sewn, while at the same time Emily read to the little girls out of some improving book in the intervals of correcting their stitches. As time passed she began to be held in great respect in the neighbourhood, and girls from other people's cottages were delivered to her sewing-class, arriving on foot clutching fistfuls of bread and

margarine. Trained girls were always in demand for situations, and Emily's began to get a very good name. The county sneered. On Sundays, however, Emily came into her own; cottagers and tenant farmers would cluster at the lych-gate outside church to see her emerge on her tall husband's arm (it was almost the only time they ever met) and the women would bob and the men doff their round hats if they possessed any. Otherwise they pulled a discreet forelock. "You are become quite the lady of the manor," remarked Leonard drily once or twice. In fact he was not displeased.

In all other ways, however, there was constant disappointment; Emily bore no children, and after a very few years, lost her pretty, appealing looks. The union was a failure; Leonard spent almost all his time in the library. The sole benefit of the marriage was, from their own point of view at any rate, Freddy's, Gabriel's, and, later on, Jeremiel's. All three brothers were enabled by it to maintain contacts with the kind of company they by now preferred to enjoy. While Angells of Piccadilly prospered

under the care of HC and a posse of hired assistants in the Houghton colours, his sons disclaimed any connection with trade; far from attempting to slice paper-thin ham like their father, they would go down to stay with good old Em at Great Quayle and ride out early to the meet, thereafter carousing in accepted squirearchical fashion and availing themselves of other hospitality whenever and wherever it offered itself.

Whether they were supposedly under her roof or not, the faded Emily saw little of her brothers. Good works by now engulfed her, and in the year the old Duchess Marchioness died at last, she had virtually adopted a motherless young Quaker girl named Prudence.

* * *

The circumstances of Prudence's arrival seemed favourable enough. She had been taught sewing and housewifery by the Quakers, who had also evidently taught her never to look anyone straight in the eye. When she first came to Emily she was twelve years old, an unremarkable child

with straight brown hair. Her complexion, and the cast-down eyelids, were like white candle-wax. When the eyes occasionally raised themselves they proved to be a disturbing water-green. Prudence was already nubile on arrival, but conducted herself so discreetly that there was none of the usual difficulty with such girls, who often became less teachable with puberty and seemed to have other ideas in their heads. Emily welcomed the young Quaker, at first, as an adjunct to the cottage children's sewing-sessions, which had become overfilled, but Emily never turned away an applicant. Prudence lived up to her name, moving about the benches noiselessly and keeping her own counsel unless to survey a questionable seam.

Her story was however unusual, if hardly unique. Emily herself had for a short time had a Quaker maid named Bethesda Fox whom she found she disliked faintly, despite all charity. The woman seemed devious, although it was impossible to pin down any particular instance of it. It had been a relief when Bethesda came at last to Emily and said

without preamble that she was leaving at the end of the month. “I have to go to look after my brother-in-law,” she announced in the terse fashion of her sect.

“Is he ill?” asked kind Emily, adding that if so she was sorry to hear it.

“No. It is his wife who is ill, my sister Abigail Penney.” Nothing further was vouchsafed, and Emily saw the woman go with some relief; for one thing, the word ma’am had been lacking from the beginning. She heard no more until, three or four years later, Bethesda reappeared with a young girl by her, carrying a tied plain bundle of belongings. The girl’s eyes were cast down.

“I’d be grateful if you was to take my niece Prudence Fox in.” No form of respectful address even yet crossed Bethesda’s lips, and it seemed to be taken for granted that there would be no refusal. However, Emily, to whom by now the world had taught a very little, resolved to ask a few questions. Prudence was invited to set down her bundle and, as it was a fine day, to take a walk meantime in the garden. Her

capped, cloaked figure walked obediently up and down the paths between Emily's flowerbeds, in the cultivation of which the latter had learnt to take some pleasure over the years.

The story was then extracted from the Quaker woman. Sister Abigail, some years since and before her marriage, had been in service as between-maid in a certain ducal household. There were guests invited frequently to stay, and once, while making the bed of an evidently licentious young nobleman, Abigail had been taken advantage of between, as it were, the pillow-cases and the counterpane. "She didn't say anything to any of us, which was wrong of her," declared Abigail's sister, suddenly becoming almost vociferous. "She left that place and came back and married Joseph Penney, my brother-in-law, and let him think the child was his. All these years he's thought that, and been as careful with Prudence's upbringing as if she was his own. Then on her death-bed, that was this very week — she'd had a wasting trouble — my sister confessed everything. Joe

won't have Prudence under his roof any more." Bethesda, who obviously fancied Joe herself, bridled righteously. "Knowing you have these sewing girls and Prudence being instructed in it, I thought of yourself." Her mouth closed with a snap. The whole recital had been made without emotion and with a glance studiously directed at the floor. Emily decided that among the first things she would try to teach Prudence — she had already decided to take her — would be to look up, at least while speaking.

This attempt was never very successful, but Emily gave a home to the poor child. Considering Prudence's parentage — the blue-blooded father was never named — she couldn't, in Emily's estimation, be treated entirely as a servant. Indeed, after a time she might become the daughter oneself had never had. Emily's affectionate heart already yearned over the prospect of having someone to love at last. Leonard, when informed as was proper, showed no interest one way or the other. He was at that time cataloguing certain editions of early herbals, which took all his attention.

Prudence, given her own small bedroom at Quayle, turned out to be an unpromising object of affection; she gave no sign of returning any. Emily was accustomed to this from her husband and stepson, and hid her hurt; perhaps she herself was, after all, too demanding. Prudence's prim coldness might well be the result of her upbringing in what Emily, the more she learned of them, considered most ungracious tenets. For instance, when the girl came down to breakfast and one duly bade her good-morning, she did not reply. Emily at first thought she was shy, but as the silence persisted, one day asked her about it.

"We are instructed not to say it," replied Prudence, head bent over her plate; she spent long periods in silence.

"Why, in all the world? It is somewhat discourteous, my dear; try to begin." But Prudence continued silent, in that and other ways; Leonard, young Quayle and the old DM decided she was a dull fool, and ignored her. Emily however kept trying; it had occurred to her over the months that in a strange way, the girl was becoming beautiful, not that Emily

had ever seen a Leonardo; but the smooth hair and placid forehead, the straight nose over the small uncompromising mouth, the long neck bent in what was certainly unnecessary humility nowadays, had their beguiling quality; also, Prudence's young breasts, rounding out below her grey gown, were growing already very shapely indeed above a slim waist; she would pay for dressing, most certainly. Emily ordered two pretty gowns to be made for her, hoping it would bring her out of herself; Prudence only wore them under protest, and herself let out her grey one when it became too tight, wearing it on all possible occasions. She was scrupulously clean, frugal and, apart from the good-mornings, mannerly enough as instructed no doubt by Joe Penney; capable of expert laundering and the execution of tiny regular stitches. Emily sighed a little, and at last let the girl do as she would.

On one occasion, however, Prudence did express pleasure. That was when Emily took her to town to visit old Mary Angell at the Marylebone shop. There was no reason why these visits should not have been more frequent

than they were; Leonard and the DM would not have cared how often Emily absented herself; but a kind of pride prevented her from exhibiting too clearly the failure of her marriage. As far as Mary knew, Em was a contented, if sadly childless, county wife, carrying out good works and providing a place for the boys to stay when they went down to hunt, or whatever it was they did. While the two women talked together and sipped tea, Prudence was sent to help downstairs behind the counter, and proved very capable indeed. "If she was a little older she'd make a good wife for Raph," said Mary, considering it. The girl was too young, of course, for Johnny, and for some reason such an outcome did not occur to his doting mother. The regrettable Belle had, last winter, succumbed in her feckless fashion to a phthisis after catching a chill in a draught. Johnny, widowed, again seemed Mary's helpless child, which was very agreeable. As for the two children of the marriage, arrangements had had to be made for young Alec; she herself couldn't manage him, and thankfully his grandparents, old

Alec and Phyll, had agreed to take the boy and train him up to be an assistant at the emporium. The girl, Vera, was no trouble to anybody except when her emotions got the better of her, and Mary, remembering heredity, had sternly warned her from the beginning to beware of men. This warning had been the better heeded because poor Horry, being by now after all a man, had one day exposed himself in the half-dark passage and Vera, unlike other children who would have kept quiet, ran bleating — she had in fact a certain general likeness to a sheep — to her grandmother. The matter had been hushed up, as neither Mary nor Cis had wanted Horry put into an institution; an eye would have to be kept, that was all.

Johnny, therefore, treated the young Quaker maiden as a father might have done, and Raph took no notice of her at all. Further visits followed, and Prudence actually vouchsafed the information to Emily that she enjoyed going to Marylebone. Otherwise, she passed the days as usual, and on Sundays had long ceased to attract attention as an

inhabitant of the Quayle pew dressed in grey servant's stuff; it was assumed that she was one more of kind Mrs Emily's charities.

* * *

Freddy and Gabriel at that time visited their sister rather less often than formerly. For one thing Freddy, in the intervals of his Aldershot posting — he had passed out of Woolwich with moderate commendation at the time — was often to be seen nowadays galloping alongside a beautiful dark-haired young woman named Skittles behind the Quorn Hunt. He was known to spend several nights with Skittles whenever possible at a nearby inn. Nobody was surprised or critical. Skittles was not accepted as a member of polite society, but she could ride like a demon and was allowed to follow the exclusive Quorn by an indulgent MFH. She could also instruct very well indeed in the arts of love, at which Freddy by now was himself adept. Apart from Skittles herself — who fascinated Freddy as she did most

young men, but who never aroused the suicidal passion in his breast evinced by some — Freddy spent much of his time in almost equally *risqué*, though no doubt better born, company. Lady Gaia Toomey might not have had to earn a girlhood's living as a prostitute round the Liverpool docks, but she had married her Irish husband Tom against the wishes of her family, who had, grimly and immediately, cut her off. Lady Gaia and Tom Toomey lived, accordingly, in a perpetual state of financial uncertainty in their small flat in Half Moon Street and, when in the country, relied greatly on other people's hospitality for existence. They also relied a good deal on such as Freddy, or rather HC himself, for loans. Freddy was generous with his father's handsome allowance, was fortunately not himself addicted to gambling, and had no unnatural vices. He was much sought after and it was thought a pity that he spent so much time and money on the Toomeys when others would gladly have entertained him: but Freddy found the couple themselves entertaining and gladly paid their more pressing bills.

As for Gabriel, he was gradually assuming importance in the City and had the strength of character not to accept, or not invariably, the Saturday to Monday invitations of famed hostesses. It was unheard of to be seen going back to town on a Sunday night, and the alternative was for such guests to arrive at the office unshaven and red-eyed off a very early train indeed on Monday morning. Gabriel had the prudence to see that his future lay in being as bright as possible on those occasions when his more sociably inclined fellows were, to say the least, a trifle under the weather. He had inherited a certain amount of HC's foresight, and his looks were presentable if unexciting. He would marry, when the time came, into a family whose connections would further his career. Meantime, he nurtured it himself.

* * *

Freddy's first sight of Prudence did not arouse any undue feeling in his breast, because at that time he was in love with a young lady whose family, despite the

honourable state pertaining to an officer and a gentleman, would not countenance the remotest connection with Trade. Freddy therefore, still mooning over the unattainable, chucked Prudence under the chin, a thing which had never before happened to her, and strode out, whistling, to Great Quayle stables to ride out to the meet and, of course, Skittles afterwards. Prudence herself did not, naturally, ride; she and Emily continued to make their journeys safely and inconspicuously in the smaller Quayle carriage, drawn as usual by two quiet and predictable bays. As time passed they were thrown increasingly into one another's company. The children in the sewing-class were growing up, had found positions, and for some unspecified reason there was a hiatus in the existing cottage birth-rate. Instead, Prudence's quiet voice would read aloud to Emily in the drawing-room when asked, sometimes from books on Quaker thought, although Emily was not the only one to find it baffling. Asked about the Inner Light, Prudence honestly tried to explain; but all Emily finally

understood seemed to be that in certain people this commodity was judged to be permanently turned off. She was never in fact converted from established leanings, nor did Prudence really try for long.

Prudence by now was as beautiful as Emily had foreseen she might become. Her walk was as graceful as a nodding flower, her figure, now that she had been induced to hold her head up properly, superb. When her smooth hair was combed out it reached her knees in a brown veil of almost Eastern sheen. When her flesh was glimpsed, which only happened by accident, it was creamy and smooth as satin. Any artist would have wanted at once to paint her in the nude, but this would have been an unlikely encounter in the circumstances. However when a jilted, jaded Freddy, suddenly arriving prior to the midst of preparations for the war in Zululand to which he eventually hoped to be sent out with the rest, saw Prudence on the second or third occasion, he fell promptly and astonishingly in love. It was, or so he assured himself, unlike any love he had ever felt before; this

was pure, a white flame; he would marry Prudence, whatever anyone said. She, by now eighteen years old, gave him no encouragement, which naturally inflamed the Angell heir's desire more than ever. She could not, must not, deny him! He spoke of it to Emily, who said she didn't know; there were Papa and Mama to consider. "They hope you will make a *good* marriage," she told him gently, thinking that it was, after all, more than time; Freddy was thirty-four, but looked less. HC, slicing away at his ham in Piccadilly, had ambitions for all his sons, as he had earlier had it for Emily herself; she stared now at Freddy's somehow unimpaired beauty in amazement, thinking of her own sad reflection in the glass. They weren't as far apart in age as all that; perhaps it was because Freddy had always taken life lightly. Emily wished, too late, alas, that she could have done the same.

* * *

HC, standing benevolently in his frock-coat, surveyed the by now accustomed

premises of the Piccadilly shop and the activities of the employed staff therein. A satisfactory whining noise overhead proved that change was passing constantly back and forth in the new cable system to the counting-house; assistants, clad in their aprons boasting the Houghton livery colours, busied themselves with serving and even with, themselves, slicing ham; HC only did this nowadays by special request from the more distinguished of the customers. He prided himself, however, on the fact that none of the young men employed could achieve quite the perfection he himself had, and still could, demonstrate; also on the fact that none of his sons, except young Jeremiel who was by now in the upstairs office, soiled their hands with trade at all, at least not here; there was of course Raph in Marylebone. HC reflected with satisfaction that if it hadn't been for that boy, the original business would have fallen apart by now, with only old Mary left, daft Horry and poor foolish Johnny, who never knew his own best interests. The strange fact that it was no other than Raph who had put into his

father's head to dress the assistants in Houghton colours instead of plain white aprons intrigued and baffled his father: it showed perhaps that Raph had a foot in both camps; he was a deep one, like oneself. It would have to be seen in any case what the future would bring. Meantime, business was doing well. HC bowed to a regularly calling viscountess, drifting past in an assembly of veils and a rolled-up parasol; and betook himself upstairs to where Jerry was duly labouring over accounts. The boy wasn't as quick as he himself had by now become, but he was obedient and thorough. It was as well to have a son in both firms. To say, as Cecily did, that Jerry had the nature of a young saint and had never given anyone a moment's anxiety was perhaps taking things too far; at some time in the future, human nature would certainly manifest itself. HC surveyed his son's bright head without trepidation meantime: his thoughts were elsewhere. If only Freddy, his pride and delight, were as stable in his accustomed ways! As for Mike, they'd heard rumours of unsuitable young women in the West

Indies, but after all a sailor could be permitted certain vagaries now and again. Gabriel was lately engaged to a young woman whose family were safely embroiled in stockbroking. Poor Horry would never be any different. As for Emily, she'd visited them the other day, with that silent girl she'd grown so fond of. The pair of them saw more of Freddy than he and Cis did, and there was a war brewing up in Zululand.

* * *

During the events that gave rise at last to that war, which meantime allowed Freddy a certain amount of prior leave, he continued to haunt Great Quayle. He followed Prudence everywhere, even to her ironing-board; and pled his cause without result except for occasional disdainful looks down her long straight nose. It was as though she hadn't ever set eyes on him properly; in Freddy's bosom was ingrained the certainty that if any woman had, she would be unable to resist. "Look at me, Prue!" he would beg, without result; Prudence merely got

on with the ironing. It was considered eccentric of her to do this, as there was already a laundry-maid at Quayle; but she had been brought up to occupy herself with such things, and never lost the habit.

Freddy began to mouth sentiments such as an actor might have declaimed on some second-rate stage; he wasn't feeling as young as usual by now; if only Prue would take pity on him! "Even if you can't love me at the beginning, I swear I will make you do so by the end," he babbled, distraught. A lock of slightly fading blond hair fell over his brow; he looked for moments like a misplaced poet. "Marry me before I sail for South Africa," he begged. "After all I may never return."

Prudence set the iron back beside the fire to heat, and suddenly raised her extraordinary water-green eyes.

"I do not," she replied in what was probably the longest impromptu sentence she had ever uttered, "consider your profession one into which I would ever marry. I disapprove of violence and war."

"Then if I — " He had been on the

point of offering to throw up everything, his career, his prospects of promotion: but after all she hadn't promised anything even if he did. "My darling girl, I spent five years at Woolwich learning to be an artillery officer, and have earned advancement since," he pointed out reproachfully. What would the other chaps say if at this moment of all moments, on the brink of war, he sent in his papers? It would be a disgrace he could never live down; society would close its doors; even Prudence wasn't worth it.

Prudence remained calm, cool and collected, however, and Freddy left Great Quayle in a more thoughtful mood than usual. His resolve hardened as he rode to town and to Half Moon Street, where the Toomeys listened at last with expected sympathy; they hoped in any case to touch him for a final loan. "Fact is," admitted Freddy after the fourth glass of his own champagne, "I know damned well there's fire somewhere in there, but I can't seem to get at it." He gazed dolefully into his glass, watching the bubbles rise and burst. "I've never met

a girl like her," he moaned. "Only wait till you see her."

Lady Gaia had already done so, on a brief formal visit to Emily at Great Quayle. She wisely said nothing, but privately decided that old Freddy would be bound to get over that colourless creature as soon as something was done about it. He mustn't be allowed to throw himself away in marriage. She would think of something; she usually could. She contrived it, quite soon.

* * *

Two days later, Emily was gratified to receive a second visit from Lady Gaia, discreetly attired in a wine-coloured travelling dress and small perched matching hat; her gloves as usual were elegant. Emily, from a lack of any inclusion in county gossip, had heard nothing of the disfavour with which Tom Toomey's wife was regarded in more particular circles; Leonard could have enlightened her, but Leonard as usual was not available. They drank tea, Prudence served sponge cake and small rataffia biscuits, and Lady

Gaia confessed presently that she had come to ask a very great favour indeed of Mrs Purslove; would she permit her charming charge to accompany oneself back to town for a few days, to stay at Half Moon Street? Perceiving Emily's somewhat startled expression, she added hastily that there was an exhibition of Pre-Raphaelite art at which she greatly desired to show Prudence to certain artists who would themselves be present at the private view. "I want them to know that they have passed by a far more encouraging subject than Miss Siddal, whose red hair is of course glorious but her profile quite inferior. I had heard already of the beauty of Miss Fox." She smiled, and her smile was Emily's undoing; it was impossible that this suddenly arrived and evidently well-born lady meant any harm to Prudence, and it was perhaps time the child saw a little more of the world. "I am afraid Prudence has not the right clothes for town," she said deprecatingly. "We live very quietly here." She wondered, in fact, who had told Lady Gaia about Prudence in the first place, but was as ignorant of the former's acquaintance

with Freddy as she was of the latter's acquaintance with Skittles.

"That is of no consequence," said Lady Gaia pleasantly. "She will dine alone with us, and we do not keep great ceremony. If necessary I can lend her a dress."

Prudence was then instructed to go and pack her overnight things, and obeyed quietly. Presently, seen off by Emily, she found herself bowling along opposite Lady Gaia in the latter's carriage, with the roads flying past much faster than they were accustomed to do with the foreseen assistance of the two quiet bays. In fact, the whole adventure was being conducted at an extremely rapid rate; when they reached town, Prudence felt herself almost hustled upstairs and into a tastefully appointed bedroom, where she was given hot water in which to wash and also time to set out her hairbrushes and nightgown. Having done this, it was already evening; Lady Gaia herself came in to close the curtains, a bright dress cast over her arm.

"I thought you might like to wear this for dinner," she said; her manner was

impersonal, and she scanned Prudence, by then in her chemise and with her hair down, critically. "You must let me do your hair tonight with a flower," she said. "We have a guest coming, and you must look your very best, must you not?" Without giving Prudence time to answer, she spread out the dress on the bed; it was patterned in garish colours. Prudence had never seen or imagined such a dress. She protested slightly, saying she would prefer to wear her customary grey, but was brushed aside.

"Nonsense, you can't appear in what you've travelled in," said Lady Gaia, and seizing Prudence's hairbrush, an ivory-backed gift from Emily, began to burnish and finally twist up her long hair into a fashionable coiffure, setting pins judiciously here and there. The final result in the glass was astonishing in its flattery. "We will put the flower in last," said Lady Gaia, and did so after Prudence was dressed. "Have you heard of the Jersey Lily?" Gaia asked narrowly, studying her own creation; it was surprising what could be made out of what had seemed rather unpromising material.

Prudence had not of course heard of Mrs Langtry, and she was beginning to be aware of unaccustomed sensations of a kind against which her adoptive father Joseph Penney had often warned her. These increased when she caught sight of herself in the provided gown. It was cut dreadfully low, and in addition her hostess had tight-laced her into the fashionable hour-glass shape, having already, to Prudence's further confusion, removed her chemise. It was almost as if there was hardly anything left at all above the waist. Perhaps a shawl was necessary. Prudence ventured to put the one in which she had travelled round her white shoulders and what was revealed below. "Not at all; you look exactly as you ought," said her hostess, and whisked the shawl away somewhere with the rest of Prudence's discarded clothing. Then she marched the girl into the small drawing-room. There, having meantime arrived, Freddy Angell, glittering in full regimentals, stood, handsome and smiling, beside their host.

Prudence's confusion deepened uncontrollably. She had been aware from the

beginning, in fact from the time he had first chucked her under the chin, that Freddy's presence must always induce in her great strictness of behaviour. Her youth having been firmly spent in the exercise of this, there remained the fact that what her mother knew, and her stepfather until latterly did not, Prudence herself had never been told by anyone. That there was unguarded blood in her veins, which must never be permitted to race, she was nevertheless aware; and it was racing now. The way Freddy was looking at her, in the low-cut dress, made everything worse. Blushes rose in an unaccustomed manner in Prudence's cheeks, bringing her to life as no Leonardo was ever perhaps brought; her colour echoed that of the rose Lady Gaia had tastefully placed in her hair. Her mouth trembled out of its primness even before wine was produced at dinner, when she managed for the last time that evening to remember her upbringing; otherwise, they had placed her directly opposite to Freddy and he gazed through all five courses steadfastly down her gown.

"I do not drink wine," Prudence heard

herself say to Tom Toomey, who in the absence of any manservant was pouring it himself. Tom, with Irish charm, assured her that the next course, known as Nabob's Relish, would be uneatable otherwise; water only made it worse, the results would burn her tongue off. Faced with this prospect — the soup had already contained some strange and bitter flavour — Prudence reluctantly allowed him to fill her glass with a delicious and heady liquid she had never drunk before; it was full of bubbles, and certainly helped the Relish down. Prudence could not afterwards remember what they had all talked about.

Her blood was pounding still, also her heart; she could feel it thud against the lacing. Behind her, Tom poured the champagne again and again into her tall-stemmed glass. The pudding was a delectable nothing, unlike anything ever met with at Great Quayle; Prudence spooned it lightly into herself, then drank more champagne. She had by then stopped protesting about anything. Dinner itself had continued, except for the pudding, to taste on the whole rather

singular; no doubt these fashionable people used some unknown herb in the cooking. Prudence downed the taste with still more of what Tom by now openly called bubbly, then after dinner there was a little glass of something fiery as well, going down the throat with ease. The world had long since begun to swim; even Freddy's godlike form, in its bright, tight uniform, grew blurred, and there might almost have been two of him. Prudence heard herself giggling. Two of Freddy! That would be quite excessive; one was enough, only one Freddy, only one, only —

"I think she will do now," said Lady Gaia, as Prudence heeled over at last under the combined influences of champagne, brandy and Spanish fly. Freddy rose with commendable steadiness to his feet, picked the unresisting Quaker up in his arms and carried her out of the drawing-room. Behind them, after the door was shut, Tom and Gaia winked at one another and frugally finished what was left of the champagne.

⋆ ⋆ ⋆

When Prudence came to herself it was morning. Her head felt as if it would split open, her mouth was swollen and dry, and she was aware of an inward hurt which was at the same time, strangely, pleasure. Staring in bewilderment at the chink of grey daylight beginning to show between the drawn curtains, she became shockingly aware of her own naked body. It was quite naked, except for her stockings. She had been undressed; and other things had happened to her. She had no exact recollection of these except that they had been shamefully delightful, that the growing remembrance of them almost banished her pervasive headache, and that she had had experiences of which in all her life she had never yet dreamed. These, which she could no longer recall more clearly than a little, had most certainly taken place: deep within her was that mysterious and intimate pain. She made herself move, and observed the cause; Freddy Angell, lying beside her likewise naked, the first naked man Prudence had ever seen. He looked like a sated god; his graceful limbs were flung out, his breaths

came easily, his unshaven face — how it aroused unexpected tenderness in her to perceive the few light lines on it! — a fallen angel's, dulled blond hair tumbled against the pillow. They hadn't, she noticed, been inside the bed all night; and there was something else in evidence, something Freddy possessed, a man's member. Prudence had never had the opportunity to stare at one before. Mundane feelings began to flood in; her whole body became a renewed blush, and she made herself turn away. What had happened was after all shameful, unspeakable; the kind of thing her stepfather had warned her about without ever putting it into words. It must never, never be permitted to happen again: and as soon as Freddy woke up it would almost certainly do so. This prospect made Prudence look wildly about her. The disgraceful dress she had been forced to wear on the previous evening was there, draped over a chair, likewise her drawers; but of her travelling-clothes there was no sign. She must however escape as best she could; delay was not permissible under any circumstances. Prudence slid,

shivering slightly and feeling her head pound most abominably by now, from the bed, huddled on the clothes somehow and with the bodice pulled up as far as was humanly possible; and retrieved her shoes, which Freddy had placed last night with commendable neatness side by side on the carpet. Then she stole, not daring to look at Freddy again, from the room, and at last let herself silently out of the flat. Had there been servants, they might well have been awake; but there were none, and Prudence went down to the street, reaching it at last thankfully. Except for marauding cats and garbage, it was still empty.

Having escaped, Prudence realised, having exercised less than her customary foresight, that she had no money. Her purse and other things must have been taken away by Lady Gaia with her outdoor clothes, and nothing would induce her to go back. She knew exactly, however, where she was going instead; she would go to Marylebone. It was a place she knew, and couldn't be as far as all that to walk. However she had found, on first descending the stairs, that her legs

were strangely weak and that walking was unusually difficult. It must be because of what had happened and which did not bear thinking of. She began unsteadily to pick her way, however, at last finding Piccadilly. Mrs Emily's carriage had gone in a certain direction from there; and shortly, in the early morning light, was the new HC sign, creaking slightly and with an angel flying above it. Prudence turned her head away, feeling slightly sick; then reassured herself. She knew the direction now; all one had to do was to follow the way the carriage had taken. In the country it wouldn't seem as far as all that.

The sight of a stumbling, dishevelled young woman in a tawdry dress, with a lopsided rose still somehow pinned in her hair, diverted such passers-by as had early roused themselves for a working day; late roysterers had fortunately gone home. One more tart going back where she came from wasn't such an unusual sight at that hour; some of them called congratulations, others hooted. However it was too early in the morning to accost her, and Prudence stumbled resolutely on.

* * *

Mary Angell, who hadn't been feeling at all well lately — after all she was a good age — was up by custom at half-past five. It was no use employing a maid if you didn't see to her, and the maid would be in at six; she lived out and was not very bright. Otherwise there was breakfast to prepare for everyone once the fire, already laid, was lit; her own toilet, the formidable lacing of her corsets, and young Vera to get ready for school, later on. A mercy Vera liked school so much; she already said she wanted to become a pupil-teacher, which was the best thing that could happen. Mary pulled at her own laces energetically — one day they'd break, at this rate — and heard a timid knock at the door. It was too early for the maid. She went down. A blowsy and exhausted creature stood swaying there whom Mary was on the point of turning from the door; but the creature cast herself on the old woman's upholstered bosom with great gulping sobs of relief, and Mary, with horror, at last recognised Emily's

discreet Quaker companion, transformed and, evidently, ruined. The shock made Mary feel dizzy.

"Please take me in," Prudence begged. "I can't ever go back to Mrs Emily again. Let me help you in the shop. I'd earn my keep." She broke down into hiccupping crying.

Mary wisely did not ask any questions, but took the young woman in and shut the door. Whatever had happened, the neighbours mustn't know. The best thing would be a good strong cup of tea. Over it, Mary had time to reflect that an extra hand in the shop might not be a bad idea; Johnny had all he could do with the deliveries now they didn't keep a coachman, and she herself could certainly use more help in the house. She'd have to talk to Johnny about it, of course; but all that could be seen about later. She packed Prudence off to bed, in a flannel nightgown of her own; it was the best place, and later on she'd take up hot water in a can.

Providence arranged matters otherwise for Mary Angell.

* * *

It was still very early. Nobody else was yet up, and after seeing Prudence into her own still warm bed Mary made herself climb, on her creaking painful knees and breathing with difficulty owing to her lacing of her increasingly stout form, up to the attic to resurrect, out of its hair trunk, a seemly gown of the late Belle Angell's; Prudence couldn't go on being seen in what she had arrived wearing. Prudence lay awake, a prey to shameful memories but feeling much better after the cup of tea. However the results of Nabob's Relish by now began to induce in her an urgent need for the close-stool, and she got up and went, clutching the flannel nightgown about her, to find it. Seated thereon, she heard a thud from upstairs; perhaps Mrs Angell was replacing a trunk. However time passed, and seeing the kettle still boiling its head off on the range, a thing Mary would never have allowed to happen, Prudence set it carefully aside and called up quietly to ask if she might help. There was no answer. Presently she ventured cautiously

upstairs, aware of her improper clothing if seen; but after all it wasn't as bad as what she had walked in through London.

Mary was lying on the attic floor, quite still and with her head turned sideways. There was a smell of stale blood. Prudence knelt down and took the old woman in her arms. Mary was alive; her breaths came snoringly and her mouth hung slack, half open. There was an opened trunk nearby with clothes in it; Prudence seized the nearest garment and cast it round herself; that would have to do. Sounds from below showed that the men were stirring. Prudence ran towards the sounds, hammering at last on a closed door.

Johnny Angell opened it, still in his shirt and waistcoat and unshaven. He had been on the point of going down to the shop to set out the cooled meats from the larder before he took his breakfast, and had not yet put in his teeth. He gaped, beholding a young woman with a white face and one of his dead wife's gowns cast about her shoulders. He recognised Prudence with some difficulty;

she generally looked tidier than that.

"It's your mother," Prudence said. "She's lying in the attic. I think it's a seizure. I didn't try to lift her by myself, but we could both get her to bed. You'd best send for a doctor." She spoke, as always, calmly and without fuss. Johnny. followed her obediently up to the attic, shamefully aware that he still lacked his teeth but that the fact should hardly be uppermost in his mind at present. They found Mary, carried her down between them, unlaced her and left her propped up with pillows and warmly covered. "I'll look after the shop," Prudence said. Her continued calm amazed him; a fine young woman, thank God she'd come, for whatever reason; Johnny didn't — his wits were still confused — think Emily was here with her, and hadn't asked. He went to rouse Raph and send him for the doctor. That personage, on arrival, examined Mary, pronounced what they all knew by now in any case, and added that a second seizure would probably finish her. "Can anyone nurse her?" he asked. Prudence replied that she could do so. Then she went off to refill the

kettle and make more tea, and stir the porridge; Mary had left it steeping on the previous evening with her usual foresight, but she couldn't have foreseen everything. Raph went down to the shop to deal with the early customers, and Prudence took her turn then after Mary was left comfortable; everyone's emotions were controlled and, though what had happened was regretted, it was silently agreed among them all that Mrs Angell had been very old; something of the kind was bound to happen soon.

* * *

Prudence nursed Mary through the nights and days until the second seizure came and she died of it. In the interval, certain other things happened. Once a sound of galloping hooves had sounded beyond the shop door; it was Freddy, his face disfigured by rage and anxiety. He'd been down to Emily's; Prudence wasn't there. Where was she? If she wasn't here, she might be in the river. What he had done had filled him, on waking, less with shame than with a slow remembered pleasure;

before he knew she was gone from him, he had reached out again to take her. It had been the most natural thing in the world to do so; her responsiveness had delighted him; their love — he knew very well that she loved him now — could be a thing of joy and redemption, man and wife made one flesh. Tags from the Bible and Prayer Book, instilled by Cis in youth, floated through Freddy's head before he opened his eyes to find the bed empty except for himself; male and female created He them; forsaking all other; with my body I thee worship. Then he had found her gone: and since then had hunted feverishly for her, in vain. She might have come here; it was after all possible.

Prudence meantime turned to Johnny, who was with her in the empty shop, and clung to him.

"Don't let him see me," she begged. "Don't even let him know I'm here. He — he frightened me, that's why I came here to your mother." He let her hurry upstairs to the unconscious Mary, dealt with Freddy — he himself had never told blatant lies before in his life — heard him

ride off, then went up to Prudence and soothed and patted her, at first as though she had been his daughter Vera when upset. However an agreeable sensation grew in him which Vera could by no means have engendered; accidentally, he found himself patting Prudence's firm round pleasant young breast. They drew apart politely, but it occurred to Johnny, thinking the whole thing over afterwards, that when Mama died there would be no one left to look after young Vera and see her off to school, as Prudence did now each morning in addition to everything else; moreover, the neighbours would certainly begin to talk at once if a young female were known to be living on the premises with two men, a child, Horry, and a maid who lived out. It seemed, all things considered, an ideal moment to grasp the nettle. Johnny did so next time they were alone.

"You need have no fear of anyone while you are with me, you know," he told her with great kindness. The fact that he had faced successfully up to the glorious Freddy, known for his ways with women, gave Johnny a heightened

opinion of himself for the time being; he forgot that he was an ageing widower whose teeth had lately given so much trouble that they had had to come out and be replaced, and that his hair was grey and getting thin. He then proposed that Prudence marry him, if she didn't mind somebody a bit older. "I will protect you," he said, his eyes resembling a melancholy spaniel's. It was this fact which made Prudence accept him; it was after all the answer, and life could be lived from now on predictably, in the way she had been brought up. She had of course already written to Mrs Emily to say she was helping at Marylebone meantime, and that lady, who happened to be in bed with a heavy cold, trusted Prudence enough not to come up herself to look after poor Mama: she would perhaps take the journey later. Nothing had been said about the episode with Freddy, and Emily no doubt thought Prudence had been sent for somehow from Half Moon Street. In a way, she had. And she liked helping in the shop.

* * *

Johnny and Prudence were married by special licence the day of Mary Angell's funeral. The ceremony was so quiet that nobody was present but two witnesses, one of them Raph. All the available Angell clan had met together for the last time at the funeral, knowing nothing about the nuptials to follow it; Johnny himself, Freddy, pale and haggard (but Prudence did not appear); Gabriel and Jerry and HC. The two shops were shut for the day and word had been sent out to Mike's ship by telegraph. Freddy, savagely looking forward to imminent foreign service, got drunk as soon as the coffin was bestowed and went off by himself. HC, leading the family as usual, stalked majestically out of the graveyard to rejoin his wife, waiting in deep mourning in their carriage. Cis dabbed at her eyes with a black-bordered handkerchief. Poor Mama! A mercy it had all been so quick, and she could have known very little after the first. A mercy, as well, that that quiet young companion of Emily's was present to look after her till she died. Poor Emily was not present today, being still unwell;

the cold had settled on her chest. One ought to go down. There was really very little coming and going now between the different branches of the family. Cecily had let her perennially proud glance dwell on Freddy's blond head for the last time, had she known it; how greatly Jerry resembled him in appearance! All her sons, except one, were handsome, and successful like their father; that was the main point.

She was still crying dutifully when HC ordered their carriage back to Piccadilly at the head of the departing cortege. Cis realised there hadn't been much time to say anything to her brother Johnny; she hardly saw him these days. He was looking much older. Strange to recall that he had always been dear Mama's favourite, the supposed hope of the firm! By now, Johnny hadn't an idea in his head.

* * *

Johnny's marriage was announced in the papers a few days later, as it happened on the same day as Freddy received

his sailing orders. Nevertheless the latter flung himself once more in the saddle and, in ice-cold fury, skidded at last to a halt outside the Marylebone shop. So she had been here all the time! So she was married to that old man, his uncle! If he had Uncle Johnny now between his hands, he'd slay him; old enough to be her father! Where were they? Where had they gone?

Raph, left in full charge of the shop, said he didn't know. In fact, he knew perfectly well; the bridal pair had gone off to Epping, following established precedent.

Freddy sailed from Southampton two days later, bitterly surveying the receding coast of England with a draped French tricolour flapping above his head, having been hoisted strictly against orders from the Admiralty. The young Prince Imperial was on board, his mother having stormed the War Office and persuaded them at last to let her son go and fight, which was his heart's desire. The Prince got himself killed shortly on the points of several Zulu assegais. So did Freddy. The news reached home in despatches.

* * *

Johnny Angell continued his honeymoon rather longer than he had originally intended. He had not previously realised the pleasures inherent in marriage, the one to Belle having been unexciting and arranged mainly by reason of unstressed rights in the Chiswick potato stand. Now, he was in a state of growing enchantment. Nothing in the outward appearance of Prudence, at least when dressed, could have given any notion of what lay within or, for that matter, underneath. It was true that on the wedding night he had made a certain discovery, and asked Prudence, very tenderly, "Are you sure all Freddy did was to frighten you, dear?" but she had maintained her usual prim and, to Johnny, by now extremely alluring silence. Whatever lay behind those constantly dropped eyelids and prudent mouth was after all her secret; and there was no doubt that she was a virtuous young woman. Nevertheless it became, as the days passed, like possessing Venus; Johnny extended his original two-day honeymoon to seven.

After all, Raph was reliable; oneself had never before taken a holiday, or had any pleasure, as Johnny now realised, since the long-ago time of Lady Rose. Rose's little ghost sighed and, shortly, vanished; here instead was exquisite flesh, the like of which Johnny had never before seen or imagined; he could not stop himself from running his dry hands over it, savouring its contours, kissing and handling Prudence all over like a Mameluke, at least one supposed so; laying her, at last, on the bed in afternoons as well, having respectfully removed her dress and heard it, as in a dream, subside to the floor. Thereafter it was paradise; she denied him nothing. He had never seen anything as perfect as her breasts; to caress and fondle them was, if Johnny Angell had known it, his apotheosis, and at least he made the most of it while it lasted.

Prudence remained calm. Whatever had happened with Freddy — and she still tried to erase that matter from her mind — this was different, to be expected, unexciting; like the sounds her formerly presumed father Joseph Penney

had been used to make through the wall while taking his prescribed rights upon her mother Abigail. This was what women had to put up with, and she might as well get used to it; besides, it was a good idea to let the old boy keep at it all he could, because she'd begun to feel queasy on the day before the wedding. Johnny had himself suggested, only yesterday, that they ought perhaps to go down and pay a polite visit to Mrs Emily, to see how she did, before returning. He didn't seem at all anxious to get back to the shop.

* * *

It was HC who, some weeks later, brought news to Marylebone of Freddy's death in Zululand. He added, as if in a dream, that the body would shortly be on its way home by sea.

They had seen how greatly he had aged as soon as he got out of the carriage. His hair now was white, except for a few strands of remaining grey; he moved stiffly and his face, which had always been lacking in expression, now

resembled a mask. They knew, from the fact of his presence here at all, that something of import must have occurred. Prudence put her hand to her breast for instants; then as if by habit drew aside her stepdaughter Vera, who stood as usual stolidly in the way.

HC removed his tall hat, came in, stood before the fireplace, and broke the news. There was a silence, then Vera began her shallow bleating. She had hardly known Cousin Freddy, and he himself had never noticed her existence; but all her life the fact of death and change were to affect Vera audibly. She wailed on, not yet having removed her school satchel from her shoulders: Prudence drew it off her absently. She herself was still devoid of feeling. Freddy dead! It was impossible; she'd last set eyes on him, naked and glorious, on the bed they'd shared with such ecstasy that time in Half Moon Street. It was a world away, her life now was quite other. She shut away half of her mind, and with the other half listened to her husband and his kinsman making arrangements. They would go down, of course, with poor Cis, whom

the news had evidently half killed, to receive the coffin at Southampton when it was brought home. "Your sister is prostrated at this time," said HC to Johnny. "It would be a comfort to her to have you with us meanwhile." He had not looked at Prudence, and she heard herself offering to come to Piccadilly. There was a sudden hush as Vera's sheeplike noises stopped; she was in some awe of her uncle by marriage, whom she seldom saw.

"I will be open with you," said HC to Prudence. "My wife prefers that you do not visit us."

He gave no reason, and made a little bow. Prudence felt rebuffed, but as was her way said nothing further. Johnny frowned a trifle in puzzlement. Why didn't Cis want Prudence there? Nobody could be more helpful. He opened his mouth to say so, but Prudence said suddenly that Johnny could go by himself to Piccadilly; she'd stay with the shop and the others, meaning Vera and poor Horry. But it transpired that Cis had demanded that Vera and Horry should both be brought also, and stay for a little; again, no reason was given.

Johnny packed a small valise full of shaving and nightgear, and kissed Prudence fondly on parting; it was the first time since their marriage that he had left her. "Raph will see to the shop," he said. "Don't overtire yourself." He thought she had been looking peaked lately. Perhaps —

"I will try to return tonight if I may," he told her in a low voice. "It depends on how Cis finds herself, and what is to be done. Do not wait up for me, my dear."

The carriage bowled off at last, with Vera, her pop-eyes round with diversion of a dreadful kind, and poor Horry, who of course knew nothing about anything; likewise Johnny and HC. Prudence returned to the house, got on with the work, made her own supper and Raph's, which they ate in silence; then went upstairs, combed out and plaited her hair, undressed herself and went to bed. She was tired, and somewhat bewildered about Cecily, already feeling grief for Freddy, and must have slept. Presently she woke, aware that time had passed and that Johnny must have

returned. There was still a faint glimmer from the gaslight in the street.

He climbed into bed, and began his usual handling of her. Prudence was not too willing; she was only half awake, and wanted to think again of Freddy; he seemed near to her, very near. Presently it seemed as if he, and not Johnny, was making love: Johnny had never aroused such response in her as now. It was almost reminiscent of the half-recalled night of glory and shame. She felt the man's member hard within her, not tentatively as was Johnny's wont but masterfully, like a young and adept lover. She heard herself cry out; and knew that she must have done so that earlier time; it all came back. The delight endured; it became almost unbearable, as if she must bite his very flesh, wrap her legs close about him. She heard his grunt of satisfaction at last, a deep male sound unlike any Johnny had ever made before. In due course she fell asleep again, and in the morning he had gone, which did not surprise or alarm Prudence; no doubt her husband had had to return to town.

She rose presently, and started to

dress herself to go down and prepare breakfast. She discovered while doing so that she had, unaccountably, lost one of her garters. It was one of a pair Emily had given her in the days when the latter had unavailingly tried to interest Prudence in pretty things: there were forget-me-nots embroidered round it, and it must have been expensive. Prudence could not understand what had happened to it; she searched the carpet unavailingly, then decided that perhaps the garter was trapped in her bodice, and she would find it that night. She went to her housewife, cut off a length of plain elastic, knotted it and used it for the time being; there was no more leisure to look, she had to get on.

There was less however to do than usual, without Vera and Horry and her husband. She found herself in the shop in mid-morning, at an hour when early customers had already been and late ones were not yet arrived. Raph had his back to her, marking prices up on packets of tea. She considered him idly; he wasn't a person one noticed much. His appearance was a faint echo of HC's. He

had a habit of standing four-square at the counter, furred arms bare below rolled-up shirt sleeves, hands placed hard on the flat cold surface, the picture of a grocer waiting to serve. He turned now to face her and she saw a smug expression in his eyes. One of his hands held some object and he suddenly opened his palm to reveal what it was; the missing garter.

Shock beat at Prudence in waves; she was slow to realise what must have happened, and yet knew she should have known. She felt dizzy for moments; her legs felt weak, like they'd done that other time. She heard Raph's hard laugh. He still held the garter, dangling it like a toy.

"What'll Uncle Johnny say if I show him this, eh? What'll he say if I tell him a lot of things? Don't make that poker face at me; you enjoyed it as much as I did, Prue, and will again."

"I will not. It was wickedness. You had no right, none, to come and — "

"To come and what, eh?" He had moved close to her. "Give me a kiss, come on." He took one, placing his arm hard about her; she felt her mouth tingle.

"Give me a bit more than that behind the door," he said. She heard herself protest weakly; someone might come in, and she — But she was no longer a creature of decisions, or not now. Her knees had turned to water; she felt him pinch her bottom, then laugh again; there was nothing to be done, she ought to walk away and leave him, but, but —

They coupled in the end standing behind the inner door; nobody came into the front shop. It wasn't like last night, but better than it was with Johnny. She knew it was wrong, but there was nobody to tell: and if she didn't do what he wanted, he'd show Johnny the garter. At least, that was for the first day or two; later on he threw the garter at her in contempt, saying it didn't matter any more, they could go on without it; and they had, later that same day, on the bed again, in daylight.

* * *

"I know," Raph assured her as she lay beneath him, "all about it, my girl. I saw you arrive that first morning,

looking like a drab with a rose in your hair and its petals falling. Who put it there, eh? It was Freddy, wasn't it? Why else did he come here for you? He gave you more than a rose; there's something in your belly, and it's too big for Johnny's." He caressed the small, unsuspected swelling, and Prudence tried to writhe away from him.

"Don't hurt it," she begged. "If you go on like you're doing, it'll be hurt." She had no idea how she knew this.

"I'm careful," he assured her, adding that he'd found the bright dress after Mary threw it out with the rubbish. "I must say I'd like to see you in a dress like that again," he told her. "All the same you're better without one." He mouthed her breasts greedily. "You're a fine girl," he admitted. The bed shook gently.

Later he said, "We get on together, you know that. There are times when old Johnny's out on delivery, or out anyway. We'll make the most of 'em. We'll do what we did in the back shop, often; and when it suits everyone I'll come up here." He got off the bed, and buttoned himself. "In the shop, tomorrow, between

ten and eleven," he told her. "If he isn't back tonight I'll come, but I daresay he will be."

Johnny came back. He seemed quiet, and not as eager as usual to make love: she turned away, glad to be left in peace. If she had known, the reason for his silence was Cis. Cis had said Prudence killed Freddy; he'd no longer cared whether he lived or died.

"He wanted to marry her," she sobbed. "Emily told me. Freddy and that creature! He was the handsomest man in England. If it hadn't been for *her*, he could have married anyone." This statement was inaccurate, but Cecily was distraught. "He would have taken more care of himself in Africa if he hadn't been in despair, knowing about your marriage. My darling boy died because of her whey face and her silences. I don't want to see her again, and Vera isn't going back to her, nor is poor Horry. I'm keeping them both here with me."

Vera's father made no protest; he was too greatly dazed. In fact it proved a good thing for Vera; Cecily, out of a nest-egg Mary had left her, paid the

fees for a new and prestigious girls' school named Pratt's, lately opened near Chiswick. Later still, as the child continued her unpredictable bleatings and proved to be a great deal more trouble than poor Horry, Cis sensibly arranged that she should board with her brother Alec and their Frame grandparents. This worked out very well. Meantime, Gabriel's wedding, which it had been arranged should take place shortly, had to be quiet, because of mourning; and in due course the ship docked with Freddy's coffin and that of others on board, and was met by the assembled family at Southampton. Johnny was there again, to support his sister, changed meantime into a red-eyed old woman. He hadn't brought Prudence, this time any more than the last. Nobody wanted trouble.

* * *

The day they brought Freddy Angell's coffin home from Southampton for its military funeral, Raph spent the time, the shop being duly closed, with Johnny's wife in Johnny's bed. He had made

the excuse not to attend the obsequies because somebody might rob the shop, knowing all the men were absent. Quietly, at full leisure behind drawn shutters, he coupled with Prudence. He was complacent; this was better than the back shop, with a good feather mattress to rely on. Johnny didn't know how to use his luck. Raph let himself reflect on what usually happened by now during the day; if the shop bell rang while they were busy at it, there was time to pull everything down and everything else up, and go out to the customer. Prue didn't fuss. If she had, he could have handled it. He knew about women. They were all the same: you had to know what you were doing, that was all.

Prudence was in fact beyond caring what any man did to her. The only thing was that what Raph did, constantly and rather well, reminded her of that night with Freddy she couldn't properly remember. It made Freddy seem alive again, somehow, especially if she shut her eyes and couldn't see it was really Raph. Freddy, a poor corpse decomposing in the African heat and with the long voyage

home; they said the Prince Imperial's valet had fainted when the lid of that coffin was opened at last, when it got to Chislehurst. Raph, oh, oh . . . the god's body, no more existing, Raph or any other man would have to do instead. As for the baby that was coming, it was certainly Freddy's. Prudence held that to her heart. Otherwise, she thought she was beginning to know what real life meant. If it hadn't been for what went on in the back shop now often, behind the inner door, life would have grown very dull: almost as much so as in the days of her mother and Joseph Penney and, one had to admit, the sewing-classes at Great Quayle.

* * *

Johnny Angell returned from his nephew's funeral in a state of forlorn sadness. The sight of the long coffin — Freddy had been six feet tall — borne into church, and afterwards to the graveyard, by bearers from the regiment, had been the least of it. Far worse was the slow effect, between first news by telegraph of the

death and now, on both the dead man's parents, HC and Cis. Johnny's sister had become an old woman, stooping, bitter and red-eyed, leaning on the arm of her husband as though he had been a solitary rock in a gale. The rocklike qualities of HC — Johnny hardly remembered the rivalries in the firm over the years — had crumbled, however; he was a white-haired old man now, staring ahead of him into a world known only to those who have lost all hope. It was evident that he had little desire to go on living after his son's death and would, therefore, shortly himself die; and then what would Cis do? Johnny could recall the vigorous ex-schoolmaster who had arrived so briskly to marry his sister and rescue Cis from a useless twilight existence, and had given her children to her joy, especially the one who was lost now to the grave. Mike, seeming strange behind a rich brown beard, had arrived home for the funeral; sturdy and independent as always, bearing on his arm — the shock had been absorbed meantime in the general grief — a mahogany bride from Tobago. Poor Horry had of course

been himself, led in by the keeper they had found since he had been removed from Marylebone. Gabriel and his new wife of stockbroking connections were respectably present; and young Jerry, who was said to be paying attentions of the same variety, had been in church with his recently acquired fiancée, who in Johnny's opinion looked a hard young bitch. Her mother had been with them, also a fat sister who looked ready for anything. Johnny consoled himself with the thought of reunion with Prudence, on whom, after all, he could safely now rely and whom he loved with all his heart.

He let himself into the Marylebone house late at night; she wouldn't be expecting him till tomorrow, but he had wanted to come home and to leave them all to their mourning and their marriage-plans. He stole upstairs, relieved himself, took out his teeth and put them to steep in their customary bowl, set down his Gladstone bag meantime and opened the bedroom door.

Raph had just risen from her. There was no doubt about what they had been doing; his flaccid penis was not

yet bestowed. Prudence lay on the bed, eyes closed, mouth more than usually soft and relaxed; her thighs were still bare beneath the rucked-up nightgown. It was, somehow, worse than total nakedness would have been. Johnny began to cry, the tears running down his furrowed cheeks. He stood there helplessly with the Gladstone bag still at his feet and the door creaking open. Raph turned and surveyed him coolly, continuing to stuff his own shirt back into his trousers. Presently he strode over to the door, kicked Johnny's bag contemptuously forward and gave the older man a shove towards the bed. "Your turn, uncle," he said. He was smiling.

Johnny, sobbing, found himself propelled without volition against Prudence's soft spread thighs. Their shape was familiar and in the strangeness, the betrayal, the horror, he found himself clawing them. He was still sobbing like a child. Prudence opened her green eyes wide, and looked through him as though he were not there. No one said anything more, and Johnny heard Raph go out and the door slam shut. He was aware of his own snuffling tears, falling now on Prudence's flesh,

and that despite everything he was having an erection. The shame of it unmanned him; he had become an animal, no longer himself, sobbing and jerking and trying to mate with a woman who had been unfaithful to him. Belle had been unfaithful as well. Everyone made a fool out of him, always, from the beginning of it. Beyond the closed door, he could hear Raph's laughter as he went down the stairs; and felt, as he entered the woman at last, the round pregnant swelling of the child she carried; whose child? It wasn't his own; they never were. He had accepted the situation. He had to: there was nothing else.

Prudence was already exhausted after Raph's transports; she let Johnny do as he would. Now that he knew about all of it things would be simpler. She'd never liked fuss and concealment. While Johnny gulped and drooled against her breasts she suddenly remembered her mother for the first time in years, and wondered what she'd have said. Nothing, probably: the answer, in any situation at all, had always seemed to be silence. She began to wonder, while Johnny finished,

if there was enough bacon in stock for tomorrow's shelves to be put out first thing from the larder; with Raph and his goings on, she herself hadn't been as particular as usual about ordering stock. However bacon went off in any case if you kept it too long. Prudence then remembered Freddy's funeral today. She wouldn't ask Johnny about that, or about anything else. All that was over.

⋆ ⋆ ⋆

HC was standing alone in his private office after closing time, watching the traffic clatter down darkening Piccadilly; below him, the gilded sign waved, emitting its faint regular creak and still shining in what was left of the light. The sight and sound were so familiar, so much a part of his working day, that HC no longer heard them. He was staring down at a letter he had received that day from Australia. It was laboriously written, giving the impression of a writer with his tongue protruding slightly from his mouth and wetting his lips from side to side as he laboured diligently over

every sputtered word. The Stranger, as he himself had once remarked, had had small instruction in the finer points of education in his orphanage. The letter was from Bendigo, Victoria. It had taken some weeks to arrive.

Dear Dad — HC winced a little; Nellie had visited her son too often and had made him unduly familiar with a situation which should have been permitted to sink quietly into oblivion. *Dear Dad, Ive made good with the money you guv me on leavin. Ive set up as a cochbilder in Ballarat not far, since I brak me leg. I bin at it now 15 year, after tryin one thing and another. I wouldn't take a wife who wasn't edicated, but till now there was nobody like that ere. Now I've married, er nam was Miss Susie Tomkins and she taught school and shes expectin. I ad to prove meself worthy before she'd ave me, bein that much older and er a lady very near.* He went on to describe how Miss Tomkins, who sounded a young woman of parts, had formerly played the organ at open-air preachings on Sunday evenings round about the edge of the bush. Once a man on the run — HC could not

comprehend the ill-spelt name, it surely could not be Moonlight — had dressed himself up as the visiting preacher and guv a sermon while the officers of the law came looking, held forth cool as you liked, and then got away. He hoped his father would wish them both happy and lots of little uns. He was, yours truly, Horace Cicero Angell, the younger.

P.S. Remember me to good ole Belle and maybe Johnny, if he wants.

Belle was dead long ago, like Freddy. It was ironical that this other eldest son should have written at the present time. He mustn't mention the letter at home. It might upset Cis these days; she'd lost her tranquil calm since they lost Freddy. HC read through the letter once more, then tore it across and across and thrust it in the office fire. It flared up briefly, then died. HC went out, fetched his hat and rolled umbrella, and made his cautious way home to Bolton Street.

Part Three

1

THE daffodils were nodding in a Hyde Park spring. Emily Purslove, in half-mourning by now for her late husband, who had died of nothing notable, helped Prudence with the push-chair young Freddy Angell no longer needed, his staggering steps the unfailing admiration of entranced passers-by. Balanced in the chair meantime was a hoop Emily had hoped Freddy would play with; but meantime they progressed along the outer paths in the sunlight, watching in the distance the riders raising their accustomed dust along the Row. Freddy, his shining curls echoing the daffodils, clutched cheerfully at a woollen ball Emily had earlier made for him and from which he would not be parted. His other hand was in his mother's.

Emily, watching them, was happy for the first time in months. It was not only the deaths of Leonard and the old DM — the latter had, one

was convinced, died of boredom and of having nothing to complain about now poor dear Leonard was no longer present in his library — but her own callous treatment by her stepson, who on inheriting the title had commenced to rebuild Great Quayle immediately and had demanded her prompt removal from the old east wing. Emily had not waited to witness the ruthless pulling down of the Tudor brickwork and the total destruction of what could never be replaced; she had not wanted in any case to see the Gothic horror rise, and had betaken herself to Marylebone, rather than to Piccadilly; Prudence after all was closer to her now than anyone, and had made no objection. It was pleasant to be living in a much humbler way again, over the shop as Emily had done when she was a girl; and although she missed her sewing-classes and little charities, there was small Freddy. He was her delight, and made up for the fact that Johnny, her brother, was by now a sad gnome with little to say for himself, out nearly all the time on deliveries, and Prudence had to have a room of her own as she did not sleep

well, she stated, since Freddy's birth.

"It is remarkable," said Emily now, watching the pale-gold curls dance, "how closely he resembles my poor nephew killed in South Africa in 1879." She seemed to have replaced the image of the earlier Freddy in her mind as he had been when he used to ride despairingly down to visit Prudence so often at Quayle; to her, now, in memory, he was again her handsome eldest brother, adored by their parents, coming and going gloriously from Westminster and, later on, even more gloriously from Woolwich; not that one had ever encountered him very much by then. At any rate, little Freddy reminded one of him very strongly. "Family likenesses persist," Emily remarked knowledgeably. She recalled Lady Rose Purslove and her remarkable likeness to Lady Emmeline; Emily had brought the drawing with her and now kept it in a drawer; after all, it was her property.

Prudence smiled her faint Mona Lisa smile. She was as devoted to young Freddy as his aunt, and had for a time, after his birth, seen herself as a

dutiful mother and even a faithful wife, so full was her heart with genuine pride and love. But Raph had prevailed on her again and their association was by now almost like marriage; Johnny slept downstairs, Raph came in to Prudence whenever he felt inclined, which meant most nights; there was no further need to make use of the back shop any more for anything but the purpose intended by its original owners. It was at present half full of packing-cases, and the assistant, who came in by day, ate his midday bread and cold beef in there. As for Alec and Vera, they were still with their grandparents at Chiswick and a good thing too. Prudence had heard somewhere that Vera had been accepted for next year as a pupil-teacher at Pratt's girls' school. She had never, after all, wanted to do anything else, and never would. It seemed a dreary sort of life, but Vera had been a dreary kind of child. Freddy was different.

He capered now in his blue nankeen trousers, pointing out two well-dressed figures approaching in the near distance and dropping his ball. "I declare it looks like Raph, with a lady," Emily exclaimed.

It was Sunday, and Raph had gone off on his own concerns as he usually did. Emily smiled; the family had long ago given up hope of Raph's ever being anything now but an old bachelor. All the rest, except of course poor Horry, were married by this time; Jerry's little wife had astonishing ideas about what could be done with the Piccadilly store. Hats — and such hats! — clothes, lingerie and shoes above stairs, and a tea-room with potted palms and a hired orchestra to play Strauss waltzes! Downstairs, of course, the real business went on as usual, much expanded. Papa seldom stood there nowadays as he had used to do; poor Papa.

Raph duly advanced with his companion, a prosperously dressed lady in pince-nez. She might have been about forty, and had a kind, rather hesitant face. Prudence meantime felt the familiar trembling of the knees the sight of Raph now always induced in her. His power over her was by this time almost that of a hypnotist: his virile thrustings, which hadn't after all hurt young Freddy while lying in her womb, caused that organ at certain times to respond with unexpected violence.

"You've got a hot tail, my girl; that's the main point," Raph would say equably. Prudence knew she needn't feel such sudden, savage jealousy of this unknown woman; after all, Raph was bound to have business acquaintances. This lady however had a broad band of grey in her brown hair which was in its way attractive beneath the poised, rather self-conscious hat. Prudence, like Emily, smiled, bowed and was introduced. The lady was a Mrs Wedderburn, from Scotland. Raph swept off his tall hat and made a small, formal bow.

"You will be the first to congratulate us," he said smoothly. "Frances has just done me the honour — " he smiled down at her — "to accept my hand in marriage."

* * *

Frances Wedderburn was the widow of an Edinburgh lawyer considerably older than herself, who had left her very comfortably off indeed. She had always had a longing to see London, and while there, in the heart of a Scots enclave situated to the

north of the city, had been introduced to Raphael Angell at the house of a business acquaintance. From then on her life had seemed to contain the excitement for which she had, in a rather humdrum and certainly childless existence, always unknowingly dreamed. Raph was the perfect escort, with the manners of a gentleman; Frances was astonished to learn that he had interests in a grocery business for the most part, though by now, of course, there were other investments as well. He had taken her driving to see the bright Angell sign waving over Piccadilly, and had shepherded her inside and, presently, upstairs to have tea beneath the palms, while the band played romantic tunes. This was delightful, and in addition the deference shown Raph by the Piccadilly staff, who knew him well, was enough to convince poor Frances, if she had needed convincing by then, that he was, as they would have put it in Edinburgh, a warm man, decidedly not after her money. Besides, she was, at her age, in love; the dry little husband she had buried last year in the north had given

her no children, and she longed for these with all her heart, particularly a little girl. Perhaps it was not too late. She had said Yes at once when Raph proposed to her in the daffodil-studded Park; and meeting, now, the delicious little boy with the fair curls, Raph's cousin, she was already tremulously wishful of perhaps a similar product of her own; Raph's young brother Jerry whom she had met in the shop had had even such golden hair, at his age naturally a little darker, but altogether angelic. Frances felt herself transported with happiness, and hardly saw the two women with Freddy except to remember to greet them with proper civility.

Prudence, to do her justice, showed no emotion. Like Emily, she bowed to the new acquisition, then bent and retrieved Freddy's woollen ball from the ground. This gesture let Prudence conceal her face for a moment, and allowed her finally to collect herself. She smiled on. Mrs Wedderburn and Emily were chattering away; invitations to tea were exchanged; Prudence merely stood there, looking after Freddy. He grew restless, providentially, and Frances

herself pointed out that perhaps the dear little fellow thought it was time to move on. She smiled, showing well-preserved teeth, her gloved hand still satisfactorily on Raph's arm. Everyone bowed again, and the pair moved off.

"How fortunate for him," said Emily, as they made their way homeward. "Such a pleasant woman. Raph has always been so greatly alone." She had a romantic nature, in spite of everything.

* * *

That night Raph came to Prudence as usual. She was incredulous, outraged; she had gone to bed after a disconsolate, furious day, beating her fists at last against the sheets and pillows; almost, she had called to Johnny to come up, as still happened at the times she felt sorry for him. Here however was Raph, still in silence; it was as though there was nothing to explain.

He established his accustomed mastery over her, in moments. She knew by now, had perhaps known long ago, that it must contain derision; yet why had he come at

all? She knew soon: after entering her as usual swiftly and hard, he continued in a way she was unused to; she cried out in protest.

"You promised you'd be careful. What are you doing?" But she knew very well; and he laughed, and did not answer for moments. "I've decided otherwise now, that's all," he told her presently. "You'll do as I say, Prue; you know that already."

She tried to free herself, and knew she could not; pinned down, passively receiving his seed, she had to endure the situation, now and later on. She knew she would rather do so than lose Raph; but what did he mean by it, tonight of all times? He didn't explain further, any more than he ever did; merely rose and left her. If anything happened, she'd have to be able to say it was Johnny's. She lay miserably, without much sleep for the rest of the night. She'd never understand Raph Angell; she'd never be able to do without him, either. A savage longing was with her already to feel his member hard within her again. Perhaps he'd come back.

* * *

Some weeks later, she found herself pregnant. Raph had been with her again several times, and so had Johnny, but, as last time, Prudence knew whose child she was carrying. The sickness was worse than it had been when she was expecting Freddy, and she knew she didn't want this baby at all; before she grew heavy with it, Raph married his Scots bride in a Presbyterian church and Prudence had her own excuse to stay away from the wedding; she still wasn't at all welcome to old Cis, who was of course present at the ceremony. Frances on the other hand was well received by the Angells; this seemed exactly the right wife for Raph, well endowed and, evidently, well connected at least by her former marriage in the north; nobody knew much about her own family and its members seemed to be dead, but Frances herself was obviously a lady, perhaps a cut above themselves.

The honeymoon was spent in Paris, after which it was tacitly agreed by everyone that Raph should not return

to the Marylebone shop; there was no need, they could afford an extra assistant, and Raph would continue to keep an occasional eye and help Johnny. Raph made the eye an excuse for continued visits to Prudence, though he was careful not to disturb the pregnancy as much as last time. He did not, for excellent reasons, intend to give Frances any children. Her money, if she predeceased him, would come to himself; this prospect caused Raph to buy up a few more shares with the expert help of Gabriel, and Raph himself had no intention of spending the resulting dividends on a crowd of brats. Poor Frances, enthralled by his experienced love-making, concluded at last, when nothing more happened, that there must be something wrong with her internally; neither Angus formerly, nor dear Raph now, had succeeded in giving her a baby, though both had tried. Frances grew increasingly plaintive as time passed, and often invited Emily to tea in the pleasant house she and Raph had found together in St John's Wood. It had a garden, and the two childless ladies would weed and look after this

frequently together, genteelly moaning as a rule about their general inability to produce anything but, perhaps, marigolds from seed. Sometimes they had young Freddy to stay, and this was diverting, if somewhat exhausting; but it no doubt helped poor Prudence, who was by now growing very large indeed at home.

* * *

There was only one flaw in Raph's plans, and he ought to have considered the possibility: the child who came to be born was not a son to inherit the Marylebone business in proper course, but a daughter. For lack of any other ideas on the subject Prudence called the child Violet. Violet had dark hair, but this might after all have been Johnny's. Her eyes, when they opened and changed colour, turned out to be her mother's, a disturbing water-green. Otherwise she did not, then or later, resemble anyone except herself. Raph saw her once, by accident, when his wife demanded almost with tears to be driven to Marylebone to see the baby; thereafter he discouraged

Frances from going there, and by that time she did as she was told by him in all respects. Raph maintained no interest in his daughter, and any prospect of repeating the situation was defeated by Prudence herself; the midwife who had attended the birth had told her there were ways of looking after yourself nowadays so that it didn't happen again, and Prudence used these whether or not Raph came to call. As a result, he contrived other uses for her, to which in the end she agreed; he had long aroused certain needs in her which poor Johnny could never satisfy.

* * *

HC was dying. He had been too feeble at the time to attend Raph's wedding and since then had steadily grown weaker. The family were, therefore, prepared to attend his expected death in force: it was almost a national occasion. The streets outside had been sanded to keep the passing carriages quiet; in the great shop nearby, black bows were waiting ready to pin up above the doors in proper

course, and it was foreseen that the funeral would be impressive and well attended. A projected memorial plaque, in brass, was already being considered for a certain location inside the store: royalty would subscribe.

Cecily sat beside the bed holding her husband's hand. She had never for one moment regretted their marriage; HC had been unfailingly kind to her; she had loved him uncomplainingly and her life, lacking him, was impossible to imagine. Cis did not try, and instead briefly raised her red-rimmed eyes to her sons and their wives, assembled in the half-dark room. Freddy, her beloved darling, was of course long gone; perhaps, from whatever Low Church heaven could be imagined by anyone, he would come to fetch his father. The others had almost ceased to interest Cecily although she had always done her duty by them. The waiting crowd seemed made up of strangers.

She returned to a scrutiny of HC's face, puffed now and altered by the sounds of difficult breathing which would soon cease. His eyes were closed and Cis

had no more notion of what he might be thinking than she had ever done. Certainly he did not seem aware of her presence. Perhaps he was thinking of his sister Theodora, whom he would after all rejoin shortly also. Cis was aware of a slight pricking of long-forgotten resentment. The years since Theo's death had been happier for her lack, two of them left instead of three to make decisions, to be lovingly together, husband and wife, as it should be. Cis fondled the flaccid hand and resigned herself to thoughts of pending death and loss. Gabriel would of course see to everything that had to be done; that was a comfort.

HC was in fact fully conscious. He kept his eyes closed for the sake of privacy, also some peace to think: after all nobody knew what happened after. He was aware of those who were present about the bed, but very few, if any, could assist him in any way any more than they had ever done, and HC ignored them. His mind remained clear, as it always had; those who thought the old were mostly imbeciles who could hear

and understand nothing after seventy-five would know differently when their own turn came. There were things concerning which, looking back, HC could reproach himself; one was the sterile arranged marriage of Jerry's fat sister-in-law. There were other things for which HC congratulated himself, a former schoolmaster, downtrodden like most of the race as he'd once been. Now, the Piccadilly branch of Angells was a respected institution, as much so as Fortnums. Mary Angell's Own Honeymoon Jam, with a gold-embossed label stuck on each jar, was still fetching the tidy sum it always had; he'd promoted sales of that successfully. A family tradition; *that* was important, although considering everything there didn't seem to be too many grandchildren. Freddy had died unmarried; a pity. Mike was far away across seas, and would no doubt in time — his father hadn't heard — produce enough piccaninnies to help in the sugar refinery he himself had lately proposed starting up in Jamaica. It would, Mike had written from his ship before he left it for good, supply

the firm with bulk priority at cut rates if assured by contract of regular custom. That was the Angell streak; well done, Mike Angell. As for Gabriel, his wife evidently had some kind of a blockage; that couldn't be helped. Raph's had been married too late, doubtless; at any rate there were none to be expected there. Raph had always been a dark horse, but it didn't signify. Emily, with the grand marriage he'd made for her long ago, had likewise had none; that was a pity, the county connection had been useful and had now lapsed. As for Jeremiel, the white hope — poor Horry was of course out of the reckoning — Jerry's marriage had been ambitious, his wife's family rich, something to do with Oriental carpets. Lisa, however, seemed to be more interested in the running of the Piccadilly store herself than in producing heirs as she should, by now, be doing. That was why he, HC, had behaved as he had done over her beefy sister Corisande, whose appetites had almost overflowed before marriage and who had certainly made sheep's eyes at young Jeremiel. To save his son — Jerry hated to

say No to anyone — he, HC, had arranged that a handsome former pupil from Yorkshire named Crewe, whom HC had known perfectly well had something wrong with him at the time, should come to London, meet Corisande, and be bribed into matrimony. It had happened, since when Corisande Crewe had been looking increasingly discontented. Well, the thing was done now, or after all not; Corisande's plump person showed no signs of becoming plumper, which meant that the carpet revenues would, in the end, be Lisa's, which in turn meant Jerry's. It all worked out. If only Lisa were less interested in acquiring hard cash! As for Marylebone —

HC became aware of a buzzing in his ears and of the increased pressure of his wife's hand. He opened his eyes, smiled at Cis, said clearly aloud "Australia", and then died. Cis, seeing it take place, leaned over and closed her husband's eyes, kissing his cheek quietly for the last time. She did not wait for the other members of the family to pay their respects to the dead man; she rose, picked up the stick with which she had

begun to have to walk two years ago now and went out of the death-chamber, her black skirts — she had never put off mourning for the elder Freddy Angell, her son — trailing after her.

Part Four

1

VIOLET ANGELL and her elder brother Freddy had been brought up by Cousin Emily Purslove in a little house on Ham Common rented by means of Prudence's immoral earnings. Emily, innocent as always, was of course unaware of these. She merely thought that the shop must be doing very well indeed; it was good for the children to be away from it, in the fresh air, almost the country. The Piccadilly branch might be the grander of the two, but an old family business was always sound, and dear Johnny was well known by now to everyone.

Prudence's subsidiary business operated privately up the Marylebone back stairs. It could not have done so had there been children running about, not to mention the sudden enquiring appearances of Emily in her dressing-gown. Emily had been delighted to be asked to take the children away and to be responsible for

them at least during the week. It was almost as good as having had some of her own; the unkindness of Great Quayle was a thing of the past. Emily had long lost touch with her stepson and his family; she had seen photographs, in a fashionable magazine, of the new DM with his stiff-necked county bride and, later, the young mother holding the resulting heir. They never wrote to her and she was invited neither to the wedding nor the christening. Ham was a compensation, undoubtedly.

Emily made a point of supervising the children's manners and of employing suitable governesses, always of course after consulting dear Prudence. In the evenings and on Saturdays, she took them for walks. Inhabitants of the place grew accustomed to the sight of a thin elderly lady in black, walking slightly behind a small fair-haired boy of angelic beauty who was generally bowling a hoop. The girl, younger and not pretty at all, being slight, unobtrusive and with mouse-coloured hair, was noticed by few. Curiosity was at first made manifest as to the identity of the party, but having

satisfied themselves that Mrs Purslove was indeed related by marriage to the noble family of that name, who never called, interest was quickly lost. The carriage which came occasionally to visit contained only the wife of Angell the grocer at Marylebone. Otherwise the small family appeared regularly at church on Sundays, with the two children clean, well dressed and behaving themselves during the sermon.

Prudence herself, swathed in furs, would drive off contentedly after each visit; Freddy was increasingly enchanting; she'd hardly notice Violet as a rule. She told herself she was fond of both her children; she was in fact saving up for a holiday with them in Paris. Emily would of course come. Prudence assessed the probable cost and decided that, by now, she could afford it. That she would turn into a business woman, which had happened, was not at all what Raph, instigator of the whole idea, had intended.

It had all started shortly after Violet's birth. Raph had announced to Prudence that he couldn't keep two women

satisfied, and in the same breath had mentioned that a good friend of his, a Mr Blackburn, would call in with him on Thursday evening. Prudence had been left in no doubt of Mr Blackburn's intentions as soon as he had been shown upstairs; and at first had protested, as was natural. Raph however promised her a little pocket-money if she did exactly as she was asked, and after all what difference did it make by now?

Mr Blackburn returned by himself, also other clients. At first Raph pocketed the cash, allowing Prudence a minor proportion which at first she used to keep in the top of her stocking. Later, with the increase of upstairs custom, the amounts grew inconveniently large, and as Prudence herself was a thrifty person with a respect for money, and no wish to waste it, she called upon Gabriel, who had by now acquired considerable influence in the City. Gabriel instructed her more than a little about the value of investments, and it was even possible, under the new Married Women's Property Act, to open a bank account in Prudence's own name and not poor Johnny's; there might

otherwise have been confusion between downstairs and up.

In the former respect, Johnny continued his lachrymose and obliging self; it was generally assumed by new customers that like his nephew Horry he was slightly lacking. He even showed the regular gentlemen upstairs when they came, knowing them all by name and acting very respectfully. Prudence, meantime, next time she encountered Raph, told him to his face that, in future, payment would be made by clients direct to herself. Raph's jaw had almost dropped, but he saved it just in time; only, this wasn't what he had planned at all. The control of the subsidiary business, now that he had two reliable assistants to help Johnny in the shop, should have been his affair entirely. He made a dignified protest, and for the first time saw Prudence's green eyes grow wide and angry.

"You've had your money's worth out of me with a vengeance, Raph Angell," she said, "and now you can take yourself off. Johnny can manage the business downstairs and I can manage it upstairs; what d'you suppose you're needed for

AS14

any more?" At this blow to his pride and manhood, Raph had attempted the usual blandishments, which had never before failed. They failed now; Prudence did a most unladylike thing, and kicked out with her knee where it hurt most. Raph staggered back, holding the place, his face contorted.

"I should have done that long ago, you swine," said Prudence, "right at the beginning. Get out, and don't come back."

Raph never did come back; he continued to accept, in withdrawn dignity from St John's Wood, such twice-yearly monies as were due to him from the shop, and kept an eye on the grocery accounts. He had, of course, other interests; for all anyone knew, he might have other whorehouses. Prudence's became a great success. The contrast between the immobility of her features and the receptivity of her tail provided a fillip to the most jaded, and it became an open secret that for a certain consideration and by strict appointment in private, Mrs Johnny's virtuous petticoats would be lifted up, after which it was worth it.

Later on, she employed assistants, like Johnny downstairs.

As for Piccadilly, it went from strength to strength under the aegis of Jeremiel's wife Lisa. Jerry himself remained virtually a floorwalker, if a superior one of very handsome appearance. The Chiswick stall was long since a flourishing emporium, run by young Alec with hired help since his grandfather had died. Alec, son of The Stranger and Belle Angell, was looking about him cautiously for a wife. His sister Vera enjoyed teaching so much that it was necessary to employ a housekeeper to look after them both, also old Phyll, now confined to a bath-chair. Alec was mean by nature, and paying out did not suit him.

All of this was never allowed to affect the quiet house on Ham Common. When Freddy was eleven years old and Violet eight, their mother called to say they were all to come with her to Paris, and Aunt Emily too. They would travel on Tuesday of next week; the carriage would collect them in time for the train.

"We can practise our French," said Violet, her thin little face brightening;

one of the governesses had taught it very well.

Freddy said nothing. He had decided to become a soldier after being taken once to London to see the Changing of the Guard. "It'll be hot in those busbies," remarked Violet. "A man fainted once."

Freddy still said nothing. Girls were silly.

* * *

Prudence, with the help of Mr Thomas Cook, who was not one of her clients, had selected a discreet hotel near the Opéra. When they arrived Emily, who had not been well on the crossing, went to lie down. The rest, having left their baggage, set off on foot to explore Paris. It was a crisp and beautiful day. They reached the new Champs Elysées, sat in a café in the open air while the children ate ices, took a fiacre, saw the great bridges and Napoleon's tomb and the gargoyles grinning above Notre Dame; and were duly intoxicated by the foreign smell of cigarette smoke, coffee, Pernod and some other ingredient without name which is

found nowhere else than in Paris. Freddy took it all as his due. Violet would never forget it.

Returning to Emily, who had recovered a little, they all changed for dinner. Violet was excited about her new petticoats, which had starched frills; she heard them rustle beneath her skirt as they all descended the stairs past a large castor oil plant reposing in a brass pot on the landing. Respectability was the keynote now in Republican Paris; a generation ago it would have been different, with Offenbach and crinolines, and gentlemen with opera-glasses raised. Prudence observed the difference as they entered the dining-room; but said little as was her way, and left the children to ask any questions of Emily; she herself felt that she had done her duty in the course of the afternoon.

They sat down, having been ushered to a table; and Prudence found herself gazing straight into the eyes of Lady Gaia Toomey.

* * *

She dropped her glance, pretending meantime to study the menu. She knew herself to have changed even less than Lady Gaia, who had hardly changed at all. Tom was with her, grown stouter and with a somewhat defeated air; his moustache however flourished. Beside them was another woman, whom Prudence did not take time to study; but young Freddy did. "There's a beautiful lady over there with diamond ear-rings," he said clearly. Skittles, for it was she, revisiting Paris, turned her queenly dark head and smiled. Then her smile grew to one of entire delight and she rose, sweeping fan-pleated moire trimmings on a grey train as she came; the others, of necessity, followed, though perhaps otherwise they would have respected Prudence's evident wish not to be noticed. Now, it was too late.

Skittles went straight to the boy. "You," she said engagingly, "must be Freddy Angell's son. You can't be anyone else. He was the sweetest bugger." Her smile, enhanced by the dancing grey-blue eyes between long lashes, fastened on Prudence while she embraced and

kissed the boy. Lady Gaia murmured introductions. Tom was less subtle.

"Didn't give us much of a farewell, did you, Prue, that time in Half Moon Street? Last I saw of you was when poor Freddy carried you out, after dinner. None of the rest of us got up next day till — " He became aware of his wife's nudge and fell silent, his jaw still hanging open. Skittles' delight embraced the entire party. She still spoke with a Merseyside accent in spite of all polish and the Quorn.

"Are you Prudence? The famous Prudence from Marylebone? Charley Blackburn says there's nobody to touch you, not even me at my best. I declare I'm a bit jealous; Charley was one of my best customers before. Never mind, it's all in the luck of the draw, love, isn't it? And these are your children. It's easy to see who the boy's father was." She patted Freddy with reminiscent tenderness. "Who was the little girl's, or don't you know, dear? Sometimes it used to happen that way, but not any more. I never had any, somehow. You must all come out tomorrow and we'll go together

and drive in the Bois for old times" —

Emily had already risen. Her face had paled enough to reveal a network of tiny broken veins, blue meantime with shock, on her worn cheeks. She said, "I am taking Violet home to England at once. Pray allow me to pass."

* * *

Violet had made no outcry; most children would have burst into a wail. She allowed herself to be taken firmly by the hand and led away from Freddy, from her dinner, from Paris, which meant already everything that she had briefly seen and that had been stored away for ever in her receptive child's mind; and apart from a vague resentment that she should be taken and Freddy left, as usual asked few questions. Emily packed in grim silence, then they obtained a carriage to the station; thereafter it was a reversal of the enchanting journey here, full of hope and promise as it had been; now, everything was grey, the Channel, when they reached it, deceptively smooth; Emily survived the return crossing with fortitude. When they

reached Dover, she put up, with Violet, at the Lord Warden Hotel for the night. The shock she had sustained about Prudence suspended all her faculties; she could hardly think what to do next, except that they must of course not return to the house at Ham, undoubtedly the reward of shame; they had best perhaps go to Bolton Street, to Mama, at least for the present.

* * *

Meantime young Freddy was having the time of his life. The beautiful lady — he found out afterwards that her real name was Catherine Walters, but that they called her Skittles because she had used to knock them down in the old days in Liverpool — held his hand in the carriage, dressed today not in the grey moiré gown and diamond ear-rings but in an enchanting golden stuff driving-dress with brown velvet trimming, and a matching hat with a seagull's feathers perched saucily on the brim. The carriage itself, with Mama seated opposite in her usual silence, and without the other two

people who had meantime somehow been got rid of, drove to all the places no ordinary visitor to Paris ever saw; notably a pretty little house in an estate near the Bois, called Bagatelle. Its shutters were drawn and Skittles explained that the last owner, a recluse named Richard Wallace, had died there three years before. "But things have happened here, always," she said, her exquisite profile turned towards the pavilion where once a statue of Diana had stood in bronze. "The young Prince Imperial — he fought along with your father in South Africa, Freddy, and they were both killed there — *he* used to be brought here with a fine glittering escort of Spahis, I remember, and ride his pony, when he was a boy your age. He loved Bagatelle so much they thought the old Marquis of Hertford would leave it to him, but he didn't. He was the meanest man ever." She turned to Prudence, whose silences she found restful. "You know, dear, he played a rotten trick on the poor White Lady, as they always called Lou Bréart because she dressed in it; pretended to marry her in England, then it turned out it

hadn't been a clergyman at all, but Hertford's valet dressed up in a gown and bands. She stayed with him all the same. Did you ever? Can't trust some men round the corner. We love 'em, though, don't we?" She smiled down at Freddy and he thought she looked more like a dark angel than ever. He was not surprised to be told who his real father had been, only pleased and interested. It was more exciting than having dreary old Johnny Angell for one's papa, shuffling about his grocer's shop with tears in his eyes. Freddy straightened his spine and held on devotedly to Skittles' kid-gloved fingers while she told him, as they drove away from Bagatelle, how in these same leafy rides of the Bois they had all used to meet together of a morning, high in the saddle, everybody who was anybody in the good old days of the Second Empire, and herself perched on a satiny black horse named Mouche. "All the gentlemen were round me, because your mother wasn't there," she said, and winked. Prudence smiled her Mona Lisa smile. They drove on to look at the burnt Tuileries. "Those bloody communards,"

said Skittles roundly. "They didn't ought to have done it, and what good did it do anyone? The Emperor had gone by then, poor devil, and the Prussians too." She stared at the blackened ruins of what had once been the famous palace of the old régime, with all its fabled glories; and murmured that the Empress Eugénie still came back to Paris sometimes, and could be found wandering about the bookstalls by the Seine, an ageing lady in gold-rimmed pince-nez. Skittles herself never seemed to age. She took them to a famous restaurant for *déjeuner*, chaffed the waiters, and over the meal gazed no longer at Freddy, but at Prudence.

"What are you going to do when you get back, love?" she asked quietly. "That old bitch won't make things easy for you; she might try to take the boy away as well once you're in England, and she'll certainly interfere with business." She flung the recollection of Emily back over her shoulder, with other inconvenient memories. "Why," she said suddenly, "don't you move in with me, to South Street? There's enough going on to need two of us. Even Mr Gladstone brings tea,

twelve pounds at a time."

Prudence's mind worked swiftly, as indeed it had been doing since the episode yesterday evening had occurred. The presences of Johnny, Emily, Violet, Cis, Horry, Raph and everyone else who could possibly get in the way filed briefly before her in absence; then she nodded. "We get on," she said simply. She then, by way of conversation, asked what had become of the Toomeys.

"Oh, they've gone off and left me to pay the bill," Skittles replied, adding without rancour that they tried it all over Europe, Paris and Rome and Florence and Spa and Vienna. Most people who saw them coming got out of the way fast. "However they've stayed together," Skittles allowed, adding that there weren't any children and just as well. She beamed again suddenly; it was evident that her mind no longer focused on the Toomeys.

"Do you know, I have a good friend in high places," she said, gazing again at Freddy. "We could get *him* into his father's school." This was probable; the Prince of Wales himself still called

at South Street, also several younger men — passionately in love, quoting certain well-known lines from *Antony and Cleopatra*.

* * *

Emily, with pursed lips, was emptying drawers in the house at Ham, where they had driven over for the day. The furniture was Prudence's own, purchased over the years, and she could no doubt remove it herself: but certain items had come with Emily from Great Quayle and she would retrieve them. She unearthed one object now and held it up to the light; she'd always kept it in a drawer in case the colours faded. It was a small oval portrait of a young girl with bright curls and immense blue eyes, wearing a velvet bonnet of the fashion of many years ago. Tears sprang to Emily's eyes; how innocent everything had been then! She turned and handed the little portrait to Violet, who was seated, wordless and obedient as usual, on the extreme edge of the recently stripped bed.

"You may have that to keep if you

wish," said Emily. She was uncertain why she had given Lady Rose's picture away, but it was perhaps time somebody gave this poor child a word of kindness and a small gift. At a recent family conference, taking the form of Sunday luncheon in Bolton Street, Mama, who had been very difficult indeed since their arrival from Paris, made it clear that at her age, she couldn't be expected to look after more children. None of the other married couples, Gabriel and his wife, Raph and his, let alone Jerry and his, had made any offer about Violet at all; granted the child was exceedingly plain. Frances Angell had appeared to waver, but Raph had turned and bidden her be silent with such icy firmness that the poor woman had fallen silent for the rest of the meal. It was almost as though dear Raph disliked little Violet personally, though there could be no reason for that. Emily scanned Prudence's daughter now, deploring any absence of redeeming features except the eyes, which were best forgotten. Violet's hair was lank, mousy and straight, her small frame skinny, her thin legs and arms meantime — it might

of course clear later — purple, as some poor children's were. Her expression was subdued, but Cis of late days had after all nagged at her unceasingly whatever she did or failed to do, though Emily had to admit the child was never troublesome. It would certainly be quite unsuitable to have left her at Bolton Street, and equally so to take her back to Marylebone, the scene of untold shame. However Uncle Johnny still had to be looked after above his shop, and Emily had decided that she herself and none other must do it; that abandoned creature who called herself his wife must never be allowed back over the threshold again. The family had agreed about *that*, if nothing else. The future of Freddy had also been raised, as it happened by Gabriel: but on Emily's having related the full gist of the conversation in the Paris hotel, it was generally felt that he was sullied by, if not actually tarred with, the same brush as his unspeakable mother, and could at least be left with her meantime until the question of young Violet had resolved itself.

It was Jerry's hard-faced little wife Lisa

who had made a positive suggestion. Vera Angell was a schoolteacher somewhere, wasn't she, at quite a good girls' school near Chiswick? Why shouldn't Violet be boarded with the Chiswick Frames, if the school itself didn't take boarders? Somebody ought to find out.

"Who is to pay the fees?" enquired Cis acidly. Lisa Angell opened her dark eyes and said surely the child's father would do so. Emily, however, was beginning to have doubts as to whether or not poor Uncle Johnny *was* the child's father, as things evidently were. In any case she herself still had a little nest-egg left over from Quayle days, where she had spent very little apart from the small cost involved by the sewing-classes. She spoke up, "*I* will pay them," she announced, and so it was settled. The child Violet had sat silently among them all, staring at the tablecloth and hearing herself arranged for as if she wasn't there.

She gazed with her disturbing green eyes at the little portrait now; it was pretty. "Who is she?" she asked shyly.

"She is Lady Rose Purslove," replied

Emily, and vouchsafed no further information about how she herself, a neglected bride, had passed the days in staring at a similar portrait of Lady Emmeline and had then drawn, from memory, Lady Rose. The less said about all of it the better. She would visit Violet from time to time at Chiswick, to make certain the child was happy. What happened if the reverse should prove to be the case failed to cross Emily's mind, which had never been very perceptive.

* * *

Shortly, following discreet enquiries by Gabriel through his City connections, it was discovered that the Prince of Wales had himself recommended young Freddy for Westminster School. After that there could of course be no further interference with Freddy's prospects.

* * *

Violet Angell did not miss her half-brother. They had never had much in common and Freddy had always basked

in any limelight there might happen to be while Violet tagged behind unnoticed by anybody. Nor did she consciously miss Ham, which was the only home she could remember. She was a quiet child who, left alone, would have been perfectly happy in a corner with a book: but from then on she was very seldom in her whole life to be left in peace. The pictures, books and other familiar things with which she had grown up had, if she knew, by then been mostly sold; there was no more room at South Street and Prudence, with Freddy staying at weekends, were made extremely comfortable there, by Skittles and her maid. Prudence collected as much money from the sale of furniture as she could: one could never be certain what would happen, and Freddy must be helped to keep up with the others at school, as one realised. As for Violet, she was evidently being looked after; Prudence had always done her best, and hadn't asked for Violet's existence in the first place. It was too much to hope that Raph would admit his responsibilities, but perhaps he would help in some way; anyway it was no longer one's affair. Life had

meantime grown unfailingly delightful, with the bawdy talk of Skittles, in business hours and out; no need to get up in the morning; gentlemanly customers, of a class Prudence hadn't, herself, truth to tell previously encountered; some of them had very famous names, but you treated them exactly the same way as usual. Altogether, though at first it hadn't seemed like it, the visit to Paris had been most fortunate. Skittles said she often crossed over there again, out of nostalgia. It was the kind of word Skittles picked up, as well as the other kind she'd brought with her. The days were no longer dull, and the nights were profitable.

Violet had meantime managed to rescue one small book of her own the day a great many things were taken away from Ham by Cousin Emily and the carrier. It was called *The Story of Little Hal* and Violet had re-read it many times. Hal had died of pneumonia at the end and had of course gone to heaven through the Golden Gate. Before that he had had a loving stepmother and a great many brothers and sisters, all of whose pictures

were separately drawn in the book, and they lived together in a manor house with a beautiful old nursery. It was all very different from what was happening now. It was certainly quite, quite different from Chiswick.

* * *

At the beginning that hadn't been too bad. Cousin Emily and Violet had arrived on a Saturday, in time for tea; tea hadn't been much because Miss Vera Angell had prepared it herself. Miss Vera — she always insisted on the Miss although, working it out, she was Daddy's elder daughter and accordingly one's own half-sister — was so schoolteachery she couldn't do anything properly that wasn't teaching, which she evidently did very well; but it was the housekeeper's day off and there was, moreover, a visitor today; a very special and, lately, recurrent visitor, who sat now with her well-polished shoes placed as usual correctly together on the ugly run-of-the-mill carpet. Old Phyll Frame, who lived with them, sat hunched nearby in her bath chair, mumbling loud

as she always did beneath a stiff cap of black net, shaped rather like a clerical biretta, which disguised the fact that by now Phyll was totally bald except for a few fog-coloured wisps. Her presence had caused the visitor to think twice, perhaps even to prevaricate a little; looking after a smelly old woman wouldn't be pleasant, but might not last long. Alec meantime, having said all he had to say, munched solidly through Vera's stone-hard scones. Miss Vera herself bridled and said coyly that they'd be better soon, she herself had never been a baker. The visitor's statuesque face betrayed no emotion to speak of at that, but she and Alec looked at one another in a meaningful way. They had just become engaged, and, as Violet learned later, Miss Cummings was the domestic science teacher at Pratt's School for Girls, where she herself was, shortly and terrifyingly, to go. Miss Cummings, by reason of the coming nuptials to Alec, would of course leave in June.

Violet was then sent out to play in the garden while the rest discussed her future. The garden was small, grimy and largely untended, but a privet hedge

surrounded it and the small white flowers of that smelled sweet. Violet picked one and crushed it in her fingers, unaware that for centuries men and women long inured to evil smells had been doing the same thing or else, if leisured enough, boiling the flowers up in their private washing-water. Inside, meantime, Violet's fate was being resolved. Miss Vera had glanced somewhat anxiously at Millie Cummings to see if she would mind having a child in the house, that was, one there already. Vera's mind shied away from the fact that *that*, as well as other things, might happen: since being scared in childhood by the sight of poor Horry's briefly exposed member, and by old Mary Angell's repeated warnings to her about men, Vera had frequent nightmares in which men always figured. The prospect of her brother's marriage however cheered her in other ways; the housekeeper here, who had tended to think she could order everyone about, could go, and Millie's excellent baking would be available instead, every day, for tea. It had been like a dispensation of Providence, in its way, that Alec had

come with Vera to the school's prize-giving last year and had encountered Millie, had observed her feast prepared for visiting parents and the staff, and had fostered the acquaintance since then and had lately proposed. Why anyone should have accepted Alec when they had a prestigious post at a school like Pratt's was another matter. Vera asked no further questions of herself, least of all looking at Alec objectively to see him as he really was, an unexciting citizen of the second or third water in search of home comforts without having to pay for them. Vera herself considered that clever girls didn't get married.

Questioned by Mrs Emily about the girl, Millicent Cummings — she liked a few chosen friends to call her Millie, spelt that way — primmed her lips over her teeth, which unfortunately were false but seldom showed. She didn't really welcome the prospect which had been thrust upon her, just after she'd agreed to become engaged to Alec Angell (who after all owned a prosperous emporium and could moreover offer her, Millie, who'd thought she would never be

married at all, the coveted title of Mrs), but didn't like, at the present almost tremulous moment, to make a fuss. It would seem most ungracious to refuse to have the child, who seemed quiet; and Mrs Purslove, Alec had told her, was related to all the best families by marriage. Millicent inclined her comely head — she was in fact a fine handsome woman, if narrow in outlook — and made no further difficulty. Mrs Emily would of course pay. "And she'll be out, the little thing," put in Miss Vera encouragingly, "with me all day at school."

She then, having absently removed the tea-things with the brisk assistance of Alec's newly betrothed, ventured out to the garden to see little Violet again for herself. An unforeseen blossoming had already taken place in Vera's untried heart, not in itself arid but barricaded from early youth against all improper feeling. This was, after all, her own wee half-sister. She could be educated carefully, especially in arithmetic at which she was evidently weak, and by the end turned into a pupil-teacher such as oneself had been, at Pratt's, and perhaps

later join the staff. Heaven itself, for Miss Vera, could hold no greater bliss; that it might be different for anybody else she never stopped to consider. She tottered now across the lawn with the swaying movement inspired by armpit-high corsets which made it impossible to bend at the waist, but as Vera could never do anything naturally in any case by now, this hardly mattered. The china-blue pop-eyes surveyed Violet with true affection in their shallow depths. Here was hopeful material, totally in one's power.

"What is little Violet doing?" The voice was still that of a sheep and always would be, a fact not unremarked by the less disciplined elements at Pratt's. Violet raised her green eyes and replied politely that she was looking at a flower. Miss Vera had spoken about her to herself in the third person. Subsequently Violet was to find that everyone at Chiswick did.

"She'll get her hands dirty," said Miss Vera now in coy reproof. Life, and her profession, encouraged her continually to find fault. She had a kind heart, however. She shepherded Violet back

inside, having made her drop the flower meantime on the grimy grass.

Back in the parlour, among discreet conversation by her elders about other things, Violet surreptitiously raised her palm to her nose. She could still smell the flower. Miss Vera smelt instead of chalk and acrid sweat; the latter showed constantly in a half-moon under her arms through her blouse. She had begun of late years to grow a slight dark moustache. One felt, however, that she was at least an ally; nobody else here was so except Cousin Emily, who went away presently and left Violet with these unknown people; silent Alec, the faintly hostile presence of the woman with the well-polished shoes, and the other very old woman in the bath-chair, making occasional noises that weren't considered polite. They talked on among themselves and didn't speak to Violet again, but she surprised a covetous brooding look from Miss Vera, as though she herself had been something being got ready to eat. It made Violet feel faintly uncomfortable.

Later, Daddy appeared with her luggage in the delivery cart. Johnny was the

only familiar sight Violet had seen for a long time, though she didn't know him very well; she was seldom taken to Marylebone. However she ran to him and put her arms round his neck, saying quietly "Daddy."

Johnny's eyes filled with tears. He was incapable nowadays of decisions and anyway no one had asked him about Violet one way or the other. He fished in his overall pocket — he'd been on delivery — and brought out half-a-crown. "There you are, to buy yourself something," he said. Then he went off, his thin neck sticking apologetically out of his collar, an old defeated man long ago. Violet stared down at the half-crown. Presently Miss Vera, seeing, came bustling to take it away from her; she'd keep it safe, she said.

On Monday, Violet was taken by Miss Vera to school.

* * *

Pratt's School for Girls had been founded some years previously by two sister maiden ladies, daughters of a newspaper

proprietor. Their parent's lapses from grace had been so frequent that his shocked daughters never married, and when making their wills in later life agreed that their by then considerable resources should go to found an educational establishment to preserve girls' purity and, if possible, encourage them to adopt the teaching profession, which the Misses Pratt had been forbidden to enter. The latter ambition largely failed, as the girls, once educated, hastily got married instead. One reason had been the daily sight and sound of the female staff of Pratt's. These ladies were all single — widowhood might have been accepted but had not yet happened — and wore voluminous black gowns which floated behind them like crows' wings on their way to the staff room or the lavatory (which was after all the same thing) for tea at half past ten, or else once a month to collect a welcome salary cheque from the headmaster's study. The headmaster was, of course, a man; it was advisable to have one in control, but he had to be married, sternly evangelical, and as unattractive

as possible. He, and the few other men on the staff, teaching such subjects as art, music and science, were collectively known as Pa except for the science master, who being very small indeed was known as Sonny. Pa Blundell, the headmaster, had his morning tea served on a tray and drank it sternly alone: but Sonny, with the rest — including a very tall mathematics graduate who arrived shortly after Violet's advent and was of course known immediately as Tiny — disappeared into a cupboard off the science lab. where there was a filched bunsen burner, and made their own tea on that, and probably told stories about women while relieving themselves. All, of course, were married, but their exercising of the functions involved in that state were not made evident except in the regrettable case of Tiny, whose wife was one morning announced in the newspapers to have given birth safely to twins. Consternation reigned in the staff room among the flock of celibate she-crows; one hadn't realised that, well, such things went on almost in the building. Tiny was studiously avoided

in the corridor for some time, until they got used to it all, and then he left, having been promoted.

Otherwise everybody filed in and sang hymns at nine sharp every morning and then Pa Blundell preached a small sermon for the day from his raised lectern. His narrow, perennially angry face, peering out above a high winged collar like a giraffe from behind its palm tree, scanned the assembly with an all-seeing eye and a mind that forgot no least detail. After the homily the pianoforte, played by the requisite Pa, struck up the *Marche Militaire* by Schubert and lines were formed in proper order, everyone filing out again to the respective classrooms. In these, history was taught with a strongly Protestant bias which very few of the listeners did anything but absorb and then forget. Violet, however, remembered. One day she put her hand up and said, after a lesson in which Miss Vera had told them how dreadful all the Popes were, and said, "But, Miss Vera, there must have been *some* good Popes. There was Saint Peter." She had heard of him by way of the governess who had taught her

French. She had not the confidence to go on and was duly crushed by a snap at the time and a prolonged bleat later, at home. None of the others lived with a teacher; it wasn't fair; it made her different, as she knew. However Vera had her good points, and long division was one of them; she drummed it into Violet so that the latter, who had no head for figures in the ordinary way, remembered it all her life, which ended long before the days when every child could carry a machine with buttons to push for the right answer: but she remembered *malgré lui*. Apart from the remark about Popes — that was the kind of thing Vi Angell *would* say — the other girls, from well-heeled backgrounds, had decided on the very first day that she wasn't one of themselves; living with a teacher, hopeless at games, and the smelly old Sheep probably did her homework for her.

* * *

That first summer there had been the nuptials of Alec Angell and Millicent Cummings, watched by an interested

crowd of end-of-term well-wishers as well as those actually invited to the ceremony. There was concealed amusement when the bride, at her age, appeared resplendent in a snowy veil and orange blossom, but one no doubt might as well make the most of so unexpected an occasion. Miss Vera, as the bridesmaid, wore pale green satin with a hat to match, and tittupped along behind on dyed satin shoes of the same shade, and silk stockings. Violet had not been asked to be a bridesmaid; she knew already that Miss Cummings — Mrs Angell as she soon would be now — didn't like her much. In any case Thelma Cummings, a niece from the north of England, who was at the wedding, hadn't been asked to be anything either, so that was fair. Moreover Violet would have died of shyness at the prospect of being in such a procession, watched by everyone. Thelma was slightly older than she was and had already winked at her in a conspiratorial manner, which gave Violet an unlooked-for sense of warmth. She still hadn't made any friends at school.

Old Phyll Frame, in her bath chair,

was borne in and thoughtfully placed near where she could hear. This proved unfortunate, as the old creature emitted — Millie was privately convinced she did it on purpose — at the most solemn moment of all a prolonged fart. Worse, at the reception afterwards she informed all and sundry that Alec, the bridegroom, wasn't Johnny Angell's son at all, only the coachman's. "Belle told me 'erself, and I'm Belle's ma, aren't I?" the terrible old crone was clearly heard to state by several invited persons in the vicinity. "Oh, de-e-ar," Miss Vera Angell began to bleat at once, in unintentional but unfailing advertisement of the whole situation; anyone who had not heard old Phyll's original statement now asked their next door neighbour what it was all about, and was told. "Oh de-e-ar, oh de-ear," the plaintive sound continued, perhaps in unadmitted mourning for the owner's own virgin state at the bridal; an outbreak of embarrassed talk burst out and the sound died, of necessity, away. Poor Johnny Angell, looking frail, was also present, but pretended not to hear. Violet and Thelma Cummings, standing

together near Cousin Emily, suppressed their giggles with such difficulty that Violet felt as if she was going to burst. Afterwards, waiting for the happy couple to go off, she was able to have a word with Thelma in a corner, and they promised to keep in touch, except that Violet knew her own letters would be read aloud to everyone by Miss Vera at breakfast. She liked Thelma; she didn't seem affected and sidey, like the girls at Pratt's. Probably her aunt thought she wasn't ladylike enough. She spoke with an earthy unfamiliar accent and was herself a big high-coloured determined creature, getting on for thirteen years old. They let their giggles subside while the going was good, then the bride and groom came out, to be pelted decorously by everyone with rice. Millie wore a wine-coloured outfit and looked faintly annoyed. "It's because she knows now she hasn't married the true heir to the emporium after all," muttered Thelma irrepressibly. She said things oneself wouldn't dare to.

It was indeed true, but by the time the truth had been made manifest the vows had been irrevocably taken: it was

too late to go back to the security of a good paid post in the domestic science room at Pratt's. During the honeymoon at Weston-super-Mare, Millie questioned her new husband closely regarding the allegation made by his dreadful old grandmother; was there anything in it? "How do I know?" said Alec; he never in any case said much. It was too early yet for Millie to find out about his meanness with, for example, the housekeeping money, but she did notice that he made wordless difficulty about paying for anything extra, like a welcome pot of tea: and there were the other things which, of course, weren't mentioned or to be approved of by properly disposed persons. Millie endured Alec's furtive goings-on in bed in a tight-lipped and disapproving silence, staying relatively immobile throughout. Perhaps if she made it clear she didn't like it, Alec's demands on her would stop. They continued, however, unabated and certainly unfruitful, even after the return to Chiswick and the pop-eyes of Vera Angell to be found watching everywhere, not to mention the old woman and the

child to have to look after as well. Millicent set about trying to run the household as she was well fitted to do, and tightening her lips permanently over what could not be helped; and so life continued on its way.

Violet would, in fact, have agreed with the returned bride about one thing: Vera. Miss Vera pried relentlessly into everything. She could even be heard creeping upstairs to look into Violet's exercise books after she, Violet, was in bed and supposedly asleep. Luckily she didn't have to share a room with Miss Vera, even now. It was one place at least where she could be private, by herself.

* * *

Emily called occasionally at Chiswick and never failed to ask if Violet was happy at school, and Miss Vera never failed to answer for her, then and at other times in general and in particular. "Yes, Violet's happy," she would say cheerfully to everyone, and Violet did not argue; in fact, she was not consciously unhappy now the other girls had stopped

tormenting her as they had on first arrival. School was there and you put up with it, the same way as you put up with whatever else happened. Violet once started to keep a diary, but it was seized upon and read and she gave it up; it was easier to hide what you were thinking if you didn't write it down. Nevertheless she was good at English, and shortly won a scholarship which relieved Cousin Emily of some of the fees. Emily was pleased, and when she died — Violet was by that time fifteen — she left the girl a small amount of money saved out of Leonard Purslove's grudging jointure and put later into shares by Gabriel. There was a condition; Violet was to take nothing to do with her mother, and the money was in any case not to be hers till she was twenty-one.

Miss Vera pondered it; the money would have paid for Violet's possible training at a university, but as things were she'd have to be a pupil-teacher after all, as Vera herself had earlier been; you worked your way for nothing and were then perhaps appointed to the staff. Vera had never quite lived these humble

origins down, and some of the crows who were actual graduates by now drank their morning tea in a snobbish and separate group, but it didn't matter. Violet should teach, that was already decided. In fact, nobody ever thought of anything else for her. As for Freddy, he never wrote except for a dutiful card at Christmas. He was by now in another world, with a separate orbit.

⋆ ⋆ ⋆

Old Cis lived on. She was seated now, as she usually was since it had become difficult these days to descend the stairs, in her second-floor room in the Bolton Street house, which had been divided into flats. Jerry and his wife Lisa occupied the ground and first floors, because it was necessary to go in and out to the business, also to entertain. Horry and his male nurse lived in the fourth. Lisa's fat sister Corisande, who had separated from her husband, inhabited the third floor with her baby girl, who had apricot hair. Cis grimly remembered meeting Jeremiel, in his nightshirt, creeping down at two

in the morning in the days when she herself had been able to move a little faster than now; she'd accosted him then and asked what he thought he was doing up there. The smooth face, so like and yet unlike Freddy's, had given its floorwalker's smile; that was all he was, and, evidently, an adulterer as well; but after all his wife wouldn't let him get at her, probably never had; the little bitch was only interested in cash returns. Cis had glared at her son, however, standing before him like Nemesis leaning on a stick, with a shawl draped over her nightgown.

"Why, Mama, I thought I heard you move, and came to see if anything was wrong," replied Jerry innocently.

"That wouldn't have taken you up to the third floor. I know what goes on. If I had any say in matters now, I'd turn that great fat creature out, to go back to the man she married."

Jerry smiled on; there would be no point in sending poor Corisande back to Frank, who was no good to her at all and never had been; he himself was very different. Cori had told him only

tonight that she was expecting his child. That had given Jeremiel satisfaction. It had been thought previously that Cori was too fat to have one, and that he himself was incapable, because of Lisa and the fact that they had no children. Morality had to be bent a little in the circumstances. Jeremiel had, on that earlier occasion, seen his mother with chivalry back to bed; at her age she shouldn't be up in the small hours of the morning. After that they had found her a lady companion. It wasn't good for her to go on seeing nobody except poor Horry, day after day.

Horry lived on the fourth floor, with his male nurse. The man would bring him down to visit Cis in the evenings, on the way back from their afternoon carriage-drive which she could no longer attend. It was doubtful if Horry perceived what went past him daily in the streets; but he was always amiable, and now and again made sounds which indicated that he was trying to speak. Cis would have him put in a chair before her for a half-hour and would try to talk to him, but there was in fact very little to

say after one had asked about the drive. Of late she'd taken to reading Horry a chapter of the Bible out loud. Miss Beech, the companion, had found her a different one from the usual, revised by a Bishop Challoner. It had certain parts the King James Bible didn't. One Cis liked particularly was the Book of Wisdom. She'd read a part of that to poor Horry only today; she could still remember the passage. *Whose land for a testimony of their wickedness is desolate, and smoketh to this day; and the trees bear fruits that ripen not, and a standing pillar of salt is a monument of an incredulous soul.*

For regarding not wisdom, they did not only slip in this, that they were ignorant of good things, but they left also unto men a memorial of their folly, so that in the things in which they sinned, they could not so much as lie hid.

But wisdom hath delivered from sorrow them that attend on her.

It was all so extremely like what went on in this house, and had in poor Johnny's, with that wife who'd ruined his life and was, they said, still doing very well for herself indeed in a certain

kind of society. Punishment would find Prudence Angell out in the end; bound to, if there was any justice.

Horry had been taken away by now, back upstairs. Cis knew very well that once she herself was dead, the others would put Horry into an institution.

She raised her eyes and surveyed the double portraits hanging on the opposite wall. They were of herself and HC, painted at a time when the boys were growing up. She herself wore her favourite lace cap with lappets and, beneath, her hair already faded, but carefully curled. She looked at her own grave painted face; what had she had then to be grave about? Freddy had been alive, and HC. Cis let her gaze wander past the folds of her dark satin gown — she'd never liked wearing bright colours — to the portrait of HC himself, handsome and thick-haired, with the remembered side-whiskers already turning grey. Dear HC. It seemed a long time since he'd left her. What had he meant at the end, about Australia?

Emily was dead now too, and Freddy, long ago. She'd been used to take poor

Horry in the carriage sometimes to visit Freddy's grave. There were so many dead; her brother Johnny had died lately in a foolish way, trying to rescue a dog from being run over, and it had happened instead to himself; they'd found him dead on the road, with the dog still alive clasped in his arms. There hadn't been much left of the Marylebone business; Alec had taken the old sign to hang outside his emporium. Violet they said had wanted to keep the dog, but it hadn't been allowed, of course. Violet was training to be a teacher, like Vera. To Cis's mind it was almost as bad as being a governess; long ago she herself had threatened, if Mama wouldn't let her marry HC because of Nellie and The Stranger, to go and be one; but she'd never have been a success. She wasn't clever; only at things like —

She stuck out her wrinkled neck now, rather like an old tortoise, and called sharply for the companion. Mary Beech came from where she sat by custom in an inner room; old Mrs Angell liked to be left mostly alone. "May I bring you something?" she asked gently. She knew

already what would be asked for; the box with shells. They'd found it in a drawer at the time of changing the house into flats. The shells were almost glued on by now. When the box was finished, she'd have to try to find another one for the old lady somehow; it kept her occupied.

Cecily sat on alone in the darkening room, her fingers occupied with placing the remaining shells suitably; once, she'd tried to interest poor Horry in it, but he'd only made a mess with the glue. One had to be careful with that: it got on to things and was difficult to remove afterwards. Cis watched the companion set out her finger-bowl with water in it, a white cloth to dry her fingers later, and a glue-pot with its brush. She selected a pink shell with a minute frilled edge, and tried it out in different places. It was, after all, a ladylike occupation. Mama had always encouraged her in it.

* * *

Young Freddy Angell surveyed himself with satisfaction in the glass; he had dressed in his scarlet tunic and braid

for the Regimental Ball. Like his father he had passed out of Woolwich with moderate commendation, but unlike the elder Freddy had not yet heard a shot fired in anger, let alone encountered an assegai. Freddy now told himself that he was, of course dying to go and fight and that the Pax Britannica, which meantime made things very slow everywhere, was bound to expire soon in the nature of things. When it did, he, Freddy Angell, would do his duty; but meantime this evidently consisted of waltzing, rather boringly, with young ladies, a variety of person in whom Freddy was not interested.

In fact, apart from Skittles whom he still adored although the poor dear was beginning to be troubled by arthritis, Freddy was chiefly interested in himself, a useful attribute at any time. He also liked other young men. This had probably been begun at Westminster, where one's father had been venerated and there had even been some talk of unveiling a plaque to those former scholars who had fallen in the 1879 war. Otherwise Freddy had taken pleasure in such innocent things

as the tossing of the Shrove Tuesday pancake and the jovial pat on the shoulder given thereafter by the stout affable gentleman who was by now King of England. That raised one's prestige; but this had been publicly lowered towards the end by an insufferable fellow named Tyson.

Freddy had liked to think that he himself excelled in drawing: he had a certain talent. In the half-remembered days of governesses and the company of young Violet and Cousin Emily, the latter had always praised his efforts although Violet hadn't said much. Here, at the art classes held by tradition in the cloisters, he, Freddy, had to hold his own permanently against this Tyson, and Tyson likewise against him. On one occasion, the same when the mater, in a light summer dress, had been present for once at the prize-giving accompanied by an unknown escort who gave Freddy a five-pound note, he had finally beaten Tyson and had moreover walked off with the art prize, a large and coveted book about the Renaissance in Venice. Tyson, encountering Freddy with the book under

his arm later on, twisted his own spotty face in an anticipatory manner. It was possible that he also envied one's looks.

"Just as well you can draw, might have to make a living on the pavement one day, who knows? Who d'you think you are anyway? You didn't have any father killed in the war. Your father was an old grocer and he's dead, and your mother's a tart." Tyson had all this from an unimpeachable source, a much older married sister who had used to shop in Marylebone while you could still get what you wanted there, but she said nowadays the Chiswick emporium wasn't the same Angells at all. Tyson sneered. Trade and tarts! The pretty boy needn't fancy himself; Tyson told him so, in even plainer language.

Freddy's arm shot out at last and he dropped the book about Venice, which fell open on its expensive face and one of the plates was never again the same. The two boys fell to wrestling on the shaved grass and by the end Freddy had a broken nose, which later on healed slightly out of its former classic alignment. Otherwise, his beauty remained legendary. He didn't

mind too much about the nose; he was tired in any case of being compared to an angel: but he would have liked to beat Tyson, and hadn't managed it.

Remembering it all now, and how the pair of them had been separated and reproved later on in the Head's study, Freddy caressed the final version of his nose rather absently. He didn't, in fact, know very much about Mama, except at weekends which Prudence reserved solely for his company. Longer holidays had been spent with other chaps, by invitation at their places in Norfolk or the Home Counties; he'd learnt to shoot. It was, so Skittles assured him, worth keeping up with the right people: she always had, herself. One remembered curiously idle and delightful days in South Street, watching from a window while the carriages came and went and Gerald, the young man who was currently in love with Skittles, hung about. Some of the best people certainly emerged from the carriages, but one didn't as a rule meet them. "They've broken the bloody windows opposite," Skittles would point out cheerfully after what must have

been a particularly hectic night; she said they'd done it from here with champagne bottles. Skittles herself would come in often during the day to talk, still in her dressing-gown. She was always friendly and interested; spoke to a chap as if he'd been a man. The mater moved always, decorous and remote, about somehow through all of everything; she never said much, in fact Freddy could count on his fingers the things he could remember her saying. One remark had been that Mr Gladstone, who often came, bought his twelve pounds of tea now at Angells in Piccadilly. However after The Shop, great Woolwich itself, was entered, there was less time to spare for South Street at least quite yet; and as for Violet, he wouldn't know her now if they met in the street. He heard she was being turned into a schoolteacher, which was certainly a reason for not mentioning her existence to the other chaps.

* * *

The fate in question had by then befallen Violet. By the time Freddy came to be

posted abroad with his regiment she herself, had they met, would have done him no credit regarding looks, though her voice remained low and pleasant despite the constant necessity to hold forth to unattentive classes. Like Freddy, Violet once stood looking at herself in the glass, but in her case dispiritedly; her hair, which as a rule stayed almost pretty for a few hours after it was washed, had grown lank again — there wasn't time and she was tired, and Mrs Alec grudged the hot water — and was screwed up in the regulation Pratt's knob on top of her head. She wore, likewise, the obligatory carefully-ironed white blouse with a high severe neck through which was threaded a black ribbon; a plain long dark skirt, and black boots with laces. She had endured the state of being a pupil-teacher by favour of the length of Miss Vera Angell's own stalwart service to Pratt's; pupil-teachers were looked down on by the graduate staff, even after one was on the staff oneself, and not often met with nowadays. Never would Violet be eligible to wear a graduate's black gown except at prize-giving, when for the

look of the thing everybody put one on. Having begun pupil-teaching at sixteen, officially with a member of staff always present in the room — but of course they always took time off, and that was when purgatory began because some of the pupils had been there when she was one herself — Violet went routinely, by now, up and down the rows of desks to supervise work; took exercise-books home to correct at nights and weekends; endured Miss Vera's bleatings to and from school, and at home about what they'd been saying in the staff room, which was dull and narrow. Teachers never seemed to get away from themselves and from school, especially Pratt's, or they wouldn't have been chosen for it. By then, though, it was the only life Violet knew.

She reflected that she was still very bad at keeping discipline: it would come with time, Miss Vera said determinedly. Meantime, although, after the first, pins were no longer actually stuck into Violet while on progress from behind, appalling things happened still; once a live yellow slug had been found by her

in her handbag when she opened it on reaching home, and another time some enterprising person scrawled all through the corrected exercises and ruined them. Boys would have been much worse, Miss Vera said placidly. Now that Violet was actually a teacher at Pratt's, she herself could virtually depart in peace, not that it was yet time, but one paid into the superannuation fund administered by Pratt's. There was a separate office in town.

Most of the salary Violet now received went otherwise to pay Mrs Alec for her board; certainly the food was very good. She kept in touch with Thelma by letter, but at times couldn't help wishing she had been allowed to do what Thelma had and taken shorthand and typing while still at school, then got a job in an office. Thelma now worked for a solicitor, and it sounded interesting. However it wouldn't have been allowed. At least, after the probationary period was over, oneself no longer had to deliver a lesson in front of the presiding teacher and then have it picked to bits afterwards before a row of smug young faces. By now, Violet was

monarch of all she surveyed, in that way, in the small room where she liked to rest her tired back against the radiator afterwards and do her correcting alone in free periods. Pratt's was up-to-date in such matters. Violet had been told she was luckier than some.

* * *

Frequent hair-washing was discouraged in the Chiswick household; it used up the hot water. Certainly this had to be garnered, because Alec Angell almost counted the coals when he came home. Luckily he was out during opening hours at the emporium, nine till six; but during the day Mrs Alec was kept busy not only with the ordinary work of the house and getting meals — Vera was no help, and Violet was for some reason never considered fit to touch a duster or boil an egg — but with looking after dreadful old Phyll Frame, which was as time-consuming, and a good deal more malodorous, than looking after a thriving baby newly on the bottle. For one thing Alec's grandmother ate

like a horse, using her two remaining discoloured teeth which happened to be sited opposite one another and of which Phyll was so inordinately proud she refused ever to wear a plate, in addition mocking openly at those who had, of necessity, to do so. This Mrs Alec endured, but there were other things even less mentionable; she put up with them over the years in the expectation that when she should die, which must in nature be soon, old Phyll — Millie's nature was too genteel to find any synonym in the initial itself — would gratefully leave in her will a small something to the person who, though no direct relation except by marriage, had sustained her declining years, fed, washed and humoured her in all possible ways. Phyll, by now almost deliquescent, seldom uttered a coherent word these days except for an occasional "Heh, heh," otherwise mumbling and chumbling her way almost passively through the remaining tenor of her existence. However she had an uncanny habit of saying clearly that she was hungry, just after she had lowered an

adequate meal and the moment anyone who might take pity on her had entered the room and could hear. As a result, Mrs Alec knew herself a martyr to misplaced gossip about her starvation of the helpless old woman left in her power. "Get us a bite to eat, love," old Phyll would moan to Violet when she came in from school; but Violet knew better nowadays than to heed her, though when she was younger she had, very rashly, emerged once from the larder with sustaining bread and butter and some meat. That had been put a stop to at once; also the too-frequent washing of Violet's hair she had briefly indulged in, which was a matter of vanity and could be for nobody's possible benefit but Violet's own. Mrs Alec would have stopped baths if she could, but dear Miss Vera Angell needed these rather often and one had best not differentiate. As it was, the other members of the household had one a week.

Violet would sometimes look back with almost mystic awe at the ceremonial involved in having a bath at Chiswick at all. There was a large piece of striped ticking kept permanently draped

over the bath which roughly fitted that amenity and left enough hanging over both sides for the person immersed to see nothing whatever of themselves during the process. It had involved, of course, undressing first under the ticking with one's head through the hole cut ready in the middle and neatly hemmed round the edges, which made them uncomfortably stiff. Having bathed in this furtive fashion, one dried oneself and put on a clean nightgown, still under the ticking, which could then be removed without scandal. Violet thought nothing of all this until Thelma Cummings came briefly to stay in her aunt's house and collapsed in loud laughter, refused to use the ticking at all, and cheerfully pranced about naked. Thelma forced Violet on that visit to think of a great many things which had never been allowed to occur to her before, and did so now with a shock like a tidal wave. "Why stay here?" was one of them. "Granted the grub's good, but why sell your soul for that?" They shared a room meantime, and could talk in low voices together, although Mrs Alec, as well as Miss Vera, had

a regrettable habit of listening at doors and then bursting in. "Why not find a place to live in with a friend of your own age, and have some fun? You've got that money Mrs Purslove left you; use it to get out of here." By the friend she meant, of course, herself.

Violet lacked enough courage quite yet; Miss Vera would make scenes, there would be gossip in the staff room and occasional frozen silences; no one who hadn't taught there could possibly imagine Pratt's clannishness. Anyway she would have to go on travelling to teach there; a lifetime's conditioning made it difficult to think of existing anywhere else.

Thelma went away soon, saying she couldn't stand Aunt Millie and old Vera any longer, and advised Violet not to go on putting up with it or she'd soon get like they had. Violet bowed her head to circumstance, but about then old Phyllis Frame died at last, followed shortly by Cecily Angell. Miss Vera, always easily bowled over by any approach to reality, wept and howled as though both old women, for neither of whom she had

had a vestige of affection or they for her, were her nearest and dearest, reft from her by death. She clung to Violet at both funerals, sobbing loudly to everyone's embarrassment as well as hers; each demise was to be considered a relief, after all, and it only remained to bestow the coffins decently. This was done, the first time beside the original Alec Frame, long mouldering in a municipal cemetery, beneath his stone urn; and the second beside HC in the Angell vault. In the interval, Phyll Frame's will was read, and Vera could have had little to hope for there, but nevertheless wailed again; and Mrs Alec's face beneath her mourning toque was a study. The dead woman had left everything she had, which after all represented several years' profit from many baked potatoes and much hard work, to found an endowment through the Prisoners' Aid Society. This was to be known as the Belle Frame Angell Memorial, and that was that.

"Oh, de-e-ear," intoned Miss Vera. And Violet stayed on with them.

* * *

She had very little idea by now of any other existence; her horizons had narrowed. She was almost reconciled to the staff room gossip, the staff room silences, the treatment of herself as an errant child still. Miss Vera had some years before advised her, with the best possible intentions, to put Cousin Emily's little legacy into Pratt's General Fund. It showed, as Vera pointed out, loyalty to the school; and it would make interest along with the superannuation money. Violet couldn't think of anything in particular to do with the legacy by then, so she obeyed.

It was not for some time that she ran into Thelma again, by accident; Vera had disapproved of their continuing friendship. Thelma, like Violet herself, was wearing a white blouse; it was summer. At the neck was a knitted tie in green, white and violet stripes. It meant Give Women the Vote. With Thelma was a tiny woman from Scotland named Flora Drummond. She talked in a way Violet had never heard before, not having journeyed far beyond Chiswick, even in school holidays; it was difficult

for Alec to take them and for that reason, his entire household stayed at home.

* * *

Violet never did become a very convinced supporter of women's suffrage; she had lived too long in a woman-dominated world, and in fact disliked her own sex slightly. However she arranged to meet Thelma again to go to a meeting, listened to Flora Drummond's story of how her life's ambition to become a postmistress in Scotland had been frustrated by men, whose hidebound regulations rejected her because she was below a certain height; and, briefly inspired, bought herself a small amount of green, white and violet wool to knit a suffragette tie. It could, of course, only be worn at weekends, never at Pratt's.

Amazingly, neither Miss Vera nor Mrs Alec spotted the situation at once, although they habitually read their newspapers. It was Alec who noticed Violet's tie one Saturday, when she had gone down to the emporium to buy writing-paper. Violet liked going to the emporium.

You could buy anything there, gleaming pots and pans and colanders and shoe brushes and face cream and chocolate. When she had been a child Alec had sometimes relaxed his meanness and had given her a small bar of chocolate on visits, but not now.

"You one of them? Better stick to your job," said Alec darkly. It was not the kind of thing to answer back about, or the place to do so, and Violet took it away with her to think over alone. She thought afterwards of what she perhaps ought to have said, what Thelma, who was afraid of nobody, would have said; how women had always been the subject sex and had had to fight for recognition in literature, in medicine, and now politics. They hadn't even been able to own their property until a few years ago; if a married woman earned any money it was by right her husband's. Thelma's voice had grown strident, relating all of it; that was the trouble. A woman, Violet was certain, shouldn't try to turn herself into a man; they were different, had their own weapons. She was uncertain how she knew this. At one point she had tried to

say so to Thelma, who smiled lovingly.

"You haven't been brought up to argue," she said. "You're rather sweet, Violet." She then did a thing which shocked Violet profoundly; came forward, reached out both hands to Violet's blouse and lightly caressed the slim breasts lying beneath. Violet shrank away uncomfortably. Miss Vera, to do her justice, hadn't ever touched her in that way. She wished people would leave her alone. If Thelma was going to go on like that, she wouldn't go out with her any more, to meetings or anything else.

⋆ ⋆ ⋆

It was however through Thelma that she at last met somebody more important to her than any woman. He ran a pacifist bookshop near St Mary Axe. It was in fact only a stall, like Alec Frame's had been at first, and Stephen — his name was, somehow, Angell and he came from Australia — lodged in a house in the street. It was his name, not his occupation, that had made Thelma mention him. "I say, I think I've met a

remote cousin of yours, or something," she said casually; she had been rebuffed by Violet's earlier behaviour and was off-hand these days. "His name's Angell at any rate. He comes from down under."

They arranged, next time they were out together, to go and see the bookshop and the possible relation; Violet thought she remembered something or other about it all, perhaps from Cousin Emily. It wasn't a very common surname. It would be interesting, at any rate, to meet a pacifist, in fact slightly daring; during the Boer War, she could remember reading, they'd been most unpopular.

* * *

He straightened up from the rows of books as they came, and saw Violet immediately. He was a stocky little man; she herself was not tall. He had a high balding forehead that reminded her of Shakespeare, a sensitive mouth and eyes like a friendly spaniel. She noticed his hands at once and, even then, knew she wouldn't mind their touching her. An extraordinary thing happened in her

mind; she found two lines float up in it.

Being thy slave, what should I do
but tend
Upon the hours and times of thy
desire?

It wasn't the kind of thing one thought of, let alone taught, at Pratt's. Thelma introduced them to one another.

* * *

"I know something of what you have to put up with," he told Violet when, quite soon, he found out that she was a schoolteacher. "My mother taught school in Horsham, Victoria. She used to come home at night laden with exercise books. I did the cooking and washing up. I still can." He smiled. He must be about her own age, perhaps a year or two younger. It didn't matter. Violet murmured that she took exercise books home as well. Thelma said "She lives with two bloody old women who won't let her speak out." Thelma was looking like a Valkyrie today, her hair blown back beneath her hat. If he wanted to look at anyone, Violet thought, he ought to want to look

at Thelma; but, instead, he had been looking from the beginning at herself. The friendly hazel eyes hadn't left her face since they arrived. She —

"Mother wanted to save up to send me to a university, but she died," said Stephen Angell simply. "My father was dead long before; he was a good deal older. I don't remember him. So, I got interested in books and in the end I worked my passage, and came here. I like London." He raised his head and regarded the tree-lined street; the planes were in leaf, their peeling bark creamy in patches and grey on the rest. "It's very green here," he said. "The grass in the gardens is plain fresh green. I can't stop looking at it when I pass by." He pronounced words slightly differently.

"How long have you lived here?" asked Violet, for something to say; only, there was no need to say anything. Steve — that was what Thelma called him, but Violet always called him Stephen afterwards, she liked it better — replied quietly that he'd been here a year, and didn't seem to be making much money.

"But you'd rather do this than teach."

What was making her so quick at replying today? As a rule, she hadn't a word to say for herself. Stephen Angell laughed.

"I'd rather draw on pavements for a living with chalk than do that," he said. "Look, it's nearly closing time, and there aren't any customers. Won't you both come in and have a cup of tea? I make very good tea."

That was the beginning of it. Naturally she said nothing at Chiswick; they merely went on thinking she'd gone out somewhere with Thelma again. It was healthy, Miss Vera had already decided, for Violet to have a few young friends, like this niece of Mrs Alec's; and she herself had a sneaking sympathy with all this business about votes for women in the news; after all, women had brains, or they wouldn't be in teaching.

* * *

While Alec was exercising his due rights upon Mrs Alec's rigid and, as usual, unwilling body after they were in bed one night she, with eyes firmly closed, was thinking not of England but of the

housekeeping books, over which Alec maintained almost as determined a *droit de seigneur* as he did over herself.

For some time now Millicent had found it increasingly difficult to make ends meet, not that she was incompetent but that Alec grew ever meaner as the years passed. It was almost impossible by now to afford even third-rate butter, and as a first-rate baker herself Millie greatly disliked using margarine. It seemed ridiculous to have married a large-scale grocer and —

Alec began to grunt, and Millicent put up with it, having her thoughts scattered for moments by unpleasant necessity. When she collected them again, it was to rediscover a solution with which she had for some time toyed; namely, putting up the board and lodging rates paid her by both Vera and Violet Angell. She didn't like doing it, but after all they got their money's worth and always had, and so did Alec. Millie made this last reflection without a vestige of humour, for, perhaps mercifully, she had none. Alec meantime finished, and turned over on his side to sleep; he seldom addressed her.

"Goodnight, dear," said Millicent politely.

"G'night." He began to snore shortly, and not for the first or last time Millie regretted her marriage. If only she were single again, her own woman, earning a moderately paid living by what she did so well! As it was, she envied the other two their monthly salaries; and that reminded her of a disturbing thing.

Once in a very infrequent way, when she simply could not endure the state of things any longer and wanted to buy herself some little treat, a secret bottle of sherry for instance, to keep in the wardrobe, or even perhaps a new dress — not that Alec ever now noticed what she wore — Millie had gone to withdraw some of the money she had put into Pratt's Fund steadily over the years, thereafter to keep it in a certain teapot on the highest shelf in the kitchen until it was spent. One didn't go too often; for one thing you had to give four weeks' notice of intention to withdraw; and for another it was difficult to find time to get away, journey into town, and be back in time for Alec's lunch, which of course he

ate at home and always spoke of as his dinner. However Pratt's office, situated in town, was open on Saturday mornings, and Millicent had contrived once or twice to slip away while Miss Vera was at home to do any necessary explaining.

While waiting in the short queue of like-minded persons — fortunately it numbered no acquaintances, one didn't want it to be publicly known to what straits one was reduced — Millicent perceived Violet Angell standing at the counter taking out some money. She was in fact near enough to note the amount signed for; £30, a large sum for a young teacher, surely almost the whole of Violet's superannuation payments to date. There had of course been that legacy as well. However there seemed no earthly reason Millicent could see for Violet's requiring such a sum; she had few expenses apart from the board and lodging, which were paid direct out of her salary, and this was term time. That sum would — Millie added up in her head the things £30 would do, and among them was the purchase, as one happened by chance to know,

of a special marriage licence, although for herself and Alec the banns had of course been called. However poor Violet would most certainly not be buying *that*. Millie permitted herself a tight smile and reflected, out of her own bitter and by now deeply rued experience, that if you did marry you lost your job. Nevertheless Violet didn't know any men, and if she did was too plain, and too devoid of ordinary conversation, to attract one. Men liked a sprightly companion. Millie glanced briefly and with faint dislike at the sleeping and temporarily sated Alec, turned over to her own side of the bed and presently also slept, but not before deciding at last to mention the matter of the withdrawn £30 to Miss Vera. *She* would investigate the matter, without a doubt; she had always liked to know every single thing Violet did, even, no doubt, whatever Violet happened to be thinking.

* * *

"But what did you want to do with the money?" persisted Miss Vera. Never

the most subtle of souls, she remained unaware of the fact that her mention of the money at all proved to Violet, if any proof were needed, that she and old Millie had been discussing her affairs again, as far as they knew about them. She herself had seen Mrs Alec standing that time in the Pratt's Fund Office queue and had pretended not to; they didn't like each other, and both were there on (by Pratt's standards) nefarious business. Nobody would think she herself was thirty next birthday. Alongside Mrs Alec's demand for raised rent it was too much even for gentle Violet. In any case she had a new reason for confidence; Stephen's love. The thought of it brought a blush to her cheeks, making her suddenly resemble a rose; a rose carrying a small suitcase. Miss Vera naturally assumed that the blush signified shame. She herself would have regarded the withdrawal of superannuation money — the legacy had long ago merged into all that — as a profanation of the Holy of Holies. The money was meant to sit there till you retired; no teacher in her senses would withdraw any of it as early

as Violet had evidently done. She said so, forgetting that Violet had not replied to her earlier query and showed no signs of doing so.

"Retirement can mean a lot or a little," Violet replied, in the impertinent manner she'd lately acquired since taking up again with that Thelma. Miss Vera reminded herself, with the distracted enthusiasm of a mother hen sitting on far too many eggs, that she'd said only last week to Violet that she must stop wearing that suffragette tie. A member of staff had noticed it on her one Saturday in the street, and had mentioned it on Monday in the staff room. In fact, it had not been in the street at all but down at the emporium, but that establishment was considered vulgar by Miss Vera, who never by any chance went there and left it out of her conversation. Violet, in the same obstinate manner and unlike her former self, had refused to abandon the tie and was wearing it again now. It was once more Saturday, and Violet said she was going to spend the night at Thelma's. She often did that nowadays; Miss Vera wasn't sure

she liked it, it made for distraction. Violet ought to pay attention to her teaching, which meant correcting work at weekends the way she'd used to do, and that way one knew where she was.

Violet had fallen silent, and Mrs Alec put in coldly that as she evidently had money to waste, it wasn't out of the question to have asked for an increase in rent. Violet, most unexpectedly, rounded on her and said straight out that she was going to stay with Thelma for good, and wouldn't be back and they could send on her things, she'd pay for that. Her eyes flashed green fire as she said it. Mrs Alec was, for once, too greatly taken aback to think of an immediate answer; later on she said to Miss Vera sourly that Violet would find a difference in her food where she was going.

"And as for superannuation," said Violet, this time addressing Miss Vera herself, "that old Miss Symonds nobody ever liked taught at Pratt's for thirty-six years after going through it as a pupil from the beginning, and that meant the whole of her life and that was what was the matter with her. Then she dropped

dead a fortnight after retiring because she couldn't think what else to do with herself, and Pratt's got the money. If schoolteachers could get themselves some other interest in life they wouldn't be as boring as they are and might even live longer." It was a long speech for Violet.

Miss Vera began to bleat helplessly, her eyes full of easy tears. They'd had a tea-party in the school hall for old Miss Symonds when she left. She'd been a landmark, one of the first pupils ever to enrol at Pratt's. There'd been a nice bit of fruit cake, almost as good as Millie used to make and never did now, and bread and butter, of course, from domestic science; and they'd presented the old lady with a handsome lace tea-cloth which hadn't even been unfolded when she was found. As for the funeral, it had been well attended, with the headmaster and all the governors present, and a wreath laid on the coffin in Pratt's school colours. Miss Vera had really enjoyed herself on both notable occasions; and now here was Violet being nasty. There hadn't been any need to

say that about teachers being boring and having nothing else in their heads.

"Oh — " began Miss Vera predictably. But Violet had already gone.

* * *

The suffragettes continued to make unabated news for themselves, Thelma Cummings among them; her name was mentioned in the papers as having chained herself, with some others, to the Houses of Parliament, disguised herself, likewise with others, as charwomen to get in with mops and brooms and then badger the House of Lords; she attended the funeral procession of the woman who had flung herself in front of the new King's racehorse, and was hustled away by police with the rest. She made speeches outside public meetings, distributed leaflets in shops and through letter-boxes, was arrested, refused to eat while in prison and was forcibly fed with a stomach tube. Violet, lying snug at nights in Stephen's arms, her smooth cheek pressed against his rough one, shivered a little because of it all and

Stephen comforted her.

"I feel so useless," Violet told him. She'd helped to distribute some of the leaflets, that was all; they said Votes for Women. Stephen had printed them in his press, which he had found second-hand and installed in the basement of the house they rented some time ago now next door but one to where he'd used to live when they met. Violet's salary had paid for new letterpress, and some of the rent; at least she'd done that, it was easier now she didn't have to pay old Millie, and Stephen did the shopping and cooking economically for them both and had a hot meal ready when Violet came back each evening from school on the tram.

She felt his hands, his familiar and beloved hands, caress her flesh gently; he was always gentle with her. "You tire yourself out enough in that job day after day," he said. "I won't have you going into danger as well. The women are violent now, deliberately; look at the way they break windows and damage property and disturb law and order." Stephen disapproved of violence, as she

already knew. She herself remembered Thelma's saying that women had put up with the situation and protested in peaceful ways for long enough without any result; now, it was time for violent means to keep the issue firmly before a still complacent public. It was true; both sides were in their way; was violence ever justified? Would more be achieved if it didn't ever happen? Stephen was writing, now, his own view on the matter, would print it himself and put it in the window of the new shop, on the ground floor. They'd painted the shelves cream colour together, at weekends.

"Do you know," she murmured against him, "that it's more than a year already?" She felt a little deceitful about staying on at school; but without her job — Miss Vera had always referred to it as a post — they'd be in the soup, as Stephen put it. As it was, they hadn't been able to wait any longer, at the time.

"The first day I met you," Violet said, stroking his forehead, "I thought you looked like Shakespeare."

"And I thought you looked like a little brown mouse, until I saw you

had beautiful green eyes. Then I knew it was you."

Laughter came then, as it often did when they sat before the fire or lay together, as now; she had experienced nothing resembling this in all of her life, this swift flame, this tender glow of contentment after ecstasy; and they could talk about so much together. Stephen knew so many things she didn't, he had read far more widely than she, had had access to books she hadn't even heard of in all the years at Pratt's. His mother must have been a wonderful woman; she'd given him every possible chance in life as long as she herself lived. Stephen seldom spoke about her, after the first time. He didn't think he would ever go back to Australia.

"There's no one left there," he said, as though the sub-continent was empty. He liked London. She was glad.

Next morning, he cooked breakfast for her and saw her off to school on the early tram. It was Monday, and a longer journey than it had used to be from Chiswick.

* * *

Mrs Alec had continued curious, when she had time to remember it, about the withdrawn £30. Vera hadn't got the truth out of that girl in the end; Violet was sly. The certainty of Violet's slyness sustained Millie in an act which was frankly criminal, but which she told herself was justified in the circumstances; a letter arrived addressed to Violet, and this was a rare enough happening for Millicent to wonder in any case where it came from. She turned it over and over, rather like a curious servant, if she had known; then took it across to the kettle and steamed it open. It was from a firm of lawyers in the City, and had been recently written.

Millicent opened her eyes. It was headed:

Earl of Quayle's Estate.

Dear Miss Angell, she read,

We understand that you are the beneficiary of the late Mrs Emily Purslove. Mrs Purslove was in possession of a small crayon portrait of the late

Lady Rose Purslove which is in fact the property of the present Earl, who would be obliged, assuming you are in possession of it, for its return at your early convenience.

They signed themselves yours truly.

Curt, thought Millicent: she'd often seen the little portrait, which Violet had annoyingly taken away with her to Thelma's when she went. Millie gummed back the envelope carefully, and being neat-handed made a reasonable job of it. Then she thought what to do next. The letter provided a good excuse to find out for oneself what Violet was up to; she'd ask Vera to come as well. It was worth taking a taxi, after lunch on Saturday. If asked, she could pretend the letter had only just been delivered. It wasn't the strict truth, perhaps, but the excuse itself was too good to miss. Vera would be grateful: she mooned about on Saturdays now, not having Violet to supervise any more; she complained that the young woman avoided her in the staff room. It was possible.

On Saturday, having seen Alec off to a providential stocktaking after lunch, they

set out. Thelma's address, where they went first, yielded no results; the landlady said nobody was here, Miss Thelma didn't live here now, she'd be with that lot somewhere. Asked about Violet, the woman denied having set eyes on her for months. By now, Vera was justifiably bleating a little. "Be quiet, and let me think," said Mrs Alec rather sharply. The best thing, although it was expensive, was to let the taxi cruise round; they might see something or someone before going home. Otherwise, Vera would have to take the letter to Violet at school next week; an opportunity missed.

But there was no need, after all. Among the crowd of cheerful Saturday afternoon couples walking along the streets was, incredibly, a figure at last they both knew; Violet Angell, with a man. The man had his arm about Violet's waist. The couple disappeared into a house in the street. They were laughing together.

"*Well!*" said Mrs Alec triumphantly; she'd felt in her bones from the beginning that something of the kind might be going on, although Violet had seemed the last person at all likely to induce it;

but young women were unpredictable, and so were men. Mrs Alec got out of the taxi, closely followed by Vera, and told the driver to wait. He waited, absently flicking his whip and chewing tobacco. Those two prissy bitches seemed to know where they were going. He'd keep an eye peeled to make sure they came back.

Miss Vera was torn between tears and genuine shock. To walk about the streets like that, a Pratt's teacher, with a man's arm round her waist! That Vera herself had never had a man's arm round hers, and never would have, was nothing to do with it; the whole thing was unspeakable. Fortified by virtue, the two women marched towards the door where the couple had disappeared and Millicent firmly pulled the brass bell almost out of its holder. Nothing happened, and she rang again, knocking loudly on the door as well. She then began to call out.

"Violet Angell, come out of there!"

A small crowd began to gather; the men were grinning. Presently the door opened and a small stocky man, the one who'd been with Violet, appeared. He raised his eyebrows politely. Mrs Alec

— she did all the talking, while Vera stood like a stout tree struck by lightning — held forth, all her bitterness pouring forth in an exhibition of rage and envy; they'd looked so happy; it wasn't decent; it was disgraceful. She told the man so, and Stephen continued polite, making ready however to shut the door.

"Mrs Angell is not available," he said. "Goodbye."

Mrs Angell! On the way home — there had been no point in waiting on the doorstep, with the taxi mounting up, the crowd beginning to be positively familiar, and oneself almost ready to go into action in some other way — *Mrs* Angell! The deceit of it. Undoubtedly the man was either lying, or else he wasn't. Either way, Pratt's must certainly be told, and at once, on Monday morning.

"Oh de-e-ar," wailed Miss Vera when told exactly what to do. "Oh de-e-ar. Oh *de-e-ear.*" A man. Violet Angell, with a man. She must be taking after her mother, after all.

⋆ ⋆ ⋆

The non-graduate teachers at Pratt's had a rota of playground duty every so often, and this was Violet's week. It was cold, so she went mid-morning to put on not only her hat, which was obligatory, but also her coat, scarf, and gloves: at least it wasn't raining. Patrolling the playground was usually uneventful; it involved mostly watching skipping-rope games from where one walked up and down, round and round, longing for a cup of tea with the rest; but there would be no time after the lines were seen inside once the bell rang again to resume classes. Violet patrolled, therefore, slowly enough to keep an eye but longing to do so more briskly, to keep warm. The children skipped, shouted or else hung about; if any girl did that you were supposed to tell her to go and play, as it wasn't healthy. Some went in and out of the lavatories at the end; they were lucky, there hadn't been an opportunity for oneself, and it wouldn't of course do for a member of staff to be seen using one. As it was, Violet was fairly certain that a certain fat apricot-haired child named Corisande Crewe, who had lately come,

was imitating her walk behind her back. Before meeting Stephen she herself would have endured this and other mockery, but now she spun round.

"You haven't the figure for it, Corisande," she called out clearly. "I wouldn't try."

A ripple of laughter sounded, someone clapped, and Corisande retreated with a face purple with the cold and more so with fury. She'd tell them at home what Miss Angell had said, and Mummy would complain. She herself didn't like Miss Angell, whom she had once asked, out loud, in class, if she was related to some grocers. "Remotely, I believe," Violet had answered coldly, and had got on with the lesson.

The bell sounded, and Violet thankfully saw the lines in and went quickly to take off her things again and tidy her hair. On the way she met Miss Vera, stony-faced. That occasionally happened; Miss Vera was aware of her dignity at Pratt's, and it was true Violet had avoided her lately; that was natural, and she'd talked instead to a new and pleasant young member of staff afflicted with asthma and too shy to

speak much to anyone.

"You are to go to Dr Blundell," Vera told her, not looking her in the eye; then walked away with her stiff rocking motion. Violet went and tidied herself; it meant leaving the class alone for a few minutes, but that was old Blundell's fault. She made herself remember that some unspecified university committee had recently awarded him a doctorate, nobody quite knew why. At the same time a sense of creeping guilt had already invaded her vitals. Somebody, a woman, had shouted her name yesterday and banged on the front door. It had sounded uncannily like Mrs Alec's voice, but it was more likely to be some trouble about leaflets; Violet herself had been accosted lately more than once by householders through whose letter-boxes she'd tried to put these, and had been told to go home and look after her husband. If only she could! Perhaps one day: she held the thought to herself, comfortingly.

She knocked on Dr Blundell's door, was told to enter, and did so, closing the door after her. As soon as she was inside the carpeted room, with the emptied tray

of tea and customary buttered toast still standing on the headmaster's desk, she knew the truth. There was a letter lying open on the desk, in Mrs Alec's writing. It had, after all, been her voice. Stephen had told her to go away. She must have guessed everything, and Vera must have delivered the letter. Now —

The narrow angry face, winged by its stiff collar, confronted her; Dr Blundell did not rise or ask Violet to sit down. He wasted no time. "I am told," he said, "that you have been cohabiting with a man. Is this true? Whether it is true or not, such gossip should not have arisen; your conduct must in some way have justified it."

She felt her colour, which had fled, rising; the word cohabit sounded dirty in his prim mouth. Without replying, Violet fished inside her high blouse collar and brought out the long narrow black ribbon on which she kept her wedding ring, and held the latter out silently. His expression did not alter.

"How long have you been married?" he asked her. Violet told him; over a year, by now.

"Then you are dismissed at once, will leave this building immediately and will repay the arrears of your salary from the day you were married. It is, as well you know, in the contract that no married woman, unless she is a widow, shall be employed at Pratt's or elsewhere in the teaching profession." His mouth grew smug; there were no widows here, never had been. They carried an undesirable aura of experience of life, and knew about such things as childbirth, and other matters. All this flitted through the good doctor's mind as Violet faced him, shocked again to whiteness. She stared unseeingly at the sight of his Adam's apple bobbing up and down, between the wings of the collar.

"I can't possibly repay the money; and why should I? I've worked for it," she said. She had indeed done so; she thought of the long hours spent correcting, teaching the girls, walking up and down supervising, walking up and down in the playground, getting cold like today. She still felt cold; it must be shock. There was no way she could ever repay the money; so after all they

couldn't make her. She said so, rather foolishly. Dr Blundell's smile grew wider; he enjoyed correcting young women, even in the present disgraceful circumstances. Shortly he would dictate a letter to his secretary to thank Mrs Alec Angell in Chiswick for her helpful information; without it, this situation might have continued undisclosed for long enough, perhaps till the young woman was actually in a certain condition. The thought of that made the headmaster blench; such a thing, at Pratt's, had never happened or been thought of, except for Tiny.

"We can take it back from your funds lying at Pratt's General Office; I imagine they may cover at least a part. Otherwise, we can take you to court."

"That would be a bit of a scandal for the school, wouldn't it?" Violet heard her own voice rising, suddenly almost a Cockney voice, a little rag-and-bone girl's, perhaps what she ought to have become in the first place. It was pointless to argue with such a man. She turned to go out of the room, and heard his voice call after her, almost screeching; he was like a spiteful old woman, she thought.

"You will not meet other members of staff again. You will go straight out of the door, and not return."

"May I use the lavatory? I've been on playground duty." She said it on purpose; the reference to natural functions would be almost too much.

He froze. "That remark is most improper. You may make use of the ones outside, if you so wish."

So Violet, after putting on her things again, at last saw the inside of the pure young girls' lavatories at Pratt's. The walls were covered with scrawls about boys and one drawing of an erect male organ. It was her last memory of Pratt's, except for the one from the General Office.

⋆ ⋆ ⋆

She went straight there, taking a tram into town. It felt unreal to be free on a Monday morning, with well-dressed women beginning to emerge for their shopping after seeing to the housemaids. Violet still wanted a cup of tea, and realised she had better not afford one in

a tea-shop; there wasn't much money left in her purse, salary day would have been Friday. She felt no compunction about trying to withdraw her money from the office after what had happened; after all, they had at least no right to keep what was left of Cousin Emily's legacy.

The clerk was unfriendly. Violet said she'd come to give a month's notice of withdrawal, and he looked down his nose after taking her name and number.

"Can't do that, it's been frozen." He looked her over; not what they were used to here, a bedraggled young woman evidently no better than she should be. "We've just had Dr Blundell on the telephone," he told her. "Take yourself off, please."

The headmaster was, at least, efficient. She'd forgotten about telephones. They hadn't had one even at Mrs Alec's, and certainly not now, at the bookshop.

* * *

She carried the packet of ham sandwiches Stephen had given her to eat for lunch home again, and shared them with him.

He was shocked and angry about what had happened, the first time Violet had ever seen him so.

"I'll go and see the bastard," he promised, and went, leaving her in charge of the shop. There were no customers, and Violet stared at the rows of second-hand books and dusted a few without remembering the titles. She ought to read more. There would be time now, perhaps. Blundell would see to it that she didn't get employment in any other school.

Stephen came home later, dispirited; he had come no speed, as he put it, with Dr Blundell. "I'm only glad you're out of that," he said. "Let's go upstairs and heat some soup."

"What did he say?"

"He said we could instruct our solicitors if we chose. We can't afford one. Let's go on up."

* * *

The days passed, and the crying lack of money began to make itself felt at once; they'd relied a good deal on her salary.

She knew she'd have to take a job of some sort; it was difficult to think what, she'd never been brought up to think of doing anything but teach. At last she thought of something; her unknown mother would perhaps help now Cousin Emily's legacy was out of reach. Violet had no idea where to find Prudence, and thought of writing to her half-brother Freddy by way of the War Office; she had no idea of his regiment. That would take a long time; she was relieved when Stephen, on being told of the long-ago meeting in Paris, recognised the name of the beautiful dark woman they had called Skittles.

"Skittles of South Street," he said. "She's famous. Try there." He was glad to think of things to keep Violet from brooding on what had happened; he himself stayed in the shop, mostly working on his booklet which would be out in a day or two. He felt a savage need to protect Violet, to compensate her for all she'd had to go through because of him; better, in a way, perhaps, if she'd never met him, except that she would still have been with that damned crew of old

maids, or else the suffragettes. Stephen hadn't time for most women; his one sight of Mrs Alec had been enough, and now he knew about her letter to Blundell he wasn't surprised. Another letter, readdressed in Miss Vera's prim handwriting, came for Violet in a day or two. It was the one from the Quayle Estate. There was no word from Miss Vera; she'd evidently cast one off.

"And a good thing too," said Stephen. He had meantime pawned his watch. When Violet showed him the Quayle lawyers' letter he said, "Tell them you'll sell his lordship the portrait, if he wants it as much as all that. It probably isn't his by now, I'd say," Violet wrote, accordingly; it was something to do, and she propped Lady Rose's exquisite face meantime up on their dressing-table.

'Sirs,

I have your letter regarding Lady Rose Purslove's portrait. As far as I am aware, my cousin drew it herself from an earlier portrait of Lady Emmeline Purslove, an ancestress whom Lady Rose much resembled, also from memories of

Lady Rose she had as a child. It was, accordingly, her property and she took it away with her when she left Great Quayle.

I am however prepared to sell you the portrait at valuation, if this is agreeable to Lord Quayle.

Yours truly,
Violet Angell

There was never any reply. Either Lord Quayle was not prepared to pay for anything, or else something she'd said in the letter had displeased him. One never knew. In any case there were other things to worry about.

* * *

Violet had been slightly conscience-stricken about troubling her mother after all these years, although Prudence had certainly abandoned her to Cousin Emily in Paris that time without protest, and Emily's will had been specific about staying away. It was not difficult to realise that Mama was not approved of by respectable persons, but this in itself

did not worry Violet greatly, despite her upbringing. However first she thought of going to see Alec Angell at the emporium to see if he would give her a job. After all, she knew where things were kept on the shelves.

Alec showed neither surprise nor displeasure at the sight of her, but no great pleasure either. In fact, now one thought of it, he was the most unresponsive person Violet had ever met; nobody ever knew what he was thinking. He was in the small office, which looked out on the main store through a window so that Alec knew what everyone was doing. The store itself was large and, at this hour, not too busy, which was why Violet had chosen it.

"Good-morning," she said timidly. "I wondered if — "

"Nothing doing," said Alec at once. His eyes regarded her sadly, like two dead fish. Violet flushed a little, and then said, "I rather hoped that because you have after all known me for most of my life, you wouldn't believe everything you may have heard."

"Can't stop 'em talking," said Alec.

"I'd work," said Violet desperately. "I got quite good at adding up registers at — at school, and Miss Vera certainly taught me long division. I could help you in the office if you don't want me to be seen outside."

"Don't need help."

"Well, then — " She was about to turn away dispiritedly; it hadn't been worth the tram fare, and she would have to walk part of the way home. Her shoes needed mending and there was a new hole in her stocking beside the ones she'd darned before leaving home. Everything was getting shabby, and she was hungry; so was Stephen. Luckily it was warmer weather now and they didn't miss the fire. She suddenly thought of Stephen's booklet; this was the day it was to appear in the shop window. It was called *Why War?*

As if he had read her thoughts, Alec suddenly called after her. "Your fancy man," he said, "is my half-brother, did you know? I heard about it at the time from old Gran. She used to talk to me sometimes, when the rest weren't there. Our father, his and mine, was a son of

old HC by the cook when he was at school. Things go on in schools, don't they?" He leered at her, and the sensation was unpleasant. She let herself out of the office.

"Well, thank you," she said. "He isn't my fancy man, he's my husband." She could have said more, but there was no sense in making enemies. She'd have to go to South Street after all. Surely her own mother wouldn't turn her away.

"Tell him to look in sometime," Alec called after her. "Steve, I mean."

"His name is Stephen," said Violet frostily, reverting for the last time to the manners pertaining at Pratt's. She would tell Stephen, but of course he wouldn't go near: nobody would want to.

* * *

She found South Street without difficulty; it was quiet and sunlit, well known and lived in nowadays by the utterly respectable of town, except, almost, for Skittles and Prudence. Skittles at least was by now accepted as a celebrity, really more or less a desirable neighbour;

everyone knew her house and pointed it out, smiling. The carriages of the great however no longer called so often; but there was a landau standing now outside, its polished body shining; Violet saw her own thin reflection pass by.

Prudence had stoutened over the years. She looked by now a fairly mature Juno, her creamy flesh having burgeoned delectably as to its upper parts. Her face was still smooth, if somewhat heavier; wide hats became her. She was wearing a gown of the S-shape that had been fashionable three years ago, and the fact that Prudence was wearing a gown three years old at all indicated trouble somewhere. The trouble was of course darling Freddy, who used up a great deal of his mother's hard-earned money and, by now, gambled heavily and hardly ever seemed to win. Prudence continued to adore him, nevertheless; he called in to see her whenever he was in town. He was not here today.

Skittles was present, with the devoted Mr Baillie at her elbow. She sat these days in a wheelchair; her arthritis had worsened of late years, begun no doubt

by the cruel damp of the Liverpool docks in old days. Skittles smiled bravely, however, and otherwise looked much the same. The maid ushered in a visitor; a shabby young woman in a battered felt hat, with a hole in her stocking. From beneath the hat's brim, green eyes blazed out at Prudence, who raised her own.

"I'm Violet," said the owner of the similar pair of eyes. "You haven't seen me since I was eight. I'm married. I've been married for a year."

She began to tell the story. "Whoops, dearie," said Skittles quietly, and had herself wheeled out of the room by Mr Baillie, who, as those in the know swore frequently to those who were not, had really married her: and the mother and daughter were left alone.

⋆ ⋆ ⋆

"I can't do a thing for you," Prudence said presently over tea. "If I give you a fiver, it's all I can manage. I'd do more if I could. Freddy needs it all; he has to keep his end up with the rest."

She smiled according to Mona Lisa,

and Violet numbly sipped her tea; after the heat and dust outside it was welcome, but her heart had again sunk. Prudence looked at her wisely, suddenly rose from her chair and went to a small rosewood desk which belonged to Skittles, opened it, and sat down. She took writing things and carefully wrote a letter on pale grey scented paper, closed and addressed it. She then handed it to Violet.

"Take it to Raph Angell," said Prudence grimly. "He's your real father. He ought to do something, and I've told him so in there. It wouldn't suit him one bit if the news came out, not now." She made a face suddenly. "Take it along today, looking like that," she said. "That should worry the trousers off him, for a start. He might even give you both the fare back to Australia."

She then handed Violet the fiver, kissed her absently and saw her off the premises. "Don't come back, dear," she said. "It's better not."

Violet then walked on to where she could find a public conveyance to St John's Wood. The tea had strengthened her, but she was beginning to feel dizzy

with exhaustion and disappointment; if Raph Angell didn't do whatever it was he was supposed to, she'd go home, and start again somewhere or other tomorrow.

* * *

"This letter constitutes blackmail," said Raph in fury. Nevertheless he tore it up, casting it with evident nonchalance in the wastepaper basket. He had been smoking a cigar and regarding, with a considerable store of first-hand knowledge, a spread-out map of Jamaica when Violet was shown in. The map itself was spread on the even larger walnut desk in the room which Raph used at home as his office. Unusually, he happened to be at home.

The map was marked in red at four points which indicated the areas of Mike Angell's sugar plantations, which were successfully managed by Mike's four coffee-coloured sons. Mike himself now lived in a bungalow looking out on Montego Bay with his now vast and waddling dark brown wife, to whom he was devoted. Raph had voyaged out with Gabriel to stay with

them two years ago and had returned home mildly envious of the situation. Mike's sons were intelligent, able and willing to help run the export business; furthermore, young Joel, the second, had evolved a mysterious means, by having noticed certain small grasshoppers which flourished in those parts of the plantation not affected by cane blight, to rectify further possible blight in young oncoming shoots by bringing in more grasshoppers. Nobody understood how it worked, but the operation itself was kept so secret that while other planters suffered and lost money through recurrent blight, particularly in a bad outbreak of it five years ago, the Angell plantations not only survived but continued to flourish. Accordingly, Mike, and Raph who had invested a certain amount of Frances' money in the sugar business, were now very rich men indeed while others were bankrupt. That was satisfactory; what was much less so was the fact that, despite copious effort in various directions over the years, he, Raphael Angell, still had no son to take over, in due course, a fifth plantation which had recently come

on the market at par.

He looked with disfavour now at the young woman who was undoubtedly his daughter. Violet did not resemble him except perhaps in colouring, but he recognised Prudence's eyes. He had not set eyes on Prudence herself since the occasion when she kicked him hard in the groin, and Raph blamed this episode, perhaps unfairly, for his own resulting sterility in subsequent years. There might be other reasons; he'd seen his physician lately. He drew on his cigar, not having had the courtesy to stub it out in female company. The young woman had some depressing tale or other to tell; he'd hardly listened.

"Not pregnant, are you?" he asked hopefully. If that was the case — evidently there was a husband — he'd buy up the vacant estate on the off-chance; might as well keep it in the family, meantime putting a manager in; but one never knew what to expect out there in that way, everybody had several fathers. Meantime Violet had flushed and drawn herself up, which improved her drab looks slightly. A schoolteacher! It

was a breed he knew very little about. However there she was; something or other might happen; children often after all resembled their grandparents; young Joel, despite his complexion, had a strong look of old HC.

"Well, get in the family way, and make it a boy, and then I might do something for you." He questioned her briefly about the husband, decided it was no use thinking of sending them both out to Jamaica to manage things there, and picked up the telephone.

"I can fix you up meantime," he said grudgingly, adding to the woman operator, who knew him, "Get me Mrs Lisa at Angells, Piccadilly." Lisa would still be in her office; she didn't go home till late. The operator knew the number by heart.

Violet stared at the black instrument with its brass fittings; she'd seldom seen one. Raph Angell — she couldn't think of him as her father — had grunted at her that there was a vacancy in accounts at Angells and he'd see. She wondered how he knew about the vacancy, but it wasn't a time to ask questions or, in

fact, to resent any he'd asked her; it was beginning to have to be necessary to put up with such things, like servants had to. She waited while Raph talked briefly to this Mrs Lisa Angell over the telephone, and put back the receiver on its hook. A little bell rang. Raph drew again on his cigar.

"Go and see her tomorrow at nine sharp," he said. "The office is upstairs."

After Violet had gone Raph drew on his cigar again and thought briefly of the reason why he knew about the vacancy; he'd set the previous incumbent, a taking little thing, up at last in a handy small flat he kept for such purposes just off Clarges Street. However picking up shopgirls had its dangers, as Raph already knew. He reflected bitterly on what the physician had said. Well, it was too late now for Frances, and that was that. She was in any case out this evening, visiting friends in Ealing. They led separate lives nowadays.

* * *

Frances came in later, had her own supper sent in, and next morning

walked through the house inspecting the unseen progress of the servants. They hadn't yet got to Raph's office, evidently, and there was a smell not only of cigars, which Frances disliked, but also of some other faint, pleasant scent; surely he hadn't had one of his women in here, that was a little too much; dear Henry in Edinburgh, whom Frances now remembered with deep affection, would never have subjected her to anything of the kind in the first place. She traced the lesser smell to the wastepaper-basket and to some fragments of torn pale-grey writing-paper that lay there, and out of a sudden fierce resentment bent and picked them up; she might as well know exactly what went on. She pieced together the letter Prudence had written, using the surface of Raph's walnut desk, whereon the map still lay, for the purpose; and stared at it for some time. Unlike the schoolmaster's wife in Belgium who sewed together, for its literary merit, a mildly synonymous missive to her husband from Charlotte Bronte, Frances did not take a needle and thread. She noted the address at the top of the letter,

kept the pieces, slipped them into her handbag, put on her hat, instructed her housemaid briefly, and then used Raph's telephone to call a cab to take her to South Street. Once there — they had after all been introduced to one another years ago in the Park — she and Prudence sat down together for a long, and most informative, chat.

⋆ ⋆ ⋆

Violet arrived home on the following evening tired, almost deafened by the constant overhead whizzing back and forth of cash containers, but triumphant. She had some money at last. Mrs Lisa, whose shrewd dark eyes — the fact of the carpet connection led everyone to assume, rightly, that Lisa Angell must have Levantine blood to be as good as she was at business — had agreed in the end to a small advance on Friday's pay. The young woman who had come to take Daisy's place seemed suitable and intelligent, but faint with hunger, and a starved employee did not give of her best. Once mildly sustained, Violet

had proved adept enough. Experience with class registers, summaries and Miss Vera's ingrained long division had helped her; she'd soon get used to the job. The fact that her name, on signing for the money, had been proved to be Angell had been received coldly, however; she was told that that made no difference to prospects, she was here to work. It didn't matter; on the way home, having got off the new electric tram, she'd bought a pound of pork sausages. She and Stephen cooked them together and mashed some potatoes that were left over as well and drank three cups of strong tea each and then made love, and that was the best part of all.

Stephen was happy too; he hadn't been able to get the printer's ink off his fingers. Tomorrow the booklet *Why War?* which he'd taken all sorts of trouble to write and print, would be for sale on the open stall. If it sold, perhaps by next winter they'd be able to rent the shop, or another shop, again. The one they had briefly occupied was still empty.

"It's because it's summer, with every-one away," said Violet drowsily, against

him. Pratt's itself would be closed now, with even old Blundell surely away somewhere or other in this heat. Violet spared a moment to wonder what Blundell's wife could possibly be like; the poor woman had never been seen, but was known to exist. What a life; her own was much, much better.

She looked down at Stephen tenderly. He had fallen asleep on her breast, like a child; he was very tired, as tired as she was herself. Now that they were both working to make a little money, there was hope again. She'd never really been without it since she met Stephen, and understood at last how to live. Hopefully the booklet would sell over the summer. It had certainly been an unusually hot one; they both lay naked, with the window wide open on its creaking cords despite the noises from the street. Violet idly remembered the date, this day she'd started work at Angells in Piccadilly, like a wheel coming full circle. She'd leave in plenty of time to get there early tomorrow: and tomorrow would be the fourth of August, 1914.

Part Five

1

VIOLET'S granddaughter Hilary Angell had reverted to her maiden name on making the discovery that she had been married, some years ago now, for her money. She lay at this moment in bed by herself, in a roomette on a Canadian train between Vancouver and Montreal, from which airport she would fly back to London. She was meantime writing notes for a freelance article of the variety she still sent by request to Ted Walsh, the editor to whom, again some years ago by now, she'd sold the LeBreton newspaper chain at a profit after struggling with it for years, writing for it herself, badgering contributors and advertisers, supporting everything for a time with her own inherited capital.

The magnificent Ontario dawn had meantime come up and Hilary watched it at intervals while still thinking. Her article was to be called THE SMILE

ON THE FACE OF THE DOLPHIN and dealt with the fact that dolphins kept in dolphinaria as tourist attractions, as they were in Canada, smiling on through forced ballet performances in arranged rows of three, were quite as unhappy as a tiger in a cage; and that their occasional unexplained deaths were certainly allied to the unexplained deaths of hens in battery cages and those of any animal kept under unnatural conditions. Hilary glared fiercely and sadly through her spectacles out of the window at the paling sky and black pines. The world was certainly in a better state in such ways than when Edward VII had shot, for sport in India, a tigress pregnant with eight cubs and been proud of it: but there was still a long way to go.

Her thoughts flew back, as they still sometimes did, to Marcus, her husband, dead last year in a helicopter crash with his latest mistress, a Hungarian evidently named Eva Festics. Hilary, who was a Catholic, prayed for both their souls each night and morning, along with the souls of Granny Violet, Grandfather Stephen and her own unremembered

father, who had been killed in the Second World War in the year of Hilary's birth. There had always, by then, been money; enough money, though a great deal of it had at first disappeared down the maw of Marcus' newspapers, which were dropping sales at the time. She hadn't known that, of course, the first time the famous Marcus LeBreton had invited her, a grubby third-year medical student at McGill, out to dinner; she'd been thrilled, naturally, and there had been nobody left by then to give her the right advice. Marcus had been persistent after that in asking her to marry him; she'd struggled on long enough to pass in the following year in gynaecology and obstetrics, but Marcus had been too persuasive, or perhaps too desperate, by then, and they'd been married before Hilary qualified. That had been a mistake she never ceased to regret. She turned her head away now, surveying the closed roomette door. "I thought you must be ill, because you always keep your door closed," the attendant had remarked brightly the other day. People on this train seemed to keep their doors open

and curtains unzipped, sitting in public all day like a row of Tussaud waxworks. After she herself had found out what Marcus was really like, it was preferable to be private.

Hilary turned over on her other side, put away her spectacles, and reached somehow — gymnastics of all kinds seemed to be necessary in a roomette — for the boiling element she'd bought lately in Peter Jones and brought from London with her, because she knew already that in Canada they simply did not make tea. They handed you, if they had heard of it at all, a glass mug full of warm water and a teabag to hold in it till the mixture coloured slightly. Granny Violet had taught Hilary how to make proper tea; she plugged in and made it now, and drank it afterwards thankfully. By that time the dolphin notes had got entangled with the bedclothes, but it was still too early to get up. Hilary lay back and, as she often did, thought of Violet, who was still more real to her, though she'd died long, long ago, than anyone since. That was the case with somebody you really loved. She hadn't

known Daddy, of course, though Violet spoke of her son with pride and told her, mostly, stories about him when he was a little boy; after that he'd been mostly away from her. As for Mummy, married now for the third time at seventy-odd and living on Long Island, she'd always been a butterfly and hardly ever met with. They sent cards to one another at Christmas.

Hilary pulled the two provided yellow blankets over herself again and lay down, thinking again of her grandmother and of love, real love, such as Granny had certainly had for Grandfather Stephen even when he could no longer speak, write or read. That had been the result of brain damage caused by stones thrown at him by a hostile crowd in the First World War because he was a conscientious objector and had lately published a booklet about peace. Granny Violet had had to go again to her horrible real father, Raph Angell, partly because she was pregnant by then. She hadn't wanted to go, she said, but apart from getting work in a munitions factory, which would have betrayed Stephen's beliefs, she was again

out of a job. Angells had sacked her because a fat woman named Corisande Crewe, whom everyone knew perfectly well was Jeremiel Angell's mistress, had walked into the store with her nasty little apricot-haired daughter of the same name, who'd been a pupil at Pratt's. Old Corisande had said she'd heard all about what had happened there and a woman with Violet's past wasn't suitable for employment at Angells, even with a war on, and she'd see that the customers knew all about it. So Mrs Lisa Angell, the one who had ended up with an OBE for putting wood chips and red ink in the raspberry jam to eke it out in wartime, had sacked Granny Violet on the spot, saying they couldn't afford to lose custom. Granny Violet had wandered home in a dazed state, not even able to pay the tram fare, and once there had learned that her husband had been taken to hospital in the last hour and would probably die. "I got there somehow and sat beside him, I don't know for how long, and held his hand, and willed that he must live," Violet had said, her resolute green eyes still unfaded. "I talked to him

as though he could hear me. By degrees I knew that he could, and that he would live if I stayed with him. I don't know how I knew. They let me stay on at the hospital. I learned to clean floors." There had never been anyone as indomitable as that thin little woman with the glowing eyes and serene smile. Later on, with the money Raph Angell at last gave her, after the news that Great-uncle Freddy had been killed on the Western Front, on hearing which their mother Prudence had lost interest in life, she'd come to Canada, bringing Grandfather with her, travelling about the country with a horse and cart as an agent for Angells, having crossed the submarine-infested seas unharmed. "It was hard going once we got there, and I had a miscarriage, which didn't suit old Raph," Violet had said. "He wanted the best of both worlds; to have us out of the way, and for me to have an heir. We conceived your father together later on, but not because of Raph Angell." The worn little face had grown radiant suddenly, remembering. "Stephen never spoke again, but his mind was here with me, always. We loved each other so much.

I know he's somewhere and that I will see him again." Her smile was lit by the love that had sustained her all the rest of her life, alone; and after the war news came that Raph Angell had died of a stroke, and following on that, his widow Frances died too and unexpectedly left Violet all her money. Violet never fully understood why; and by then it was too late for Stephen. However she had been able to bring up their son and send him to school, a proper school in England. Timothy Angell had joined up at once when war broke out a second time. "He wasn't like his father," Violet said. "He had his own ideas, always. He said Hitler had to be fought. I suppose it was true. I think that perhaps Stephen would have been proud."

No doubt they were together somewhere now, Violet and Stephen. Violet hadn't lived long enough to know about Hilary's marriage. If she had, she might have seen Marcus at once for what he was, "but I don't suppose I would have listened," Hilary admitted: not at the time.

It was daylight now. She swung herself

off the narrow bed, briefly opened the door and curtain — it was necessary if you wanted to stand on the floor to pull up the bed — found the end catch which had at first bewildered her, and cranked the bed back against the wall. Then she remembered she had left the dolphin notes inside, unhooked everything, fished them out and went through the whole thing again. She wasn't always as disorientated; it came from trying to think of too many things at once. She caught sight of her reflection in the provided mirror above the basin; worse without lipstick and eye shadow; she didn't bother about much other stuff on her face. Having washed and dressed, she then sat down in the armchair the folded-up bed made, finished the dolphin article, decided it would do, and began to think of the next project; a novel, her first. It was to be about Lady Emmeline Purslove. Hilary had never forgotten that curious discovery some years ago in Ireland, and anyway she'd always been interested in history. It would pass the time to write it.

* * *

The flight was on time, Hilary reached the flat, went to bed and slept for two days after posting Ted's final article — it had to be got off as soon as possible, one dead dolphin less, perhaps, and fewer under stress which was even worse — then got up, made breakfast and ate it, went out and walked presently along Piccadilly. She saw herself occasionally reflected in the shop windows as she went past; a large blonde woman like a Valkyrie, no longer young but probably looking younger than she was. She still didn't feel any age in particular, and never had; perhaps nobody did. She passed Angells, with the flying angel triumphant above its gilded sign; people often said it resembled the late Jeremiel, but that he hadn't exactly behaved like one, from all one heard. Then she turned down St James's and went to the London Library. There didn't seem to be anything specific there about Lady Emmeline; Hilary hunted about the various shelves without success, then looked up the Peerage in the reading-room. Lady Emmeline had died in 1790

giving birth to a son who inherited the Quayle title; such deaths weren't unusual in those days. The husband must have been very much older; an arranged marriage, without doubt, and probably a heartless one. There was not much else about the Quayles, who seemed to have kept themselves out of the limelight since their emergence in the seventeenth century; no politics, no exploits, only the address given as Great Quayle, the predictable clubs of the present Earl, and the information, separately looked up by Hilary, that the Earl's father, the current Duke Marquis, lived on a Hebridean island, evidently retired, and made a hobby of agriculture. She'd write to the island first.

Meantime she turned up towards Piccadilly again and decided, as it was by then mid-morning, to look in for coffee at Angells. Apart from its well-known restaurant, the branch — together with Chiswick it was by now, of course, HC Angell, Sons, and Company — was these days the supermarket of supermarkets, unrivalled anywhere in the world at least for its wine department, which resembled

a library; and also on the ground floor, extensively set out on shelves, display cabinets or elegant deep freezes, all manner of goods exotic and plain; cock pheasants, chocolates, mincemeat, tea, coffee of all kinds from all lands smelling delicious and specially ground; preserves; especially Mary Angell's Honeymoon Jam, supposedly the original recipe by now but still not quite what it had once been before both world wars. Hilary bought herself a jar for, as it were, old times' sake. Cousin Justine Angell in Ireland, who'd been a Fiske before her marriage as a great many of them were, was dead now, but she'd remembered old Mary Angell and heard her speak of her husband Fred. Hilary had therefore sought out old Fred's tombstone when she stayed with them a few years ago at Leskinfere, the scene of the battle in 1798 and, before that, in the Gaelic, menacingly, the Hill of Men's Heads. She had stared at the by now lopsided tombstones of old Fred, older Horace — extraordinary how the name persisted in the family! — and certain others. The present Horace Angell, Justine's son, who

farmed at Leskinfere and owned the graveyard field among others, and his wife Peggy had entertained Hilary most hospitably at the farmhouse, and to repay them a little — they never had time to come to London — had taken them one day, with old Justine, to a nearby and wonderful converted eighteenth-century mansion, now a deservedly famous hotel, for lunch. Downstairs there had been a great log fire burning and portraits on the walls that had no doubt always hung there. Among them had been the one of Richard Fiske with Lady Emmeline. She'd known the former from school books and the latter at once, because Lady Emmeline was the image of Lady Rose, whose little portrait Granny Violet had given Hilary before she died and had told her the story. There could be no mistaking the beseeching expression in the great blue eyes, the bright curls cascading, in this instance, beneath a *sang d'aristo* cap with a tricolour, such as they'd worn in the streets in the French Revolution and later adopted for the attempted freedom of Ireland under Lord Edward Fitzgerald. Lady Edward,

who had been very beautiful, had been an illegitimate daughter of Philippe Egalité. Perhaps Lady Emmeline had known her and her ideas, and that was how she had come over here and was now, quite evidently, holding the hand of Richard Fiske, who with his well-known apricot hair was nevertheless directing operations in the battle where he'd been killed, and in course of which they'd thrust pikes through a hedge and thereby finished off the English commander and a good many of his men. The hedge was still there, alongside a great tree. Horace had shown it to her only the other day.

She asked old Justine about it all, over wonderful crab soup so fresh you could still taste the sand. Lady Emmeline's white arm, the one that was free of Fiske, was pointing with some reproach towards England. Justine however was cross and said the whole thing ought to be forgotten. Hilary persisted, nevertheless, through the excellent Irish roast beef and some fluffy pudding or other that followed. She had a reporter's nose by now, and if you didn't ask old people what they knew it would soon be too

late. As it was, she'd extracted certain things from the unwilling Justine, and would use them in the book.

She sipped her coffee at last in the upstairs room Mrs Lisa had once caused to be made bright with potted palms and an orchestra. Now, there was only a centrepiece of regrettably plastic flowers, and the orchestra had been paid off long ago. There were some customers, however, seated at the cloth-covered tables; Angells was a fashionable morning port of call. Hilary had already considered leaving some money in her will to the London Library to found a coffee room of its own.

* * *

Percy Titus Leonard Grandison Fitzhardinge Purslove, fifth of Quayle, sat in the smaller study upstairs doing accounts with a small push-button machine of the type used in schools. Since the public had been allowed, for fiscal reasons, into Great Quayle at certain times of year strictly laid down and adhered to, concentration anywhere downstairs was

no longer possible in the season. There was, for one thing, the constant whine of vacuum cleaners after hours; otherwise the dust raised got into everything. Brown the agent, who might possibly have helped matters, had his hands full with letting the summer cottages and getting ready the illustrated brochure for next season. Marjory, as usual, was out.

The upstairs study was however situated pleasantly enough in one of the four pepper-pot turrets whose exuberance embellished the neo-Gothic horror Quayle's great-grandfather had chosen to perpetrate in his otherwise undistinguished day, and which was much admired by the populace, who had never seen anything quite like it and now paid handsomely to do so, paying also for using the car park. Considering all this, the Earl, raising what was no doubt a pure Saxon gaze — he had been described in the New York papers, in a brief and unwelcome blaze of publicity some years ago now, as the typical retiring English aristocrat — stared unseeingly down at parterres filled meantime, for survival's sake, with begonias. Every evening in season the

gardener — one kept of course only a single man nowadays, even with the grant — was seen to ferret among these for lurking cigarette-ends still thrown there with disgusting regularity by a Philistine public, who also walked on the lawns although requested, by clearly phrased and frequent notices, not to.

The Earl was a small man with a protruding stomach. This, most unfairly, was generally held to be due to secret drinking, but the Earl was, in this and other ways, abstemious and led a blameless life. The unfortunate protrusion was in fact due to the negligence of the midwife at Quayle's birth, who had forgotten at the time to put on a binder. This omission had in itself been due to the fact that after it was all over more or less, Quayle's late mother, who like his ancestress had been inbred, had given way to an additional and totally unnecessary spasm which had caused the good woman to hurry back to the bed to see if it was twins after all. The result of all this was all the more bitter because at Harrow, Quayle himself was naturally made fun of; and only lately his son and

heir, a schoolboy with a rampant sense of the ridiculous but not much tact, had cheerfully informed his offended parent that the villagers had always referred to him as Percy the Pear. It had taken a positive effort to walk, on the next necessary occasion, the short distance down the public street to the estate-office to see what Brown was doing.

The estate-office had formerly been situated, rather more conveniently, in the stables, which with the original library — its removal at the time would have caused everything else to subside — was all that remained of the old Tudor house where Lady Rose and Emily had lived and had been, at their separate times, unhappy. Quayle brushed all this out of his conscious awareness and recalled instead that the stables were now filled by a suddenly made available Queen Anne coach from somewhere else that hadn't room for it. The public paid extra to see this and also a few military uniforms in a glass case. It was worth it, even allowing for dripped ice-cream, empty plastic cups and half-eaten beefburgers, all of which had certainly been purchased at one of

the two nearby Portakabins unwillingly erected by Quayle on the estate when it was decided to open the whole thing up to make a pound or two. The first Portakabin was a café also selling food to take away, and the second contained a multiple series of lavatories. Quayle had refused to label these toilets and as a result, the public remained confused.

The Earl was thinking resentfully of all this when the telephone rang. Quayle, irritated — he would have to start the button thing again from the beginning — picked up the instrument and immediately heard the soft distant roar of Hebridean seas. It was, of course, the DM Quayle set his well-filled teeth slightly. His father, having in his time grown weary of being Lord Lieutenant and all the rest of it, had turned over everything to him, Quayle some years ago now, and instead lived happily on an island in the far north by himself, breeding Ancient British pigs in former danger of extinction to whose welfare he devoted far more interest than he had ever seemed to do, in remembered youth, for Quayle. The breed had been in danger

of dying out, as the DM had pointed out reasonably at the time, and this bloodline evidently wasn't; but that was of course nothing to do with the matter. Quayle himself, who was devoted to duty of all kinds, had undertaken the rearrangement with his usual thoroughness and would greatly have preferred to have been left in peace to get on with it. However the DM kept ringing up to ask how things were getting on and the present seemed to be one more such occasion. Sometimes there was other news; a boar named Fred, for instance, had got away somehow in a boat and thereafter married every available Middle White sow all down the West of Scotland, hiding expertly all day, and it had got into the newspapers when Fred — he had almost become a national hero — was finally discovered and shot, far from home, by enraged bacon farmers at last. That was when the papers had described Quayle himself as retiring; he had of course given no information to reporters.

"That you?" roared a voice, above the sound of far tides milling round the Dutchman's Cap and Iona. Quayle

raised his own voice, which tended to be inaudible on committees, and replied civilly. The fact that the old boy had taken full advantage of his own well-known devotion to duty made him, as usual, bitter. It must be pleasant on the island at this time of year. He himself had not had a holiday since the takeover, as he supposed they called it now. In any case the DM didn't like visitors; he preferred pigs. Last time a boat had called in with trippers and the DM, silver moustaches flying like banners, had rushed down to the jetty brandishing a gun. Thereafter it was rumoured that he had gone mad, a rumour no doubt started by himself to keep more people away.

"All right down there?"

"Absolutely," replied Quayle, keeping a stiff upper lip; no mention of begonias, cigarette ends or ice-cream passed this phenomenon or ever would. The draw-back was that there seemed no other relevant information, so talk at his own end was sparse. He enquired politely if his father was, likewise, all right.

"No. I've had a letter from some

bloody woman novelist. Says she wasn't sure whether to write to me or you, and was tryin' me first."

"What does she want?" enquired Quayle frostily; such persons were of their nature *non grata*, and generally had blue-rinsed hair and pink notions. His father's next statement actually made him blench.

"Wants to write a book about Lady Em."

"Good God."

"Better stop it, if you can."

"Certainly." Quayle had no doubt of his own ability to stop anything; one merely issued orders to the purpose. The DM talked on at his end of the line.

"Wanted to know if there was a portrait anywhere; thinks she's seen one in Ireland. Find out where, and buy it up. Don't tell her about your aunt's Gainsborough."

"Positively not. Most certainly not. I shall warn Aunt Penelope."

"Well, it's up to her, of course; the picture's hers by the arrangement. Don't want the whole thing to become public, naturally. Discourage these people. They

go away in the end." In this latter statement the DM was, unusually for him, mistaken. He added, "I'll ring off now. Beautiful weather up here. Got some shootin' yesterday over on Mull. Seven in the first hour, three later on. Not many left up here this year. Marjory and the boy well?"

"Oh, yes, very. She's out playing golf, I think." He had privately wondered if anyone, even Marjory, could play as much golf as all that; there was that painter feller who'd rented one of the cottages. Marjory was Quayle's second wife, a good deal younger. Well, one kept a stiff upper lip. Control was the thing, and keeping up standards.

The telephone barked something incomprehensible and then the line went dead. The Earl continued to stare rather disconsolately out of the window at the begonias. He'd forgotten to enquire for the DM's beloved pigs. It was as well to keep on good terms with the old boy, after all. He should have thought of it in time, but it wasn't worth ringing back.

He got up, walked out of the study and through the smaller drawing-room

into what had formerly been the Young Ladies' Corridor. There on the wall was a space where once had hung the Gainsborough painting of Lady Emmeline Purslove, secret mistress of Richard Fiske, taken away at the time of the change-over by the DM's only sister, who fancied it. It was most unfortunate about the painting in Ireland. That might give away anything at all. This novelist must be discouraged at all costs. No doubt she would write to *him*. Quayle thought what next to do: there wasn't, after all, much question.

* * *

Hilary had received no reply from the DM, and had not waited for one; perhaps he was old or eccentric, probably both, or perhaps again they'd delivered her letter to the wrong island. Before writing to Great Quayle — after all she had a certain amount of information already, and knew what Lady Emmeline had looked like, though not yet how she came to be wearing a red cap like a *sans-culotte* or why she had been

portrayed in Ireland — to be going on with, Hilary had started writing her book; with Lady Emmeline seated gazing into her glass at her own reflection as a very young girl, and sadly contemplating the arranged marriage on the morrow with a kinsman much older than herself. Having thought of everything feasible in such ways, Hilary repaired once more to the London Library to gaze hopefully, but without direction, at the table of publications in the Reading Room. There, among other erudite temptations, reposed the current Fiske Folio, with an address in St Mary Axe to which to apply for membership.

The fact of the Folio's existence was not surprising. Every schoolgirl — at least, in every properly run Catholic school — knew as much about Richard Fiske as others possibly did about Byron. Fiske, granted, had not been a poet; but he had stood up in Parliament to defend Maria Fitzherbert when Charles James Fox commenced to roll her in the kennel, as she herself described it later on, by

openly denying her rumoured marriage with the Prince of Wales. Prinny's supporters had pulled Fiske down and had made so much commotion that, like Disraeli much later on, he could no longer be heard. Fiske had stormed out of the House, gone straight to Maria with apologies about the whole shabby business, and had shortly — it was not evident exactly when — betaken himself to Ireland, being next heard of in Lord Edward Fitzgerald's rising for Irish independence, and had been killed the same year, 1798, fighting the English at Leskinfere. What had happened after that Hilary knew quite well, as Fiske was some sort of collateral ancestor of her own; in the Catholic church over there they still prayed for his soul on the anniversary of his death. Hilary was glad Granny Violet had, to her own great comfort, joined the Church in her old age and that she herself had accordingly been brought up in it; Mummy, married and widowed in the war, hadn't cared one way or the other and soon married someone else. But on the whole subject of marriages,

it was still difficult to disentangle the behaviour of Lady Emmeline Purslove. Had she deserted her old husband to join Fiske in Ireland, becoming a kind of banner for liberty in her own right like lovely Lady Edward Fitzgerald, bastard daughter of Egalité? The date of Emmeline's marriage had been 1781, when she was twelve. Her son had been born in 1799. The rising had been in 1798, and had collapsed in that same year.

"All of which is very interesting," said Hilary to herself aloud. It was certainly time to write to Great Quayle. Also, she would join the Fiske Association. It was true that the Folio had contained very little of interest except advertisements for hotels near Bigginthorpe, where Fiske had been born. However it was stated that the annual Fiske Fiesta (members only) would take place there this year on the twenty-eighth of September, after the usual champagne breakfast at a hotel. That sounded interesting as well. She would go to St Mary Axe tomorrow.

⋆ ⋆ ⋆

She took a cab there next day. It was raining and Hilary wore her red plastic hat. At the address given there were steep stairs up which, as no lift seemed to be in operation, she climbed. A brass plate on the third floor finally said FISKE ASSOCIATION. Hilary rang the bell. Presently a woman opened it who reminded one of the early figureheads on a ship, but this one had sunk a long time ago. Her voice was harsh.

"*Well?*" Perhaps she thought oneself was a canvasser, or perhaps she didn't pay bills. "I want," said Hilary with slight hauteur, "to join the Fiske Association."

Agatha Poynton-Dennings, presiding director of the last-named, did not alter expression as a matter of course; she never did. "It's better to write," she said quellingly.

"Well, I'm here now," said Hilary, adding encouragingly that she could write a cheque at once.

Agatha, who was of course known to all and sundry as Aunt Aggie, beckoned her rather ungraciously inside to a small office. Hilary sat down on a chair. "No,

don't sit there," said Agatha, "sit *there*." She indicated a second chair exactly like the first.

"Is there something wrong with this one?" enquired Hilary, who had a contentious nature developed by circumstances. Aunt Aggie drew herself up. "There's nothing *wrong* with it," she replied; it was merely, as everyone who was anyone knew, that she liked to have the upper hand from the beginning, and this unknown woman who had arrived, most inconveniently, to join the Association must be put in her place *at once*. Hilary smiled, stayed where she was, and brought out her cheque book. On the opposite wall, apricot hair bright against a background of general greyness and a stone tower, hung a portrait of Richard Fiske. Hilary knew him from schoolbooks. He was gazing into the distance as usual. She started to say that she had seen another one of him in Ireland, directing the battle; but something told her this woman would snap up information like a parrot with sunflower seeds and, like the parrot, without thanks. Hilary made out the

cheque, therefore, Agatha took it, walked over then to a small desk and made out a membership card. "The programmes will be posted later," she said distantly. "Did you say the name was *Angell*?" She held out the card with her usual expression of slight disdain; then it brightened.

"Will you be joining the pilgrimage to Bigginthorpe?" she asked, in the tone of one offering the last empty seat in a coach to Lourdes. Before Hilary could agree — it sounded interesting, at any rate, and there would be champagne — Agatha added "That will be extra, naturally. We no longer run the vintage steam train; it became too expensive."

Her eyes grew wistful; the steam train had been her greatest triumph, and dear Lord Quayle had come. Hilary was meantime staring at a photograph on the desk of Agatha herself in youth, on a horse. It gave an aura of county origins which one somehow knew, from experience in the newspaper trade, to be spurious. No doubt she'd hired the horse.

* * *

Pym Court, London, S.W.1, 30th June.

The Earl of Quayle.

Dear Lord Quayle,

I am working on a novel about your ancestress, Lady Emmeline Purslove. I myself have a very distant connection with your family through Emily Purslove, who brought up my grandmother Violet Angell, her much younger cousin, who in turn brought up myself. Hilary thought at this point of mentioning Emily's drawing of Lady Rose, then decided against it; Granny had after all said the Quayles had tried to get it from her at one time. *I wonder if you have a portrait of Lady Emmeline at Quayle, or any kind of other information about her? I will pay for any photocopied material, or else I would come by arrangement and see what you have, if so.*

I enclose a stamped addressed envelope. Hilary had reflected on the faint scorn such enclosures always seem to raise, but with the price of stamps what they are

there seemed no reason for Lord Quayle to have to provide one. The DM had kept his. Hilary signed herself the Earl's sincerely, then posted it.

No reply came, and in despair she searched the telephone directory for other Pursloves. There were three. One was a non-starter, the other possible, the third hopeful; Purslove, Lady P, who lived in South Kensington. Hilary rang her up.

⋆ ⋆ ⋆

"Yes, of course you may come and see it," said Penelope Purslove, hesitating slightly. She then added that because of security, they had to ask for references. She also gave the number of the photograph of the portrait in a national art catalogue; however Hilary decided to go and see the original for the sake of colour. She took the little portrait of Lady Rose with her. It would be interesting to compare the two at last.

Lady Penelope opened the door herself. She was a slim woman in her sixties,

with strong features and pretty silver hair, curling naturally. She shut the door quickly after Hilary had entered. "I have to be careful here," she said, while traffic sounded outside in the busy street. Hilary produced her reference; she'd got it from Ted Walsh the editor, who had remarked drily that he was usually asked to say the person concerned was safe to leave alone with the petty cash. Lady Penelope scanned it briefly, then looked at Hilary.

"I think I've heard of you," she said hesitantly. "I don't mean Piccadilly." She flushed becomingly. "I go there, of course, it's a very good shop; nothing like it except perhaps Fortnums. Come into the drawing-room."

They went into a white-painted room, and there on the wall, at last, hung the Gainsborough portrait of Lady Emmeline Purslove. The great blue eyes looked out of the canvas without expression. She had a wide hat tied with a veil under her chin, and wore a wedding ring.

"He loved painting transparent stuffs," said Lady Penelope. "Gainsborough, I

mean. He even made Queen Charlotte look attractive in that way, in the one with the dog at her foot. Of course it was painted before things got difficult for her."

They discussed paintings and Queen Charlotte briefly, then Hilary drew the talk back to Lady Emmeline. "She didn't have a very happy life, I'm afraid," said Lady Penelope. "She died young, and her husband — they say he was rather odd — lived on for a great many years afterwards, and never remarried." She looked again at Hilary and decided not to relate the story about the glass-domed coffin. Hilary took the plunge. "I know Lady Emmeline went to Ireland in 1798 at latest," she said, "because I've seen a portrait painted of her there. Of course it may have been a memorial one, painted later on."

That was a lead, but her hostess didn't take it up; either she knew something or else she didn't, but in any case it was no good asking further. Hilary produced the portrait of Lady Rose and they both agreed that there was a likeness. Lady Penelope then suggested they have

tea, and while they had it the blue eyes gazed down on them, as those in portraits can. "Yes, it used to hang at Great Quayle," said Quayle's aunt, adding that she had chosen it when everything changed hands there and her brother went off to his island. "It's quite a responsibility," she said. "One hears of such dreadful things, robberies, and they go, the paintings I mean, to strongboxes afterwards owned by some eccentric rich person and never again see the light of day."

"Well, I hope that doesn't happen," said Hilary. "I'll keep quiet. I won't even mention you in the preface." She decided that she liked Lady Penelope Purslove and wondered why she had never married. No doubt it was the war. She herself went out again into the busy street.

* * *

When she reached home there was a letter waiting from Lord Quayle. He'd taken a month. It was quite brief.

Great Quayle Estate Office,
31st July.

Dear Miss Angell,

Lord Quayle regrets that the Quayle archives are never made available to amateur enquiry.

Yours sincerely,

J. Brown, Agent to the Earl of Quayle.

That, as Hilary told herself at once, was enough to spur anyone on. She wrote again immediately.

Pym's Court, SW1. 2nd August.

The Earl of Quayle.

Dear Lord Quayle,

I would have appreciated being answered by yourself rather than your agent, and to have received a reply a little sooner. In the meantime I have progressed with my book and have at least seen the Gainsborough portrait of Lady Emmeline where it now is. Apart from this, there are other sources than your archives which I can follow, but I would greatly prefer to have assistance

from yourself If you have a positive objection, will you say what it is? I will certainly do my best to co-operate in any way I can, apart from abandoning the project.

Yours sincerely,
Hilary Angell

This time, she did not enclose a stamp. However she rang Lady Penelope up in a day or two to ask about two small points regarding the Gainsborough; had it been painted at Great Quayle, and could it possibly be a posthumous portrait? The possibility had occurred to her, but Lady Penelope was out or away, so Hilary wrote. To her regret a polite letter came a few days later to say that the writer could give no further information. It had been handwritten but the envelope was typed, with the postmark Quayle.

Pym's Court, 10th August.

Dear Lord Quayle,

I am amazed at the thoroughness of your discourtesy; without doubt you have something to hide. While, no doubt, in

law families may keep their secrets, a writer may also legally pursue all available evidence about his or her chosen subject. I propose to do this, and in the meantime your behaviour has confirmed me in the opinion I have always held, namely that titles are of no value unless they are earned. In the second generation they should, in my opinion, be withdrawn unless the recipient has proved his worth, by distinction or by some form of public service, before the age of forty. I remain,

Yours sincerely,
Hilary Angell.

That, without doubt, put paid to further dealings with the Purslove family; she'd already written to thank Lady Penelope and to tell her not to worry further. Meantime, as though one bell set another of the same note chiming in her mind, she suddenly remembered where she'd heard the name Poynton-Dennings before. There had been a bounced cheque, during her own early struggles with the newspaper chain, signed by one Alfred of that name, from, of all

places, Victoria, B.C. Agatha must have raised herself up by her suspenders since then, one way and another. It was all increasingly interesting.

⋆ ⋆ ⋆

Agatha Poynton-Dennings, whose real name was Agnes Lyons, had meantime stayed in a state of mild irritation after Hilary's visit; that enormous woman had broken the rules. The rules were that people, the *best* people, found out about the Folio, scanned it, perhaps even went to some of the advertised hotels (which gave Agatha a rake-off), then wrote, preferably on crested paper, to enquire humbly about joining the Fiske Association if there was room. That woman had burst in in a plastic rain-hat and had sat down immediately. She sounded Canadian. Angell. Grocers; perhaps some connection, one hadn't asked, of course. There was perhaps some other mention of the name.

Agatha was about to take down *Who's Who* from where it stood on a shelf just beside the immortal portrait of Fiske,

when the doorbell rang. It must be Mr Folly. Having no humour, Agatha did not say to herself that it might be folly to open, folly to deal further, folly to have dealt at all. In any case, it was plain common sense in this instance; the man had been of immense help to her. It was doubtful that, without Folly, one would have progressed as far as one undoubtedly (except perhaps of late years) had.

She opened the door, and on this occasion a faint grimace, which might have been the beginnings of a smile, made itself seen on her dilapidated countenance. They did not kiss. Mr Folly was a large man in a brown suit, with long and rather greasy hair worn in presumed emulation of Fiske. His name had originally been Solly in the shortened version, but once, a client — Folly never now called them customers — had inadvertently scrawled a mildly eighteenth-century S in protest on a cheque, and the name's owner had decided, with his usual perspicacity, that to call oneself Folly instead might give, in the insurance business at any

rate, some no doubt perverted sense of added security. Folly Incorporated had now progressed from the shallows to the deeps in that respect, and Folly himself, with the rich and fruity voice which had been developed in the first place by calling the odds at Newmarket, now read out the minutes at the AGM of the Fiske Association with flair and confidence before a distinguished audience. He had meantime, on Agatha's advice, taken elocution lessons.

* * *

The pair had much to discuss. Fiske was by now big business, and so — this was clear in the minds of both Folly and Agatha — must remain. The slight decline prevailing in cash returns after the episode of the vintage steam train some years back must be halted. There were other aspects, naturally. Over the years of Agatha's sole directorship there had steadily sprung to life the Fiske Fiesta, held annually if possible at Bigginthorpe itself but if not, at some other stately home in better repair. There was the Fiske

Folio, with occasional contributions by a don; one must stir him up. The fact that such entries were rigorously screened and vetted by Aunt Aggie made the stream of directed creation somewhat slow, but it was there and only had to be, as it were, undammed; one must write another pleasant reminder. There were the Fiske Lectures, financed to a certain degree by a bequest from a grateful participant who had tottered out shortly to die, and meantime had changed his will; Agatha had been much younger then. The price of tickets was not, of course, included in the subscription, and the party held afterwards was extra as well. The prestigious milieu in London's West End, a former cinema, was advertised as being near the very spot where Fiske himself, by then of course very drunk indeed, had preached a sermon on the right of free speech from a tub in Piccadilly and had then retired with Molly Moggs on his arm to the lodging they briefly occupied together near the Haymarket. There were Fiske cream teas on the terrace of the House of Commons, by arrangement with the local M.P., who would show

participants (without extra charge) the actual spot where Fiske in 1785 had uttered his celebrated comment "Christ God, can't an Englishman speak his mind aloud?" before he was pulled down by previously instructed Whigs. There were minor lectures, open to Special Members only, on all aspects of Fiske's life and work which could reasonably be dredged up now censorship was a thing of the past. These were illustrated, as far as possible, with slides. Afterwards there was a little party, and this was where Agatha really came into her own. The party was very expensive indeed, so that only the well-heeled could afford to book in advance. One rebelliously inclined Special Member had described the whole thing as sheep and goats. This was of course unjust. Vulgarity of that kind, or in fact any complaint at all, caused Agatha to threaten actual expulsion from the Association. As by then everybody wanted to belong to it, this threat was effective except in one case, a man with a beard who popped up every year in a tiresome way at the AGM and told everyone most people met

afterwards for next to nothing in a nearby pub. As he then always sat down, one could hardly expel him for intemperate behaviour, but sooner or later she'd get him, and they both knew it.

For Agatha, like many persons who have discreetly come up from under, only admitted the Very Best People to genuine social interchange. The rest received a brief acknowledgement of their membership programmes, and a timely reminder of subscriptions falling due. These helped to pay the telephone bill. The rest paid off by its own momentum, or had done up till now.

* * *

Hilary, galvanised to rage by Quayle's behaviour, thought of other means. She wrote to her stepfather, Elmer K. Wint of Long Island. He was a retired Wall Street operator and knew everybody. Hilary explained her problem; it was exactly the kind of thing that would interest Elmer K. who had very little else to do nowadays. To do him justice, a reply came almost by return.

Butterfly's Rest, Amityville,
Long Island, N.Y.
10th August

My dear Hilary,

It was a great pleasure to hear from you in course of your busy life. Honey Doll sends her regards. She's down at the pool this minute. She is amazing for her age, never idle like myself.

I sent your problem to a good friend of mine, Tom McCormack, publisher, New York. He called this morning from there and I hasten to write what he told me, which he says isn't much but may be of help. He remembers an old girl some years back called Rosiebird P. Sydenham, who was just plumb crazy about this Fiske and had written a book about him. Tom remembers the suggested title was FRANKLY FISKE. She'd even been over to England and ferreted around this place Bigginthorpe and paid money to the villagers there to tell her what they knew, which can't have been much by then. Tom says he couldn't touch the book, as for one reason this character Fiske never penetrated the States, though Rosiebird

relates several things the villagers in England may have made up out of their own heads, such as that Fiske was helped to escape from Baghdad on a camel by the chief wife of the Grand Turk, which is unlikely on the face of it, though you never know.

I asked Tom what could have happened to the manuscript and he said he hadn't a clue, but mentioned one publisher Rosiebird seemed to know in the U.K. called Magnus Grant, who had also prudently turned down the book in the end. You will know where to find him If he is above ground.

Honey Doll as I say sends her love. Look in on us sometime. We'd like to know how you fare these days.

Your affectionate stepfather,
Elmer K. Wint

Hilary spared a brief thought of equally affectionate despair for her almost unknown mother, whose real name was Joanna. Then she looked up the Year Book to find the firm, if it still existed, of Magnus Grant. It was still there, in, of all places, Piccadilly. This made Hilary

scan with more attention the long list of vice-presidents of the Fiske Association, at which she had glanced only briefly on receiving the relevant literature from Aunt Aggie at the time. Among the Law Lords and CBE's represented was one Magnus Grant. Hilary had already thought the mention of the name rang some bell in her mind.

* * *

She had meantime received a further communique from Aunt Aggie to say that the pilgrimage to Bigginthorpe would take place this year after all on 18th September, that an overnight stay at cut rates was available at a certain hotel, and that early booking was advisable to avoid disappointment, as there would be the usual memorial champagne breakfast. Hilary sent a cheque by return. Meantime she had looked up Fiske in the DNB to refresh her memory, and had discovered the information that he had been born at the expected address in 1757. Thereafter he had been privately educated and had later been sent down from Cambridge

for undue dissipation. Having likewise dissipated his fortune, he thereafter became a friend of Fox and of the Prince of Wales, and was said to have been present at the latter's marriage to Mrs Fitzherbert, by whose influence Fiske had already become a secret member of the Roman Catholic Church. This fact was conveniently discovered after his awkward speech in the Commons, where Fiske had meantime represented his home borough ably enough but was thereafter disqualified on grounds of religion. In dudgeon, Fiske then joined the efforts of Lord Edward Fitzgerald to obtain Irish independence, and was killed near Wexford in the rebellion of 1798. There were no quoted references.

* * *

"Would it be the older Mr Grant or the younger that ye were wanting?" asked a voice, in soft Highland accents strange to hear over a Piccadilly telephone. Hilary said it was probably the older; that was usually safe, they knew everything the younger ones did and perhaps a bit

more. "He will only be in these days on a Wednesday or a Friday afternoon," the voice answered, and Hilary made an appointment to see old Magnus Grant on the ensuing Friday.

She was ushered upstairs from what appeared to be a prosperous enough publishing house, full of parcels and busy receptionists, to an upper floor. In a small room behind a desk sat Magnus Grant, senior. He was a big Highland Scot, of a considerable age which was not at once made evident as his hair contained not a single thread of grey. They greeted one another, but Hilary's eye had at once been drawn to an object lying beside others in a glass case against the wall. It was a faded red cap with a front shaped like a parabola, resembling the ones they'd worn in ancient Greece: and its colour had once been red, *sang d'aristo*, the colour of the French Revolution and of briefly attempted Irish freedom. At one side was still pinned a faded tricolour. It might of course be anyone's, but as things were —

"Is that," said Hilary, who never beat

about the bush, "the cap Lady Emmeline Purslove wore in Ireland, when she was there with Richard Fiske?"

"My God, woman," said Magnus Grant, "you must surely have the Sight. How else could you have known?"

* * *

She had told him about Ireland, the portrait there, her book about Lady Emmeline, the difficulties with Quayle; he grimaced at this but said nothing. Hilary then asked about Rosiebird P. Sydenham and if she was still alive.

"Sadly, she is no longer with us," said Magnus Grant. "I was in fact her executor. She left me the cap in her will, with other things discovered in her travels. She was a graduate of Bryn Mawr. There is something else here which may be of interest to you."

He plunged into a drawer of his desk and drew out a thumbed manuscript. "There is an awful lot of nonsense in it, but if you will let me have it back in due course I will lend it to you," he told her. "It is like Sir Walter Scott, who made

up what he wasn't certain of and had no evidence for, and left no record one way or the other. Neither did Rosiebird: she never bothered to put in where facts ended and her imagination began. For that reason alone we could never publish it. You must use your own discretion about what you find in there."

His eyes, very bright, were regarding her keenly. Hilary thanked him, rose to leave, and paused beside the glass case.

"May I touch the cap?" she asked. "She was married at twelve years old to a man she couldn't possibly have loved. The time she wore this may have been her only one of happiness, even ecstasy. I'm quite sure Rosiebird went as far as Ireland."

He let her hold the cap in her two hands, holding open the case silently. Hilary touched for herself the limp and faded thing which had briefly confined Lady Emmeline's bright hair.

* * *

Afterwards, she recalled the other things Magnus Grant had told her. He was,

like most mildly distinguished people, a member of the Fiske Association, but said he didn't have much to do with it these days and certainly wasn't going to Bigginthorpe again. This sounded discouraging. It would have been pleasant to see a known face there; Aunt Aggie hadn't been at all friendly at the two meetings she had so far attended, and to Hilary's annoyance had entered her name on the membership list as H. Engels. Hilary was fairly certain it had been done on purpose, but could see no reason for it other than her own enquiry regarding Victoria, B.C. Anyway it didn't matter. She went home and read through page after page of Rosiebird's hopeful imaginings about Richard Fiske; and at last came on certain treasure trove. It was only a copy, but it couldn't be anything but real.

Leskinfere,
date I know not, in the year 1798.

My Heart,

Pray join me here when you and Lady Edward are done talking women's talk

together. I will have horses sent as far as Enniscorthy, but can contrive no nearer; matters here are grave indeed and they say an English force is marching upon us by way of Clugh where the farmer and his sons will aid them, certainly. The poor folk here are up in arms, but the better fed know their masters.

Guard the child lying in you, for God's sake; I know well it is mine, and if matters go ill it can inherit Quayle, there being no other for him.

Till we meet, my love as always.

Your R.F.

There was a footnote to say that the writer had rescued the original from a damp cottage near Leskinfere, where it had been kept in a chimney between stones, and on being handled for copying had crumbled into fragments.

If all of it was Rosiebird's imagination, she had a good one, Hilary decided. Certainly she must have been across to Leskinfere, and perhaps while there had also found the cap. She herself must tell Magnus Grant about a great many things when she returned the manuscript.

Perhaps he'd agree to publish her own book on Lady Emmeline; he didn't appear to think much of the present Lord Quayle.

* * *

Among the future speakers bearded by Agatha for Association meetings and put on the programme list last month had been the Duke Marquis, and his talk had borne the intriguing title ANCIENT BRITISH BOARS; FISKE'S POSSIBLE INVOLVEMENT. Hilary had decided that she must not on any account miss that one, and was accordingly very disappointed when, having been delayed in setting out for Bigginthorpe by an unexpected telephone call from a friend, she was in time to open the second post, which did not as a rule arrive till just before noon. It stated that there was a change of speaker on the date and that the don who had written a most interesting article in the recent edition of the Fiske Folio would speak instead, subject to be decided later. There would be the usual reception afterwards and early booking

was advisable, charge extra.

Hilary, late as she was — she could drive fast when necessary and would make up time on the road — sat down and scribbled a hasty note to the DM hoping that it was not her presence that had deterred him from coming. *I am interested in animals and especially in Fred*, she wrote, *I thought it was a low trick to trap him at last with a sow in season, knowing he'd come out of hiding. I heard that a man went off drink for life in Ayrshire after meeting Fred on the bridge one night after the pubs shut; he thought he was seeing things, like Tam o' Shanter. Anyway I'm sorry you are not coming, but I dare say it is a tiresome journey from the island. My book on Lady Emmeline is coming on very well*. It was; she left it with some regret, having incorporated much that she had meantime sifted out from Rosiebird's less diffuse maunderings. The DM might as well know that his own failure to reply had not deterred her, Hilary, from going on with the project; it didn't do any harm to make the aristocracy aware that it didn't have the last word every time.

In fact the DM had not yet, as far as she was concerned, uttered any word at all; but no doubt Quayle had been in touch. It didn't matter.

Hilary got out the car, drove very fast along the motorway, and arrived at Bigginthorpe in time, as she had planned, to look at it in private first before the crowd got there tomorrow morning following the champagne breakfast.

* * *

Bigginthorpe, or what remained of it, was sited some few miles from the arranged hotel. Apart from a notice at the road-end, one might have missed it; the notice had evidently been put there by the Fiske Association in 1980. Across an expanse of grass kept short at reasonable intervals by the District Council, a second and humbler notice said ABBOT'S TOWER. Hilary turned her car into the park, and paid at the machine; there was nobody about. The tower itself was of plain grey stone, and roofless; it might have been any age. A small plaque outside stated that it was here Richard Fiske had

often sat with friends and constituents, drinking champagne out of a human skull prior to the date when Byron was said to be doing the same thing with claret out of a similar receptacle at Newstead, several miles off in a different direction. Inside the tower was nothing notable except shadows, and Hilary came out again into the autumn sunshine; fortunately it was not raining today.

She had been trying to work out, on the drive, her own tenuous relationship with Fiske. It certainly existed, as the family's apricot hair, passed down through old Fred Angell, appeared in Fiske's portraits and was known — it was still a tradition at Leskinfere — to have identified him when his body was found at last on the battlefield. There had been several cross-matings — Hilary tended to think of all breeding in terms of dogs, which she liked on the whole better than people — down the centuries, and she herself accordingly had a good deal of Fiske blood. However, Granny Violet hadn't been particularly interested in that side of the Angell family and most of what she had had to tell concerned Stephen's

father, The Stranger, and his long-ago doings in Australia and elsewhere. Later on Hilary had discovered Cousin Horace, still farming at Leskinfere as his fathers had done before him long before the famous Horace who went to England and founded the firm with Walpole's help after the South Sea Bubble burst about 1720. Young Horace — he wasn't so young now, of course — had even begun to dig into old church records to try to disentangle the Fiskes and the Angells in general and in particular, but the calving season kept coming round and he had drawn to a halt meantime; they kept in touch by letter at Christmas. However Horace had proved, so far, that one branch had come from Bigginthorpe at the time of the Civil Wars and had inhabited a parcel of land granted to them long before by James the First and thereafter neglected, being mostly bog. Richard Fiske had belonged to the remaining English branch, but obviously kept up an acquaintance with his Irish cousins. The whole thing was extremely complicated but if Aunt Aggie liked her better, she'd certainly have been asked to

give a talk about it all by now. It wa
trifle more àpropos than wild boars an
mythical centurions called Fiscus.

Hilary paused at yet another plaque, this time slightly larger. It lay flat among the grass-blades in the sunlight.

Here lie the bones of Richard Fiske, politician and freedom fighter, retrieved from Ireland by the Fiske Association and reinterred here at his birthplace at a ceremony in 1980. R.I.P.

Hilary's mouth firmed a little. Aunt Aggie was certainly a very determined woman. She herself would wait and see what happened next. There was no need, after all, to meet trouble halfway.

* * *

The ticket for the hotel dinner (extra) at which Folly and Agatha were both to speak, had said clearly Dress Informal. Hilary had however packed a long brocade Angela Gore creation and in some rebellion wore it. Perhaps this was why Agatha glared at her on entry; everyone else was in a short skirt and looked suitably humble. Agatha was

herself trailing about in psychedelic frills. Hilary went up to her; she was a little tired of the prevailing situation.

"I'm sorry the Duke Marquis is unable to come," she said conversationally. Agatha almost swelled, froglike, then suddenly resembled Glenda Jackson playing Mrs Siddons, if it ever happened.

"He *and* Lord Quayle," she intoned audibly, "*have refused to come* because of the presence of *certain persons* at our meeting."

She glared and then swept on, and Hilary, without much surprise — Quayle at least would have been expected to behave like he had — found her own way to where a drab woman in a plum-coloured afternoon dress and spectacles was going round distributing the new copies of the Fiske Folio. Hilary took one, smiling at the woman, who happened to be the widow of a celibate vicar of Puseyite leanings in Oxfordshire. It never did any harm to smile.

"There's no doubt Agatha *is* the Fiske Association," breathed the widow, evidently a devout follower.

"Oh, absolutely," agreed Hilary. She

then sat down with the Folio and a purchased glass of sherry, cash bar. On opening the former, she saw as before that it contained mainly advertisements, and one erudite article by a don. Hilary took out her spectacles from her evening bag; all about her was talk, but she preferred meantime to read and drink her sherry. Shortly she was interrupted by Mr Folly himself, in a black tie. He said he was collecting the money for the Folio.

"I thought it was included in the subscription," said Hilary audibly. Several persons looked round in surprise and hope. Mr Folly's mouth closed like a purse prudently snapped shut, then opened again. "*That,*" he said gravely, "couldn't be afforded. It would be necessary, if so, to raise the annual subscription."

Hilary then held out her copy. "I don't think I want mine, then, at that rate," she said, in the voice occasionally used for difficult former contributors and advertisers. "There isn't really very much in it." The article by the don she had by then sized up.

Mr Folly smiled gently. “You’ve handled it now,” he pointed out. Hilary shrugged, and paid. It wasn’t that she didn’t have the money, but it was, as people always said, a matter of principle. It was like the travel agency she’d used to book the Canadian transcontinental train journey, which had had its halts here and there; it had turned out that nothing was really paid for in the end except the fare.

Besides all that, the article itself had been mere wishful thinking on the part of the don, who had evidently once been an archaeologist. There was certainly no such tradition in her family of descent from the Roman centurion named Fiscus who had probably been stationed on the banks of the Varumna (Garonne) and had, with slightly less probability, married a Bronze Age chieftain’s daughter some centuries before the Conquest. Later on their Norman descendants of course fought at Hastings and settled as landowners in England with a name that over the generations turned into Fiske. Aunt Aggie must have bullied the old boy into writing it.

* * *

Dinner was a success, although Hilary had of course been placed with her back to the speaker and had at first not recognised her name as on the card as, again, H. Engels; she had complained about it quite uselessly and it was certainly done on purpose. Aunt Aggie made a long-drawn-out speech and Folly a short fruity one. After that everybody got slightly drunk (wine included). The psychedelic frills swept past again on the way out and Hilary, anxious to remain polite, remarked that the whole thing had been very well done. Agatha did not reply. Perhaps the single mention of Victoria, B.C., had remained unforgotten, as well as the matter of the absent DM and Quayle.

* * *

The champagne breakfast next day was excellent, and most people attended it despite the indulgence of the night before. The vicar's widow, to whom Hilary gave a lift afterwards as far as

the car park at Bigginthorpe, repeated bibulously again and again that dear Agatha *was* the Association, she was, she *was*, she *was*. Hilary parked the car. She then assisted the mildly swaying widow to walk towards the small plaque on the shaven grass which she herself had examined on the previous day. A small crowd was already gathered there. Way was soon made for Folly and Aunt Aggie; the former looked rather ill. Aunt Aggie, whom nothing seemed to destroy, made another speech, her harsh voice ringing out confidently on the still air.

"Here lie," the voice croaked, "the bones of Richard Fiske, to whose memory we have so very — so *very* lately drunk." A voice from the back said doubtfully "Hear, hear." "The bones were," continued Agatha, undeterred, "discovered by Mr Folly and myself on the site where Fiske died in Ireland defending liberty, and were reinterred here by the Fiske Association, which we had of course already founded. They lie now in peace below the ground on which we stand."

Here there should have been a respectful

silence, but Hilary interrupted; with one thing and another, she had looked forward to this moment. "But they don't," she said clearly. "Richard Fiske is buried in Ireland, at Leskinfere, beside old Fred Angell my ancestor. I've seen his tombstone, dated 1798, and it hasn't been disturbed." She refrained from adding how they'd found Fiske after the battle and identified him by his apricot hair; the point had been made, and heads were turning. Agatha gave a macaw screech.

"That is *blasphemy*," she shrieked. "I've had nothing but trouble with you from the beginning. The bones were found in an *Irish bog*, near the battle. I was *present*." She failed to add that she had in fact remained in the car; such sights weren't pleasant, and she had left it all to Folly, who had come back later with the bones in a provided sack and had told her how a farmworker had led him to what he'd sworn in a heavy Irish Jewish accent were the actual bones of Fiske, not in the bog itself but deep among some nearby primroses, inextricably entangled — he'd done his

best in such ways — with those of a young woman. That, in Folly's opinion and also Agatha's, had clinched the matter; and anyhow nobody in England was going to ask any questions. She said none of this coherently, however, but continued screaming and was presently led away. Several persons began to walk away also, but others stayed, notably the vicar's widow, who vainly proffered Aunt Aggie some aspirin from her handbag.

"Bogs," announced Hilary without pity, "preserve bodies very well, certainly from the late eighteenth century; look at that man who was dug up lately in Jutland from something-or-other B.C. If it was bones you found, they were somebody else's and we only came here for dinner and breakfast." She turned away, after a glance at the vicar's widow to see if she wanted a lift back to the hotel; but that lady stared stonily after the departing Agatha. A remnant of the Association would no doubt survive, like the man who brought the banner home from Flodden.

Before they actually reached the park a man with a beard overtook Hilary.

"Good thing somebody spoke up at last," he muttered. "Had it coming. Would have done it myself long ago, but hadn't any proof. Folly's another of them." Hilary did not wait to identify this cryptic remark, but smiled and drove away alone.

On return to the flat, there was a letter from Agatha by special delivery, requesting Hilary's resignation from the Fiske Association. Hilary decided to ignore it. People were always being asked to resign, someone had told her.

* * *

"I wish I could have met the DM," said Hilary some days later over lunch with Ted Walsh the newspaper editor, who was visiting London. "He might have been more forthcoming about Lady Emmeline if I'd met him in person." There had still been no reply to her letter commiserating about the late Fred, but no doubt the DM never wrote letters now at all.

"How's the book coming on?" asked

Ted, who would have asked Hilary to marry him if he hadn't had a wife and children already in Nantucket. They ate melting guinea fowl in a subtle sauce and Ted remarked, as the restaurant had been his choice, that the chef here was British for a change. "Aunt Aggie pesters everybody to come and speak," said Hilary thoughtfully. "She certainly didn't pester *me*." She hadn't answered about the book; it was stuck for lack of first-hand detail.

"Well, you spoke anyway," said Ted, forking a small new potato into his mouth. "We could use a really exclusive animal article for the paper chain," he said. "Would you get on to the island? He isn't easy of access."

"He certainly doesn't answer in writing, but I could try telephoning if I knew his number. It's probably not in the book, though."

Ted however had methods of getting hold of private numbers. Later that day Hilary heard over the long wire, as Quayle had done much earlier and oftener, the roar of Hebridean seas. A voice answered, evidently in process of chewing something

which had meantime got in the way of its moustache.

"I'm sorry to interrupt your meal," said Hilary, and told the DM who she was. "I've come on quite a bit with the book about Lady Emmeline Purslove," she added. "I've found out rather a lot, in fact probably everything." One might as well be honest.

"Well," said the DM without expression, and waited.

"This is about animals, however," said Hilary, "particularly Ancient British pigs. Was it because of myself that you didn't come to speak at the meeting? I'm sorry, if so."

"No, it was because the damn' woman pestered me and said she wouldn't let me off on any account. Damned impertinence. What do you want?" He sounded as if he was going to ring off, so Hilary put in quickly that her article was to be particularly about Ancient British pigs, treating especially with the cunning of Fred in escaping his murderers for a matter of almost a year, among the hills and forests, but coming down at night to walk

openly past the pubs, no doubt on principle.

"Annabella's farrowin'," said the DM absently. "She's one of Fred's daughters. Had difficulty with her last time, narrow in the passages. They get inbred; it's natural enough, so do we."

"I nearly qualified in medicine long ago," Hilary told him. "I passed in obstetrics and gynaecology, quite well as it happens." The memory of Marcus rose for the last time, then fled. "I could come and have a look at Annabella if you like," she said. "When's she due? I expect it's difficult to get a vet on time, they're busy."

"No manner of use when they're got," said the DM, most unfairly. He added, "If you like to come, I'll tell you a good deal more about Fred at any rate. Nobody else remembers or cares, but he was almost human. He got away by divin' under the tarpaulin for turnips while they were deliverin' stores by boat, then went to sleep. Natural enough. Everythin' else he did afterwards was natural as well. It was murder in the end." There was a silence.

"He got all down the west coast as far as Galloway before they shot him," said Hilary reminiscently, "and I believe all the litters were striped. The bacon farmers got out that damned sow at last and — well, you know the rest. He ran for a hundred and twenty yards, pouring blood, then dropped. I'll certainly come and have a look at Annabella. Perhaps one will be like its grandfather."

So it was arranged. She flung a few things into a suitcase. It was an extraordinary feeling, but she felt that at last, in some way and for some reason, she was going home. There was a flight at five-thirty; she could just catch it, driving like hell and leaving the car at the airport. She could hire another car in the north, then take the ferry, or perhaps he'd send a boat. She looked quickly round the flat before leaving; she felt she didn't care if she never saw it again, but it was always like that on any interesting assignment.

* * *

The two hundred and seventy-fifth anniversary of the founding of Angell,

Sons and Company took place at last by prior arrangement in a tree-lined square in Bloomsbury. Most people crowded inside the large erected marquee, as the wind was cold. The orchestra, who sat perforce outside on a raised platform and wore evening dress, suffered, especially the women players; but in any case the wind carried away most of the music. It was fortunate, as everyone kept saying, that there was no rain. Inside, on a second platform behind flowers and the portrait of the original Horace in his full-bottomed wig, sat royalty, having arrived suitably late and not being expected to say anything today. An assembly of mayors, their wives, and other notables were already poised to form a guard of honour at Exit B. Meantime everybody was enjoying themselves with wine and canapés, both of these naturally brought from Piccadilly. It was in fact almost like being in Angells itself, except that the wine was mostly uncorked by now. Chiswick, the smaller branch, was of course represented, along with the other directors; but it had been difficult to try to trace any actual Angells

themselves. Nobody could get in touch with Hilary LeBreton, who was said to have married again somewhere in the north; the Jamaican branch of the family seemed to have merged some time ago into the general population of that fertile island, and had not replied to the firm's invitation. One figure, however, stood out by very reason of its vastness; old Corisande, Countess Marciewiecz, at present romping through her fifth nuptials at ninety. The Count was not present. The Countess — she was whispered to have been got, on the wrong side of the blanket, early in the century by way of the late Jeremiel Angell, CBE, and it must be true because her hair was still distinctly apricot, no doubt with help — had thrust her disagreeable thrice-upholstered face into that of Aunt Aggie, whose Fiske Association had recently been wound up but one still asked her to certain events from habit. One or two persons overheard what the two old ladies were talking about, evidently with venom; something about some woman who had *dared*, after all that, to become a *double peeress*. Those who knew anything at all

about the history of the great store were at a loss; HC Angell had had six sons, but where was the aftermath? No notice had been taken of the rumoured earlier branch of Angells in Ireland; one had to draw the line somewhere, because of numbers.

The present General Manager, whose name happened to be Bakhtiari, raised his glass to the memory of the founder in his great wig, gazing serenely out above the famed Houghton livery; and then to the firm. The firm elicited the more enthusiastic reception of the two. Most people didn't know a thing about old Horace Angell and it had all been a long time ago; but, meantime, everybody had to eat.

Other titles in the Ulverscroft Large Print Series:

TO FIGHT THE WILD
Rod Ansell and Rachel Percy

Lost in uncharted Australian bush, Rod Ansell survived by hunting and trapping wild animals, improvising shelter and using all the bushman's skills he knew.

COROMANDEL
Pat Barr

India in the 1830s is a hot, uncomfortable place, where the East India Company still rules. Amelia and her new husband find themselves caught up in the animosities which seethe between the old order and the new.

THE SMALL PARTY
Lillian Beckwith

A frightening journey to safety begins for Ruth and her small party as their island is caught up in the dangers of armed insurrection.

THE WILDERNESS WALK
Sheila Bishop

Stifling unpleasant memories of a misbegotten romance in Cleave with Lord Francis Aubrey, Lavinia goes on holiday there with her sister. The two women are thrust into a romantic intrigue involving none other than Lord Francis.

THE RELUCTANT GUEST
Rosalind Brett

Ann Calvert went to spend a month on a South African farm with Theo Borland and his sister. They both proved to be different from her first idea of them, and there was Storr Peterson — the most disturbing man she had ever met.

ONE ENCHANTED SUMMER
Anne Tedlock Brooks

A tale of mystery and romance and a girl who found both during one enchanted summer.

CLOUD OVER MALVERTON
Nancy Buckingham

Dulcie soon realises that something is seriously wrong at Malverton, and when violence strikes she is horrified to find herself under suspicion of murder.

AFTER THOUGHTS
Max Bygraves

The Cockney entertainer tells stories of his East End childhood, of his RAF days, and his post-war showbusiness successes and friendships with fellow comedians.

MOONLIGHT AND MARCH ROSES
D. Y. Cameron

Lynn's search to trace a missing girl takes her to Spain, where she meets Clive Hendon. While untangling the situation, she untangles her emotions and decides on her own future.

NURSE ALICE IN LOVE
Theresa Charles

Accepting the post of nurse to little Fernie Sherrod, Alice Everton could not guess at the romance, suspense and danger which lay ahead at the Sherrod's isolated estate.

POIROT INVESTIGATES
Agatha Christie

Two things bind these eleven stories together — the brilliance and uncanny skill of the diminutive Belgian detective, and the stupidity of his Watson-like partner, Captain Hastings.

LET LOOSE THE TIGERS
Josephine Cox

Queenie promised to find the long-lost son of the frail, elderly murderess, Hannah Jason. But her enquiries threatened to unlock the cage where crucial secrets had long been held captive.